Copyr

ISBN: 9798653637162

Clea Galindo floated, suspended, nineteen metres below the surface of the Flores Sea, close to the steep underwater descent of Batu Bolong. Clea relocated to Indonesia four months earlier to research her PhD on the conservation of Bargibant's pygmy seahorse, *Hippocampus bargibanti*. Spotting the tiny, camouflaged creatures between the wafting nudibranchs and peach-pink corals was her passion, her purpose, and her burden. After long fruitless hours in the turquoise waters she had finally found a herd. The jubilation at such a discovery disguised the euphoria, the first warning signs of nitrogen narcosis. Narcosis occurs when nitrogen is inhaled at high partial pressure, the feeling roughly translating as one Martini, on an empty stomach, for every ten-metre increment below twenty. Her motivation to follow the trail of tiny bubbles down into the murkier depths was encouraged by the toxic effect of the inert gas, coaxing her, glibly. Clea lost sight of the sea horses after three Martinis. After four, the water turned dark and cold and she giggled in her mask, realising she could no longer see the diamond blanket of sunlight above her head. After five Martinis she started to hallucinate. Fire bursts of neon colour and alien fish. When did flowers start to grow under the sea? By eighty metres the delirium had consumed her, and she was lost to the current.

Six minutes later, lightning scorched through a huge, isolated Oklahoma redbud tree. Its current splintered through the ancient branches and into the man sheltering from the downpour beneath the broad, waxed green canopy. Pain stretched across his face in a twisted, open-mouthed grin but his heart stopped before the blood vaporised in his veins.

Two seconds later, at two thirty-five am, a pan of vegetable oil reached boiling point in the kitchen of the house at the top of Gardiner Road, Gibraltar. The violent ignition spat fire upwards and outwards. A pathway tore through the dining room, living room and then up to the first floor. The spindles of the oak banister like kindling to a campfire. Gerard Grey, aged nine, was consumed by smoke as he slept. Death came cloaked through a paralysed, fitful dream full of blackened freesias and flame red roses. He drowned in the smoke.

Thirteen seconds later, fifty-five year old Reggie Pires collapsed suddenly in front of the vast ornate window frames of the Cafe Alegria on Praça da Alegria, Lisbon.

Doctors would later diagnose a sudden cardiac arrest (most probably a coronary artery rupture) and reassured his family that it would have been, almost certainly, without pain. And it was. In his final moments he felt the warmth of the morning sunshine and admired the glaze of the sugar on the pastries in the window. He died in the short space of time between his eyes rolling backwards towards the blue sky and his knees cracking upon the cold cobbled stones.

Strong fingers closed around her neck. Cold strong hands. She clawed at a stubbled, familiar face.

Golden snatches of twilight in the darkness. That smell. The smell of him.

Darkness.

1

Running would have to bloody well do. I always hated baths. I could never quite equate stewing in my own dirt to relaxation, no matter how perfumed the water.

I couldn't use alcohol to switch off anymore. The initial calming wore off too quickly these days and I couldn't stand the dry mouth paranoia at the bottom of the bottle. At eleven thirty it was probably too early anyway. I really wanted to speak to Sam but after the shit storm of our last conversation I couldn't bring myself to pick up the phone. The news was a depressing series of deaths and it felt like every radio station played it's ad break at the same time. So, a run it would be.

The cold November air stung my dry eyes as I crunched out half-arsed lunges in the gravel of the front garden to get the blood moving in the muscles in my legs. Warming up under the cloudless sky felt futile so I started out towards the common at a slow jog; past the small Victorian parade of shops across the road and onto the hilly grass slopes.

'Run off the rage. Just run it off, Isla.'

That's what Dad always told me when I was angry as a kid. Just get out in the countryside and run it off. He and I spent so many hours running together through muddy trails in the Lake District, around lakes, up and down hills. Running and talking, running in silence, running together.

Before he died.

Although shivering and doing that embarrassing jogging-on-the spot at the crossroads while the traffic rolled past didn't necessarily constitute running. A silver VW people carrier crept to a halt at the red light. A little girl, bundled into a padded child's seat, slept open-mouthed in the back; the steam of her sleep creating a cloud on the cold glass pane.

The little girl's tiny features made me think of Jessica, the woman in the hospital bed. The woman who slept open-mouthed in the hospital through tiny rosebud lips. When I met Jessica that was one of the first things I noticed, just how small her features were. Tiny ears, tiny mouth, gamine and tiny and fragile.

And broken.

The VW people carrier moved on at the green light and I sprinted over the crossing, past the twinkling gaze of the neon Jesus looking out from the corner shop. My legs felt stiff from twelve days sitting down. Twelve days and sitting behind a desk, hunched over my laptop, cross-legged on my sofa. Twelve days since that day in the hospital. Twelve days of witness identification, passive data, CCTV footage, interviews, fact-finding, verification, staff meetings, briefings and roughly four hours of fitful sleep each night. Twelve days of piss all.

I weaved through the gated slalom of the park entrance. The cold metal of the park gate reminding me of the cold metal frame of the hospital bed. Her thin wrist. The hospital bracelet. I pictured her tiny torso propped up with four thin pillows, covered in swathes of green, watermarked sheets. Auburn, elfin hair laying fuzzy against the green pillow cover.

Run off the rage, Isla.

As the park opened up before me, a side wind blew a cold gust into my face. The woodland pathway lay to the left, with icy humps of tree roots tangled in the mud. I decided against a sprained ankle and turned down the concrete pathway through the centre of the park, taking me past the café in the centre. The café was usually overflowing with young mothers, boisterous dogs and old women. I hadn't washed off yesterday's make up yet and imagined most of the mascara would be sweat-streaking its way down my cheeks by now. If I was lucky it would be too cold for them to be outside, I couldn't face the judgement.

No such luck.

An old lady cradled a steaming mug underneath a glowing heater. She craned her neck, deliberately and slowly, to peer at me. I felt conscious of how tight my running leggings were and how dishevelled my hair must have been. Growing up under the glare of the Catholic church always made me cautious around older people, like I felt that I needed to show that I knew that cleanliness was next to Godliness. As if one look at my messed up hair would reveal instantly that I didn't give a fuck about cleanliness or Godliness. I hadn't believed in either since I was seventeen.

The crisp air and the old woman's judgement stung my face but it was the feeling from the hospital room that sat heavy in my gut. How I felt when I first saw Jessica; standing in the doorway as she slowly turned to face me, expectant with the hope of a police woman who might be able to find the man who had beaten her half to death. The weight of her head was clearly a strain on her slim, bruised neck. In turning to me, she'd revealed the full extent of her facial injuries. The contorted right side of her face was a horrible shade of blue-purple, greening at the edges. Her right eye was nearly completely swollen over. Glossy, blackened skin covering a blood-shot, watery eye. A knick scarred across the bridge of her nose from where they had to reset it.

Jessica's face had been the first thing I saw every time I stop-started sleep. I saw her as I brushed my teeth, washed conditioner out of my hair. I had promised her I would find the man who had done it to her and I was fucking angry that I hadn't yet. After twelve days I felt like me might never find him. I wavered between wanted to punch a wall and punch myself.

Run all of that off? Not a chance.

Browning leaves littered the concrete path between

nearly-frozen puddles and dog shit. Crisp packets, cigarette-ends and cider cans surrounded one of the benches on the left. I sat down with my head between my knees.

My notations on the initial interview were spread out on the coffee table back at home. I was supposed to be on annual leave but I didn't have anywhere to go. I could't go off on a romantic break with Sam. I couldn't face travelling back up to the Lakes to see Mum. So I'd just sat at home and read them. Looking over the pictures of Jessica's broken face. Reading back our first official interview. At this point I felt like I didn't even need to open the folders, I knew those conversations by heart.

'When did you first realise that someone was in your flat?'

'I noticed something. Something different about the flat, the bouquet. And then a noise. I tried to turn but he was already right next to me. And he just, hit me, he hit me in the face.'

Jessica was so strong throughout the whole interview. Bluntly outlining the details, removing emotion and providing clear details. She had recounted her movements on the day pausing only briefly to wipe the tears pooling at the inner corner of her right eye. She explained how she had met friends for brunch in Clapham Junction. Left with the others but travelled home alone to Clapham South. She bought some magazines at a Best One on the corner of Abbeville Road and then headed back to her one bedroomed flat. She wore new noise reducing headphones to walk home and kept them on as she walked from her bedroom, to the lounge, at the rear of the property. The revised Blondie album blurred out the sounds of the man waiting for her inside her own home.

Maybe that was the reason I'd left my headphones on the metal tray in the hallway. I loved listening to my music as I ran. Sam and I would run together and we would chat in the same way Dad and I did. Pushing out thoughts through heavy lungs forced me to filter them, helped me to focus on the important stuff. But on the days that Sam didn't fancy running I would listen to music. Really loud, aggressive music. Electro beats drowning out my laboured breath as I pounded the ground in that heavy-footed, inelegant way Sam used to take the piss out of.

I had been a policewoman for a bastard long time, and met some frankly awful human beings but something about the assault case made me scared. Scared or angry. But in any case, since I met Jessica it felt too dangerous to wear my headphones around the house. It felt dangerous to block out the world.

I stood up from the bench and stretched my arms above my head. Stretching the concertina of my ribcage both ways. I attempted some triceps dips on the bench but could still sense the judgement of the café crowd in the distance and ran on towards the other side of the common. I thought back to the notes I knew by heart. The conversation I relived with Jessica overnight, every night.

Jessica had only faltered when I got to the *offender* questions. *Location* and *victim* lines of questioning had been thorough. But I needed to know about *him*, her attacker, what reasons he may have have had for such violence. I couldn't understand the pure rage of the attack without a seeming end. Why hadn't she been raped? Why hadn't anything been stolen? And, truthfully, why he had stopped so short of just killing her. He had certainly tried to choke her and wasn't interrupted. He had every opportunity to take her life.

'Can you think of anyone at all who might want to hurt you?' I asked.

After a long pause, her face had finally creased into tears. Shaking her head as best she could. Thick spit gathered at the corners of her mouth as the sobs grew louder. I'd hugged her tightly over the metal barrier of the bed. Not the most professional move. The cold bar dug into my ribs. I shushed out the best comfort I could on the top of her head, breathing back the lingering scent of vanilla hair product. I could see the clipped cuttings of her hair on the top of her right ear and on her neck. I was too close.

I remembered her huge brown eyes.

Too fucking close.

I bit my lip and started off at a jog. I could manage another fifteen minutes and then head home.

I turned along the wooden sign-posted running route, ducking below a low hanging oak branch. The gravel skidded beneath me and I almost fell; I carried on and pushed against the tension of fatigue in my thighs. I liked the burn. I sprinted until my chest hurt then stopped again once I got to the foot of the hill, breathing heavy and skywards with my hands clasped over my head.

I would have gotten more out of Jessica if it wasn't for that interfering nurse, who was only, 'checking in to make sure everything is OK?'. Jessica nodded and smiled at her but the nurse had continued, looking at me, 'I can always ask the police to come back later if you want?'

The pause in concentration jolted Jessica out of the memory and I knew I wouldn't get any more out of her. Her family had since insisted on full recuperation and the psychiatrist at St George's concurred. In truth, I shouldn't have left the biggest question until last. I shouldn't have been so scared. But I couldn't bring myself to say it. To look into those wide glassy eyes. Why didn't he just kill you?

'Tell me Jessica, precisely *why* are you still alive? Why *didn't* he rape you? Why did he break into your home and *not* steal a thing? Why did he stop strangling you after going through the trouble of beating your cheek bone almost clean in half and squeezing your throat until the blood vessels exploded in your eyes?'

There was no clear sexual motive, according to the medical report. Nothing was secreted or stolen. It had to be something much cleaner. Simply to kill. But he'd stopped. And

I couldn't understand why. We hadn't found any potential offenders. No one had seen anything unusual. Twelve days of nothing.

I'd promised her I'd find him and I hadn't.

I sprinted up the hill until my throat hurt and stared out at the London yellow-bricked terraces through the naked oak branches. I took my phone out to check the time just as the call came through. I took in a sharp lungful of air and answered, swallowing against the heart beat to make sure that my voice was strong and sturdy.

The voice on the line spoke clearly and urgently.

'DCI Fletcher, we need you to come now.'

2

I ran home and showered as quickly as I could. The warm water felt like needles on my pink skin. I dressed in the cleanest outfit I could find, after discounting two shirt dresses from the armchair that were far too wrinkled. I stepped into brown brogues and dragged a brush quickly through my hair. I couldn't wait around to dry it so I left it wet. Whether I let it dry naturally or blow dried it, it didn't make any difference to the end look. Poker straight, near black. Never held a curl or a braid, to my Mother's dismay.

I turned the radio off in the car as the news bulletin spoke of another teen who had been stabbed in London. I rang the control room back so that the details were clear in my head. A 29 year old woman had been found dead by her boyfriend, we had PCs and SOCOs on their way to the scene with a crime scene manager in place. Upon arrival, I would be the most senior police officer and therefore the Senior Investigating Officer until Jim or another more senior DCI arrived. Typically, in a homicide the appointed SIO would be the most senior DCI but as Jim was at a conference in Westminster, they needed me to head straight to the crime scene.

The crime scene manager was already with the victim and I'd agreed with control that if we needed additional resources I would make the call once I'd spoken to him. I knew Lester would be setting up the crime scene parameters and coordinating the forensics teams but I wanted him to have my number in front of him in case any fast track actions kicked out in the initial sweep. We were almost forty-five minutes into the Golden Hour. That key hour after the discovery of a crime.

As I drove there, I mapped out the surrounding streets, building out the cordons and plotting which streets would need witness interviews. I drove down Balham High Road and clocked the CCTV cameras pointed down at the entrance to the tube. The traffic wasn't too bad considering it was a Sunday and it only took me twenty minutes to drive there, pushing the boundaries of what was within the speed limit. I drove in silence. I didn't want the radio to interfere with my thoughts. I only had the patience for a conversation with myself and I barely had that.

I turned off from Trinity Road into the crescent of Crockerton Avenue. Almost every residential road between here and Earlsfield were filled with similarly grand three-story houses. Red brick terraces with bright white fringing. Quaker style blinds in almost every window. This part of Wandsworth sat on the wealthier end of the scale. A tribe of organically raised, floppy-haired children in expensive pushchairs. If the victim had lived on Trinity then neighbours' statements would almost certainly be useless; living on such a busy stretch afforded anonymity to the people living side by side. This cul-de-sac however served as a catchment. Neighbours lived eye-to-eye here and aside from the occasional wrong turn there would have been a familiarity to the regular visitors; even in London there must have been someone who noticed a stranger. God. Unlike the tiny village I grew up in. Everyone knew everyone's business. Even in the vast countryside there was nowhere to secretly smoke without your Mother finding out before you'd had the chance to buy chewing gum and spray on cheap perfume.

My hands shook as I opened the car door. I considered nicotine gum but decided against it. Even such a small dose of nicotine made me agitated and I had quite enough adrenaline in my system. I was going to see a dead body. A woman who was once alive, and now wasn't. And even though the control room did not have the specifics, they had told me the corpse had been interfered with. Despite the doom-mongering assertions in the national newspapers, this area of South London did not see a great deal of bona fide murders. I had only seen two dead bodies in my time at Wandsworth CID and neither of those had involved any kind of interference.

The top of the street was swarming with eyes of neighbours; some congregated in clusters along the street, some peering through upstairs curtains. A little girl twirled her hair, looking up to the group of adults at the edge of the cordon.

DC Robert Whalley and DC Patrick Ryan stood guard at the police tape. Nodding as I approached. I knew both men reasonably well and knew they worked well together. Whalley stood a good foot taller than Ryan and didn't they just get grief for it at the station.

'Ma'am.' said Ryan. Whalley nodded in unison.

'Morning, lads. Is Lester in the house? You were first on the scene?'

'Yes ma'am.' Whalley answered, 'we called it in almost an hour ago. Greta Maiberger, 29.'

'She dead on arrival?'

He nodded. Lips pursed.

'Who called us in the first place?'

'Boyfriend. He's already been taken to Lavender Hill.'

He looked at my wet hair for the briefest moment.

'I've written down detailed notes,' he said, 'and will put the report together back at the station. But she it's definitely not an accident. Not looking like that.'

My eyes moved to the house. Adrenaline surged again. My hands felt cold and my feet felt heavy.

I knew Whalley, having worked with him on a spate of burglaries back when I first joined CID. He was a great candidate for the MIR Office manager, especially if he was first on the scene. Those details would be imprinted on him. I crossed the inner cordon of the crime scene as Lester came out from the ornate front door. He crossed the muddying patch of grass using the common approach path to meet me in the centre of the front garden. The white suits of the forensic team scurried around him. A camera bulb flashed at the window. A strobe in the grey darkness of a November morning.

According to the last birthday card I'd seen snaking a glitter trail around the office, Lester was sixty years old. He had hollowed cheeks, a sallow complexion and brilliant, turquoise eyes.

I gestured over his shoulder to the alleyway at the side of the house.

'How wide have you set the parameters at the rear?' I said.

'Two gardens either side. Plus the alley.' he said.

Sounded about right.

'Who have we got from forensics in there?' I asked.

'Seven from the forensic science department but no pathologist as yet. Four SOCOs. No specimens have been taken from the body. No swabs. The body hasn't been moved. '

The camera flashed again, illuminating the misted rainfall: making glitter out of drizzle.

'We've got Chris Jeffries taking photographs.' he said.

Bloody Chris Jeffries. I shivered involuntarily. Wet hair, cold day, old fears.

'Where is the body?' I asked. I was ready to see her. Desperate to see her.

'In the living room. First room on your right, when you enter the flat.' he answered.

'Thanks. I'm going to go and look at the body and assess inside the house. Then, between us, we can set the CSM strategy. DCI Greaves might be here by that point and I'd like his input before we address the witness or media strategy. Although...'

I turned to address Whalley.

'If anyone from the press shows up or calls can you come

and find me straight away?'

He nodded and I turned again to Lester, who took a stride closer to me, leaning in.

'Sounds like a plan to me. I'll go and coordinate the uniforms.' he said. He turned his shoulder to Whalley and Ryan and lowered his voice.

'It's unpleasant in there. Not seen anything like this in a while.'

I smiled at him and turned towards the house. I stepped carefully over the last steps of the common approach path. Galvanised metal, November rain, and well-worn brogues did not make for easy footing.

I could see no immediate signs of footprints or disturbances. To the side of the house stood an assortment of black dustbins, filled past the brim with angular cardboard and over-stuffed rubbish bags. The contents of one bag lay fox-strewn down the pave stones towards the side gate. The alley at the side was an obvious escape route, this might have just been completely random. The postcode could practically rule out a drug or prostitution motive. Although brothels were definitely not how they used to be. This was a nice street. Yes, it neighboured Tooting and probably saw the occasional burglary but it was expensive. People paid to feel safe and this street was supposed to be just that.

The flashbulb strobed again. Odd what you remember. I thought back to one of my first-year lectures on flashbulb memories. How a uniquely traumatic event could cause the human body to go into observation overdrive. I knew each detail of today would be a flashbulb. Sure as shit.

I pulled on plastic gloves and stooped to put plastic booties over my shoes. I leaned against the doorframe of the neon pink door with heavy wood and beautiful stained glass inlaid in each quadrant. I stepped onto the ornate, victorian tiling of shared hallway. There were two magnolia doors with ornate brass letters which distinguished the two maisonettes. Distinguished the two sets of humans living behind each door. Why had you chosen door A? Why was this the life you wanted to end and not the life behind door B? Was this a random decision? Or did you know when you opened that bright pink door?

Door A, to the left, opened almost directly into the living room at the back of the house. The carpet, which must have been replaced recently, forced the heavy pine door to stand ajar in its own friction. Then I saw it. I saw her.

The body. Her body.

Jesus.

Chris moved in front of me, obscuring the view of the blood. He leaned awkwardly over the victim, squinting into his obnoxiously-large camera. Everything about him was obnoxious.

The forensic teams nodded at my arrival in sequence. Finger-print dusting, taping, itemising the contents of the immaculately decorated living space. Oyster pearly whites, silver gilded photo frames, black and white images of Paris and a huge vintage poster advertising absinthe hanging above the fireplace. The fragrance of lilies lingered. Soft pink cashmere blankets draped over a grey woollen sofa with cushions, purposefully arranged in a row. The room hadn't been turned over, at least not quickly. It if had been taken apart then it had been put back together carefully. This definitely wasn't a burglary.

'Chris, are you almost done with her?'

He turned on his left heel and almost fell backwards over the crouched SOCO behind him.

'Isla, hey.' he said.

My nostrils flared at his over-familiarity. He pretended not to notice. I could smell bleach on the air.

'Yes. I covered the head first. Pretty grim right?'

I moved to the left of her. Folding my arms, nodding agreement.

Chris turned to address a PC, a chubby red-headed guy I hadn't ever spoken to but knew to be Police Constable Stephen Davies. Davies ushered Chris out into the hallway and then followed him out. I wondered if Davies had picked up on my disdain and moved him away from me on purpose. Regardless, I was happy to get the prick out of my face. I wanted to focus on Greta. The dead woman in front of me with the flowers in her hair.

Her body lay in the centre of the room. Perfectly *placed* in the centre. Dainty feet with neon blue toenails pointed towards the mantel piece. Her thin, cleanly-shaved legs bound together with brown parcel twine at the ankle and knee. She had no ligature marks on her ankles and the delicate single knots on the twine indicated they had been bound after she stopped struggling. The knots were delicate with long loop bows.

Her skin was incredibly pale – not post mortem pallor, more a sign of an Anglo-Saxon lineage. Milk cream skin with no freckles, moles or blemishes. There wasn't even a knick from a razor on her hairless legs.

She wore a plain, oversized white tee shirt, pulled down neatly over her hips to mid-thigh. Her hands were placed over one another on her lower stomach, fine gold rings covering her forefinger and thumb. Cotton blue nails. Disproportionately large breasts for a small frame falling heavy towards her armpits. Did you touch her? Did you feel the swell of them beneath you? Did it turn you on?

Obvious bruising covered the majority of her slender, pale neck; purple smudges between finger-sized red welts. Her face seemed serene. Rose pink lips slightly parted and eyes restfully closed. There had been no immediate signs of trauma. No obvious blows to the head, even though this is where he had obviously taken his time. I crouched down to get a closer look and noticed the saline trace of dried tears at the outer corner of the right eye.

I stood up too quickly and my vision blurred. I felt pale and hoped the bustling room wouldn't notice. What kind of human could be capable of this? The man, and I was certain it was a man, who had killed this woman had killed her and then mutilated her head. Decorated her hair. The facts of it sat like oil on the surface of my water belief system.

Her mid-length, golden-blonde hair was fanned out upon the floor. In and around the thick halo of curls lay a semi-wreath of flowers. There were small lilac petals, delicate yellow daisy heads, damson dipped freesias, blue spray carnations and gentle wisps of Gypsy baby's breath. A handful of blood-red roses planted bloom-upward with their thorny stems woven into the pale curls. A corpse-sized rendition of a Mucha print laid out for the viewing public.

The deep, viscous stream of crimson at the top of her forehead was still meandering down the curves of her temples; dripping into the pools of blood behind each ear. The scalpel cut along the edge of her hairline looked steady handed, professional but there was something so forced, almost desperate, about the way in which the scalp was pushed back. Fat folds of skin gathered at her crown. Her skull a brilliant white against the colours of the blood, and the flowers.

The weight of my eyes anchored me to the carpet. I swallowed against the dry pulse in my throat and realised how tightly my jaw was clenched. Tongue rammed against the roof of my mouth; molars grinding against molars.

I forced the sick back down my throat. Not today.

Carl Mayhew, the coroner, stopped me from making it all of the way outside. But the cold air in the hallway felt good against the flush of blood behind my eyeballs. I didn't often cry, only really when I was angry, I couldn't help it. I cried when Sam left, and when Dad died. But I'd be damned before I cried at work. I wouldn't cry for Greta when she needed me to be strong.

Carl practically pushed me out of the way to get through to

her. His speech was measured but forceful, he spoke to me but didn't take his eyes off the corpse.

'I've spoken to Lester, I'll process her now and get her out of here as quickly as possible.'

I let him pass into the lounge and stood close to him.

'I'll come back when you've had a chance to assess the specimen recovery.' I said, 'Let me know the best removal route and I'll sort it out.'

He nodded and hurried past me, I could practically hear him thinking. So many tapings and swabs to be made. I knew Carl and how he liked to work, and I liked how single-minded he was. We needed time of death as soon as possible and I wanted her wrapped and out of here. It wouldn't speed the process up for me to loiter at his shoulder and I needed to get more information from the CSM and the attending officers.

The bile burned acidic in my throat. I might be sick after all. I stood next to the neon pink door and inhaled slowly and fully until my ribcage was pressing against my bra strap.

I focussed on the thick wet grass and swallowed against the taste in my throat. At the edges of the small lawn stood a sparse row of pink tulips being pummelled in the rain. I wondered if Greta had planted the bulbs. I hoped she had been alive long enough to notice them bloom before he killed her. Before he did that to her.

I opened a thick black umbrella and stepped out. The perimeter of the crime scene had been extended, cutting off the road completely at the entrance. Lester stood beneath a newly-erected white tent, dictating actions to the team of SOCOs. They needed to move as cleanly and swiftly as possible. We needed to get her out of there and to the hospital. Her poor family.

I motioned for Whalley to meet me in the tent.

'Give me the detail.' I said.

'The boyfriend, Blake Wallder, made the emergency call

at eleven nineteen am. Initially called for an ambulance but controller sent over two PCs after talking him through preservation of life checklist. DC Ryan and I arrived at the property at 11:42am. We entered through the open door at the front of house, announced ourselves and found him sat in the doorway to the flat. Upset. Ryan stayed with him while I checked the flat. I checked the body for life signs, confirmed death back to control, and then checked the rest of the property.'

'And someone has taken him to Lavender Hill now?'

'Yes.'

'But before he went we took all details leading to discovery.'

'Right. And no one else went into the house before Lester and the team arrived?'

He shook his head.

'No ma'am, aside from the three of us, it's preserved.'

'Next of kin?'

'Mr Wallder gave us their details. Isobel and Joachim Maiberger, both retired, living down in Devon. She is British, he's German. Greta was born in Munich but moved to the UK with her parents in 1986. We've got local police in Devon on their way to them now.'

'Great.' I said, imagining how those police officers would be trying so desperately to find the right words to phrase it. To explain to Isobel and Joachim that someone had killed their daughter, slashed her scalp and threaded flowers through her hair.

'I'll sort out a family liaison officer to meet them when they get here.' I said.

We would definitely need a major incident room up and running, I considered a mobile office but figured the distance between here and the station in Battersea didn't warrant it. We just needed to preserve the periphery now.

'Can you get Ryan to kick off the MIR back at Lavender Hill?'

He nodded again.

'Did you ask the boyfriend whether he found the body like that, with the flowers? Did the emergency call make any mention of the corpse being in any other state than the one we found her in?'

'No.' he answered, 'On the call he seemed shocked, kept questioning what to do, talking about blood and flowers. The controller did a really great job for us.'

'And how about you, you get any sense from him? Any gut feel?'

'No ma'am. He was shaking and sobbing when we arrived. He had blood on his right hand.'

He must have steadied himself to check her arterial pulse. Making him left handed.

'And when you first entered the property there were no other neighbours in the hallway?'

He shook his head. I wasn't all that surprised.

'Have they all been alerted and moved out now?'

'Yes. They are giving reports and have taken enough belongings to stay out of the property for the evening.'

'What kind of crowd do we have?'

'Young professional couple. Early twenties I'd guess.'

He took his notepad out of his pocket.

'Mike and Daisy Roscoe. They are in the flat opposite. The second floor occupants didn't answer and according to the Roscoes they are in Thailand.'

'There is only the one flat up there?'

'Yes. The ground floor is split into two. Top floor is a two bedroomed flat in the eaves of the loft.'

'How many PCs do we have on scene?'

'Six for now. More en route.'

'Good. We might not need much more. Are you happy leading the witness statements?'

'Yes ma'am.'

I nodded. It wouldn't take long before someone from the press showed up. I could live without any details of this being shared on social media or the bloody Mail online before her parents had been told.

'And no one from the press yet?' I asked.

He shook his head. I looked over his shoulder to the cordon at the top of the road. The huddle of neighbours had seemed to dissipate in the rain. A few men stood gathered under golf umbrellas.

'Right. Thanks Whalley. Get cracking on the neighbours, I need to speak to Lester.'

A black Prius pulled into the cul-de-sac and I could make out Jim's shadow leaning through to point the driver where to pull up.

(EVE)

At ten past eleven on that very same morning, thousands of miles away from Crockerton Avenue, a small blonde child named Hazel Duggan ran into the path of an oncoming car on Ninth Street, Etobicoke, Canada. The car, a grey Nissan Altima, was driving at fifty-two kilometres per hour. Hazel was seven years old and knew no fear or sadness or remorse, only the joy of rummaging through leaves in her Dad's back yard and the thrill of chasing Gracie onto the roadway. The force of the impact threw Hazel twelve yards in distance but the trajectory had been upward and in her last snapshot of sight Hazel had captured the tree lined street, the row of neighbouring houses in the Toronto suburb, and the ashen face of the lady behind the wheel.

Three whole heartbeats later, a fourteen-year old girl injected heroin for the first time. Jenny, Munich born, had found herself in a squat in the outskirts of Berlin after being kicked out by her foster parents. She wasn't sure on which surname felt like hers so she rarely used one. Her death was not a drawn out or fearful experience. The heroin had won as soon as the plunge on the needle moved. A slow, warm and winding ribbon snaked through her veins until the mark of dull, detached ecstasy drew across her face. She was not aware that she was dying but her breathing slowed straight away. Her eyes closed as she fell back onto the hand-woven rug draped over the futon. It was only when her friends noticed her twitching hands and blue fingertips that they realised something was wrong and by then it was too late. Three junkies wading through the sea of their own respective highs would never be able to reach out for the reality of *the phone* in time to make a real call for help. Jenny had not fought her last moment; the drug coaxed her warmly towards it. In the deepest parts of her subconscious there was a desperate willing for the moment to come. An acknowledgement that this was always going to happen, always be this way, alone, without a surname, miles away from where she was born.

3

DCI Jim Greaves was not a small man. He unfolded his six-foot six frame out of the black Toyota Prius and lifted the collar of his thick woollen coat. Beneath it, he was wearing a pale blue shirt with a red striped tie, held in place with a silver tie pin. His thick, black beard was the neatest I had ever seen it. Sharp at his square jawline. The raindrops splashed off the matte dome of his shaved head and streaked down the fogging lenses of his horn rimmed glasses. It was bloody good to see him. He nodded his good morning to me. Jim was a Yorkshireman and he didn't waste time on pleasantries. My candour was one of his favourite traits about me.

He strode over to me and stooped his tall frame under the umbrella.

'Homicide, Jim, a bloody weird one. Looks like strangulation but she's been messed with postmortem.' I said, 'Decorated.'

'Decorated how?'

He stooped his head down and I lifted the umbrella. I had gotten used to craning my neck up to engage with him. It wasn't like I was going to ever start wearing heels.

'Flowers. She's been cut from ear to ear along the scalp. Skull exposed, what looks like a full bouquet of flowers woven through her hair.'

Jim puffed out his cheeks, containing the air behind pursed lips.

'You've set the strategy with the PCs?'

I nodded.

'Need input from me on that?'

'Not at this point. I've got them interviewing the neighbours. I spotted some CCTV on Trinity and back on the high road so will get them onto the council.'

'Lester and I have pushed the crime scene parameter back the length of the gardens. We haven't seen any signs of fleeing the scene and I don't think he could have been interrupted. He took his time.'

I realised then that he must have been with her for a while. The precision of the cuts, the smell of bleach at the crime scene. This was a confident first kill.

'Right.'

He wrapped his coat around him with his massive, hairy hands and crossed his arms. I don't think I had ever seen him use an umbrella himself. It would look like a kids toy in his hands. The rain had turned into downpour; fat raindrops slapped on plastic sheeting and car rooftops.

Jim raised his chin to acknowledge Lester as he approached us, walking away from the house. Lester responded in kind and then proceeded to talk his team through the next phase. I trailed slightly behind Jim, taking two strides for every one of his. I noticed an elderly neighbour two doors down had turned her armchair out to face the crime scene. She now sat staring at us through the slats of her colonial-style shutters. It reminded me of how Mum had moved her wingback chair to the bay window, just so she could see the cars driving up the lane. I wondered at what age you stopped caring about being so brazenly nosey.

Jim and I had worked together for a very long time and I knew he wouldn't want to be in the weeds of the detail until he had seen the body. I also knew he trusted me. It didn't mean that he didn't still scare the shit out of me sometimes.

Jim took his coat off at the door and we were both handed a fresh set of shoe wraps. The SOCOs had set up a coat and umbrella stand in the hallway with thick, clear, bobbled plastic. I handed over my heavy raincoat and quickly twisted my hair into a bun. I wiped the rain off my face with sleeve and steadied myself to look at her again. I could still smell bleach.

Jim stooped under the frame of the doorway and stood over the body with his hands in his pocket. The SOCOs had moved out of the primary room, leaving Carl and his deputy working on Greta.

'How quickly do you think we can get her out of here, Carl?'

Carl was bagging each flower stem out of her hair into individual containers, shaking his head. He paused and looked up-. He looked concerned, and completely ignored Jim's question.

'Have we found her next of kin?' he asked.

I answered.

'Yes. They're not local. Isobel and Joachim Maiberger. She's British, he's German. Moved to the South Coast a few years ago. We've got a couple of Devon PCs on their way to them now. It will take them a good seven hours or so to get here.'

He stood up and adjusted the slack on his trousers, rubbing the top of his right knee. He turned to Jim and answered his question.

'I reckon maybe another hour or so. At least we don't have to deal with her folks heading straight here.'

I thought about the car journey ahead for Greta's parents and felt sick. That alien blanket of grief weighing heavy on them. The neon blur of motorway lights and street signs. I knew that quiet grief. The hope that it might all be a huge mistake but knowing, in that new and real place, that it wasn't. Poor bastards.

Chris snaked through from the rear of the property. He made a scene of scrolling through the images on his camera and then nodded gravely at us. Such a pantomime of a man.

'DCI Greave. Good to see you.'

He stood between me and Jim, his body turned fully to the more senior DCI. Prick.

'Sir. I've taken as many angles as possible of the body. Once the SOCOs have bagged the flowers and are ready to move the body I'll come back into the room. I'll go and focus on the front exterior.'

He motioned to walk outside but I placed a hand on his shoulder.

'Chris, can you make sure you touch base with Lester before doing anything else?'

He stopped and acquiesced with a smile that went nowhere near his eyes.

'Of course, DCI Fletcher.' he said.

He only ever acknowledged my title when Jim was around. It bothered me, but I knew Jim didn't care about Chris. I held the bird print curtains open with the tip of my pen to make sure Chris followed orders and then turned back to Greta. To her body. To the mess of what was once a woman.

The pool of blood under her head had browned. The viscous streams either side of the cut had dried a rusted red behind her ears. The process of bagging up the flowers had caused the fat fold of skin back over the top of her head, covering up most of the exposed skull. She was pretty. I wondered if her boyfriend told her that. I hoped she thought it herself. I hoped she had been happy. That she had seen her tulips bloom.

Jim and I left Carl to talk over the content I had from Whalley. We stood in the small galley kitchen which was just off the main lounge. I looked over the assortment of holiday destinations mapped out in fridge magnets. Her kitchen looked like it had been stocked in a health store, sachets of spirulina, bee pollen and raw cacao. An expensive food mixer and a bulky looking juicer stood next to a baby pink toaster. I looked down at the frame of the French window that led into the garden and noticed an upended woodlouse, curled and frantic, in a groove of rotted wood.

I explained how Greta's boyfriend had found the body and that he was being taken to the station for questioning. Jim and I agreed that we should head straight there and start asking questions. Leaving the forensics to the experts.

We left Greta with Carl and walked the the white tent where Lester was coordinating more members of his team.

The rain had stopped. The air felt thick; there was more to come. With the coroner on the scene and the witness statements underway up on the street it didn't make sense for us to stay there. I was keen to make sure the MIR was being set up properly back at the station and we needed to assemble the team of specialists as quickly as possible. I wanted a behavioural analyst as soon as we could get one. Jim was just as keen to get back to the station, he turned to me.

'I got a car here from Westminster, you alright to drive us back to the station?' he asked.

'Of course,' I answered. 'I want to make a start on the interviews. I want to hear what the boyfriend has to say for himself.'

We got into the car and drove past the solemn faces of the uniforms manning the cordon. The downpour had cleared the last of the neighbours away. An old, pastel ice cream van tinkled and chugged its way past us and I pulled out onto Trinity.

I always drove much more carefully when Jim was in the car. Not that he had ever made any comment about my driving, or made any indication that he was checking my mirror-signal-manoeuvres. Jim reminded me of Dad, both stoic and warm-hearted and imposingly tall. My Dad started to teach me to drive three days before my seventeenth birthday. The first time I sat in his driver's seat my feet didn't even reach the pedals.

The traffic wasn't too bad as we drove through Balham.

Bad weather normally pushed people into their cars but maybe they had all decided to stay at home this Sunday. Jim cleared his throat.

'First thoughts?' he said.

'Without stating the bloody obvious, Jim, its definitely an unusual homicide.'

'I want to speak to the boyfriend and the immediate friends and family but it doesn't feel like a domestic. It's too planned.'

He hummed his agreement. I carried on.

'We need to speak to the BIA straight away. And we need the post mortem to be pushed through as quickly as possible.'

Jim carried on nodding but he looked concerned. He turned to me and undid his tie.

'We should probably get a loggist of some kind for the investigation. Something like this normally gets the attention of a senior chief officer. I could live without any bastard admin worries.' he said.

'Of course. I am going to ask Whalley to run the MIR and I'll make sure he assigns one.' I said.

'And we will need to get someone else to look over that Fox case. I can't have you spread too thin.'

Shit.

Jessica Fox. The woman in the hospital bed. I hated the idea of handing over Jessica's case. I hated the idea of telling Jessica and her family that my priorities had changed. I hated the idea of someone else taking over. But I knew it. I had to focus on this. I thought back to the conversation I had had with Derek Fox, about how I had looked into his small earnest face and made him a promise. I hated breaking promises. I needed to tell Derek, and Jessica in person and I needed to make sure that their case was given utmost priority. Christ, maybe someone else at the station could actually find the bastard.

We made slower progress towards Clapham Junction, owing to the stream of traffic bleeding out from the road works on Bellevue Road but I was able to speed up as we turned towards the police station at Lavender Hill. A comfortable silence filled the car as Jim and I chewed over the details in our heads. We would each be compiling our list of questions, motives, the way in which we wanted to question the boyfriend.

I thought about Greta. Her life, her death. I thought about her boyfriend, Blake Walder, sitting in the police station. I gnawed at the knot of skin on the inside of my mouth, where cheek met the lipline. In the way that Sam used to say was sexy. I pushed all thoughts of Sam away.

Could Blake have killed her and made this look like he was the loving boyfriend? The statistics didn't lie about the majority of murder victims being killed by someone they knew. And there was certainly a precedent for theatrics from a killer courting the police, the public, and acting like a grieving partner. There was definitely an air of the theatric in the way Greta's body had been presented. But I didn't think it was Blake. Having never met him, or spoken to him, or having the first person account of how he found her body, I knew even then that he wasn't my man.

We pulled to a standstill at the red on the corner of Northcote and I looked up at the lilac-grey sky, drumming my fingers on the wheel. I wanted to speak to Blake. I just needed to order the chaos of questions first. I needed coffee, then answers.

I always needed answers. Answers for Jessica, answers for Greta, answers for Dad.

When I was eighteen, someone ran over my Dad and left him for dead. I found him at the roadside, tried to resuscitate him. I dialled 999 and stood sobbing into the warm summer evening and waited for the ambulance to tell me what I already knew. Someone had run over my father and left him to die at the side of the road like a fucking animal.

I thought about the faces of Isobel and Joachim Maiberger and the face of my Mother. All painted the same ashen shade under the glow of hospital lights. We never found the driver of the car that hit my Father. We buried him and we grieved and we tried our hardest to move on with our lives. I wouldn't let Greta's families questions remain unanswered. Not if it killed me. The red light turned amber and I turned onto Northcote.

The clock on the dashboard glowed a dim orange in the darkness of the winter's evening.

4

Lavender Hill police station stood as a brutalist monolith at the junction of Lavender Hill and Latchmere Road. A monstrous, concrete block casting an angular shadow over the parade of shops. A shivering smoker in a tight dress and a man's blazer stood at the base of the steps leading to the entrance, peeling off fake eyelashes with long red fingernails.

At the reception desk, a thick-necked man signed for his belongings: wallet, phone and a monogrammed, signet ring. He gripped the carnation of charge paper in his left hand. The whites of the reception rooms walls had aged mustard and there was a distinct smell of stale coffee and cleaning products.

Behind the triple-bolted doors at reception and through the starkly-lit corridor, DC Ryan spoke with two uniformed officers in hushed, deep tones. DC Robert Whalley straightened his posture at our approach and smiled. Jim took a right into the gents as Ryan handed me a folder. I opened it and saw it was a summary of the CCTV footage from around the time of the killing. Quick work.

'Thanks, Whalley,' I said, 'Quick. I'll take a look later on but anything stand out?'

'I'm afraid not, ma'am,' he said.

I didn't expect there to be.

'Where is Mr Wallder being kept?' I asked.

Whalley indicated where Blake Wallder was waiting and then led us onto the major incident room. I double checked that the request for a behavioural science analyst had been directed through Opsline and then skimmed through the findings of the

CCTV review. At first glance it looked like Whaley was right, fuck all.

A junior PC sat tapping furiously at her keyboard, peering down at the scribbled notes in front of her. She stopped to turn the sheet over and absent-mindedly readjusted the crucifix necklace around her neck. I wondered if it was a fashion accessory or her communion gift. My own gold crucifix lay in a velvet box in a shoebox somewhere underneath my bed. I couldn't remember the last time I had looked at it. I hadn't worn it since my confirmation.

After Dad died, I packaged up everything belonging to the Church and kept it in a neat box that has travelled with me, only to be stored under my bed at every rented flat. I stopped believing in God that Summer. That drove even more of a wedge between me and Mum because after Dad died the only place she found solace was the church. We both wanted to help each other. We both grieved. But my place of solace was anywhere I could drink and smoke in peace. And after I lost my virginity to a neighbour I didn't care about I found solace in other people's bedrooms. But for Mum it was always the church. And she couldn't operate in my place of solace any more than I could operate in hers.

The typist with the crucifix resumed her typing and I carried on up the corridor.

'Isla, doesn't look like anything on the CCTV?' said Jim.

'No. Ryan was just saying that there wasn't anything. Nothing looked out of place, just a steady stream of cars and vans. Fair amount of ambulances too.' I said.

'And Blake was definitely on Trinity at eleven am?' he asked.

'Definitely.'

I knew that he would be. My intuition told me that his story was true but I resolved to enter the interview room without any biases or preconceptions.

'He's in room one if you're ready Jim?'

Jim downed a glass of water with a wide mouth, wiped his mouth with the back of his hand and nodded. I bit the tip of my tongue, hard. Something I always do before interview. Something about the stimulation made me feel alert, and meant I had plenty of spit to stop my tongue from sticking to the roof of my mouth. I became very conscious of how I sounded on recording the first time it was played back in court. Horrifying.

We walked across the incident room towards room one. It was much quieter in there than I expected. The phone calls wouldn't really pile up until after the local news that evening and the officers involved in the witness identification strategy session were off completing the preliminaries. Jim and I agreed that with the boyfriend being the only significant witness, we both needed to be present in the room.

'You up for starting the questions?' I asked.

'I am indeed.'

In interview room one, Blake Wallder stared blankly at a white plastic cup. His eyes were puffy. His thoughts lost in the murky swill of his vending machine coffee.

'Mr Wallder?'

The heavy door latched closed behind us.

'I'm DCI Jim Greaves, this is DCI Isla Fletcher.'

'So, you're the guys in charge?'

'We are that.' said Jim, immediately turning up the volume on his Yorkshire accent.

I loved how quickly Jim could make people warm to him just by firing up his accent. He made people warm to him, open up to him. It was a powerful way to disarm them before he asked the shock questions. Jim pulled no punches. With his team, his suspects. He took a seat across from Blake and continued.

'Just to explain that to you a bit more formally Mr

Wallder, I'm the Senior Investigating Officer, or SIO as most people will call me.'

'DCI Fletcher here is the Deputy SIO and between us we will head up the homicide investigation. Our team will catch whoever 'as done this, I can assure you.'

He motioned for me to sit, and I pulled out the chair. The screech of metal chair legs cut to every cold corner of the room.

'I know you have given my colleagues quite a lot of information but we wanted to double-check some details with you. I know it's been a difficult time. And this isn't, by any stretch, an interrogation.'

The hunched man sniffed and nodded, he spoke with a cracked voice.

'Of course, anything you need to know.'

His face seemed earnest, eager to please, broken. His grey sweatshirt was deeply creased with damp patches smeared at the sleeve. The cuticles on both thumbs looked raw and a bloodied tissue sat next to his coffee. He seemed believable. But I didn't want to be biased. There was every possibility that this guy had killed Greta. We had to rule him out, and if it wasn't him, we had to ask the questions that would help us to find our man. My man who killed Greta.

I'd always been able to tell when someone was lying, even as a girl. At university I thought it might have been eye movements, micro movements in the facial muscles, but I'd since come to accept it as something a little deeper. Female intuition, my ex called it. Not something I would utter out loud. I could not let the world know that I believed even a small amount of that kind of bullshit.

I couldn't imagine how it must feel sitting in Blake Wallder's seat. How it must have felt to open the door to his girlfriend's home and find her dead, mutilated, decorated.

I had found the body of my father, someone I loved, but to find the body like that.

Jim announced the interview into the recorder and folded his hands over the closed file of papers on the desk in front of us.

'Tell me what happened. Talk to me about this morning.'

Blake sniffed and nodded. Staring at the file, half glazed. The room smelled of his sweat.

'I was supposed to meet Jee, Greta I mean, at ten. By half ten she hadn't shown up, or answered my calls. I thought I'd just go around and see if she was OK. I got on the 155 at Clapham Common and walked from the bus stop outside DuCane Court.'

'So that was at ten fifty according to the initial report, correct?' Jim asked.

He nodded. He had definitely been asked these questions earlier, his answers sounded practised.

'And how long did it take you to walk there?' Jim asked.

'About ten minutes or so, I walk really quickly but I kept trying her on my phone.'

'So you get to her road at 11:05?' Jim asked.

Blake nodded and continued.

'I pressed the buzzer a couple of times. I knocked on the front door too, just in case the buzzer broke. When I didn't get an answer I thought I'd just try myself.'

He gathered up the bloody tissue from the table and dropped it into the empty coffee cup.

'And did you often let yourself in to Greta's flat?' asked Jim.

Blake's posture straightened. He hadn't been asked that yet. He shook his head quickly.

'No. Not often. I mean, I don't know. I guess I knew something must have been wrong. I've never known her to not answer her phone.' he answered.

'How many times would you say you had let yourself in

before?' Jim continued, 'How long have you had a set of keys?'

'Only twice or so before. I had the keys when we were friends, just in case anything went wrong or she locked herself out of the flat again. She didn't mind me having them. We spoke about it when everything became official, I asked if she wanted them back.'

'Official?' I asked. Making sure the recording was perfectly clear.

'Yes. When we started going out properly.'

Jim stopped pressing and asked for more of his story.

'So, when you entered the main entrance to the house did you notice anything unusual? Did you gather any post from the welcome mat?'

'No. I didn't see anything, I don't think.'

I made a note. With the neighbours abroad it was something to verify in their statement.

'How long had you known Greta?'

'About a year or so, maybe a bit longer.'

'And how long had you been seeing each other romantically?'

'About three months or so. It's complicated because she hadn't really officially broken up with Max when we got together.'

'Who is Max?' I asked.

'Max Greenfield. Her ex-boyfriend. He moved over here to be with her, which made it more difficult for her to break it off with him. She hated hurting him, hurting anyone.'

'And what does Max do? Where does he live?' I asked.

'He's an architect. Lives in Oval. Or he did at least. Greta said he was going to move to East London after they broke up.'

'So,' I clarified. 'You were friends with Greta while she was dating Max Greenfield and you and her started dating before she and him broke up?'

Blake nodded.

'But she wasn't like that. She hated hurting him. We just fell in love I guess.'

I don't know how quickly I bought that. Greta might just have wanted to fuck someone else. It had only been a few months.

'How did Max react to seeing you both together so soon after the break up?' said Jim.

'I honestly couldn't tell you. I only met the guy once when they were going out, and after they broke up I didn't want to pry. Not really my place I guess. But I do know he called her a few times, drunk.'

I made a note. Max was definitely next on our list. This kind of killing didn't seem to be the action of a wronged ex. It was too clinical, too planned. It wasn't a scream of rage or a cry for reconciliation, it was something much scarier than that. But I did want to speak to the man who moved his life over to London for Greta only to be rejected. If anything, he could tell me more about the kind of person Greta was, who she used to hang out with, where she might have met the man who killed her.

'Did Greta tell you that he called her when he was drunk?' I asked.

'No, I was there when he called. She answered the bloody phone every time, even at one in the morning. I could hear the music of a club or something in the background so know he must have been pissed. But they spoke in German so I couldn't tell you what they said. Didn't last long in any case.'

'Did it annoy you when she answered his calls?' I asked.

'No.'

Well that was a lie.

'Really? If it were me, I'd be pretty pissed off.' I said.

'Well, maybe a bit. Look. I felt sorry for the guy. She

wasn't happy with him. He knew it.'

'Aside from Mr Greenfield can you think of anyone who might have had any issues with Greta? Or anyone who might have taken a shine to her?' Jim said.

Blake shook his head slowly. Eyes locked upwards, suspending a sheen of tears between raw rims. Jim looked down briefly at an image in the interview aide. He took a moment and then changed direction. I could see that he was approaching it with sensitivity.

'Is there anyone who might have had any reason to buy her flowers? Any cause for celebration?' asked Jim.

Blake raised his left eyebrow a fraction and flattened his lips into a narrow line. Shaking his head.

'No. Her birthday is in April.'

'No promotion? No recent success?' I offered.

Blake shook his head more vigorously.

'And you didn't buy her flowers? Or know her to buy them for herself?' asked Jim.

'No. She liked wine more than flowers. Champagne.'

'So for clarity, you hadn't bought her any flowers recently?' asked Jim.

'No.' Blake's eyes narrowed, 'Why, do you think Max had?'

Jim opened his hands, showing his palms.

'No not at all, Mr Wallder. We are just clearing up the details.'

'You think whoever did that to her bought them?'

Blake's face became more animated, 'You think that sick fuck bought her fucking flowers?'

'Mr Wallder, we really can't say. It would just be speculation at this point. But if you didn't buy them for her and she wasn't prone to buying them for herself then we need to look at how they ended up where they did.'

I thought back to the hair fanned out on the carpet. The woven stems and the thick cut in her scalp. Blake must have thought back too. His eyes creased and he slumped over the table. He wiped a string of snot from the tip of his nose onto the sleeve of his sweatshirt and straightened up onto the plastic backrest.

'I couldn't even tell you what half of those bloody flowers are.' he said.

I believed him.

He tried to drink from the plastic cup and screwed his face up at the bloody tissue.

'Let us get you a new cuppa, Mr Wallder. And some new tissues.'

Jim opened the door a fraction and asked PC Parish to bring in fresh coffees. Blake sat with his hand together on the table, almost as if they were handcuffed. I fought the instinct to take his hand but not the need to reassure him. I was more confident that he hadn't killed her and felt sorry for the guy.

'Do you have anyone coming to collect you, Mr Wallder?'

He blinked slowly and looked at me, nodding.

Through the crack in the door I could hear muted noises from the reception desk. It was unusual to hear any voices through the heavy-set doors, someone was screaming.

From the depth of the station it was difficult to make out the words but they were definitely the coarse screams of a man. I asked Ryan to keep an eye on the witness and moved quickly to the first set of security doors. The desk officer was stood placating a tall, thin man with rimless glasses. When the man saw me through the second security door he raised his voice.

'Is he here?', he shouted, then louder, 'Have you got him?'

Whalley rushed over to me and addressed the question clearly painted on my face.

'Max Greenfield, Ma'am.'

I closed the door behind me and moved to the front desk.

I spoke clearly, 'Mr Greenfield, this outburst really isn't going to help us, or you.'

He stared at me. I continued.

'We will get you signed in and then we will come and talk to you. We are doing everything we can. We have a process. And we do want to speak to you.'

Max shook his head, and slumped his shoulders.

'He did it. I know it,' he looked away, '*Du Hurensohn*.'

I noticed Chris, the crime scene photographer, standing in the corridor, staring. Not at the commotion, but at me. He didn't shift his gaze when I noticed him. I considered reprimanding him but I did not have time for his shit. I looked at the clock over his shoulder, then glared back at him to drive home the point: he would not intimidate me.

Max was talking at a more controlled volume as he filled in the forms, he offered out an apology for losing his temper. He spoke English in a clipped, grammatically-German way. He looked very different to Blake, taller and leaner. Artistic-looking. But Blake was definitely the more attractive man. That must have stung. But I couldn't conceive of a scenario where cheating would lead to that degree of violence. But then, I couldn't conceive of any scenario that would lead to that.

PC Parish helped me to escort Max through to interview room two. I placed a hand on his shoulder and asked if he wanted a water. It was astonishing what a simple act could do for rapport-building. Men seemed to open up to me much more if they thought I was gentle. He smiled at me but declined. He seemed to settle into the chair. I asked Parish to keep him company, stepped out in the hallway carefully; I did not want Max to realise that Blake was across the hallway. That was almost striking distance. I closed the door as carefully as I opened it. The hallway was quiet.

I looked at my watch and considered when best to hand

over my reports on the Jessica Fox case. I wasn't too concerned about speaking to the new DC, or DCI, but I wanted to tell the family myself, and explain that we would still find the person who had assaulted their loved one. I hoped I could convince them more successfully than I could convince myself.

I really wanted to speak to Derek Fox directly. I owed him that much.

Jim was stood quietly at the top end of the corridor, staring at his phone with a pinched, concerned look. He looked up, and upon spotting me, tucked his phone away and pushed through the doors. Jim had been preoccupied recently, wedded to his phone, burdened.

'All ok?' I asked.

He nodded. I didn't believe him.

'Nowt to do with the case. Just that bloody son of mine.'

I smiled as compassionately as I could. I had nothing to contribute. I had no idea what it meant to grow and nurture another human. Jim had three boys, all gaining on him in terms of height and willpower. But they were all good boys, he and Jean had always done right by them and I didn't want to pry into the specifics.

'We've got the ex-boyfriend across the hall. Room four.' I said.

Jim gestured to interview room one.

'I think we are almost done in there?' he said.

I agreed, 'it would be good to get Blake out of here before we speak to this one,' I said.

'Do you think he had anything to do with it?'

'No.'

'Me neither.'

43

'Let's not rule him out entirely. But let him go home.'

I looked at my watch, 'I'm going to need to let Mr Fox know about the case reassignment today, but I don't want Mr Greenfield to have any more time to think.'

'Good shout', Jim agreed, 'Let's go and give him 45 minutes or so to see what he has to say for himself, that should give you time afterwards to speak to Jessica's family?'

Perfect. I cracked the knuckles on my left hand, rolled my neck.

I asked Whalley to wrap up the admin with Blake Wallder and escort him home. It was time to speak to the angry ex-boyfriend. I looked at my watch, noted it was seven p.m. and made a promise to myself to call Derek Fox before nine.

On the other side of the world, at almost the exact opposite corresponding point in Northern Quebec, Cecelia Liszka stepped out of the Arctic ice pattern shift research tent. Her eyes narrowed against the violent, Arctic outflow wind. She was tired. The heat of her third coffee iced in her throat. Her eyes watered cold streams that jerked and traced the shallow path of crow's feet with each gust, bleeding into the edges of her blonde hairline. She was so tired. Ce had drawn the short straw in having to trek out to the observation post but at least the cold air was clean; living with four men in close quarters for four months with a university-issued air filtration system was becoming less and less appealing. Ce missed home. For the first time since accepting the postdoctoral post, the homesickness felt tangible. If it had been any other morning, Ce would have noticed the shift in ice tension and would have almost certainly avoided the cracked ring that opened into the Arctic waters. But, on that particular morning, preoccupied with thoughts of home, she stepped out into the thin ice with her full weight on her front foot. Her body immediately entered cold shock response; respiratory gasp, peripheral vasoconstriction and sympathetically mediated tachycardia. Despite the training, Ce fought to swim, then panicked. Heat escaped from her armpits, groin and chest thirty-two times faster than if she had been on land. Blood loss diverted from her limbs, shutting down all non-urgent organ functions until it felt like all she had left was heart, and head.

Ce lasted four minutes.

5

Max was a talker. It was late when we left the interview room. He told us about Greta's life before they moved to London. The small flat they shared in Munich before her agency moved her to the Shoreditch office. I sat in the MIR and looked over the notes from the interview, his description of her, and the findings from the social media review. Greta was an account manager for a trendy advertising firm and had lived in London for four years. She worked near Liverpool Street, lived in Balham and tended to socialise in Shoreditch, Notting Hill or Chelsea. Her Instagram feed was a series of expensive brunches, rooftop views, filtered selfies. There were recent images of her and Blake but it looked like she had deleted all of the pictures of her and Max. It seemed as though Greta had moved on from Max quite cleanly.

The social media review also identified someone who seemed like a close friend, a woman named Uma Dixon who had been tagged in posts with Greta dating back both relationships, between London and Munich. We had been able to reach Uma through her Facebook page and we made plans to invite her in for an interview. I always found female friends to be a useful resource in understanding the true nature of a woman. Well, I found this to be true for people like Greta and Uma. Women who forged strong relationships with other women; not like me. I'd always been close friends with men. I found the lack of emotions with men to be safer, I liked having friends who didn't need any emotional investment from me. I could just pitch up, chat over a drink and leave. I didn't need to share secrets or go on shopping trips. But I could tell instinctively that Greta told Uma her secrets. She will have definitely told her about cheating on Max with Blake. I wonder if Uma counselled her against it, or whether she encouraged her to leave Max. One of many questions.

Max had not moved on. I looked through his instagram profile: a series of architectural images, sunsets and pictures of Greta. In the interview room he had told us how Greta was strong-minded and ambitious, how she had moved to London six month before he could. He described her great beauty, and wit. He spoke with love. Max knew that she had cheated on him with Blake but did not blame her, he blamed Blake. He hated Blake. I believed that he loved Greta. I couldn't imagine him killing her. But I guess there was a precision to her death that you could ascribe to an architectural mind. There was definitely a structure to the scene.

I wanted to talk this over with the behavioural analyst. I had a tangle of thoughts about the pathology of Greta's killer and wanted to unpick them: Strength, clinical steadiness, artistry. I thought about the network of people who's lives would have overlapped with Greta's and how he found her. How he picked her. Why he killed her.

It was too soon to expect anything through from the coroner's office. I sent out an update to the family liaison officer, scanned over the notes from Whalley's report and remembered that I hadn't phoned Derek Fox. I resolved to calling him first thing in the morning and checked over my emails. i received confirmation that the BIA had been assigned and could expect to meet with him tomorrow.

The MIR was beginning to clear out as people petered out home. I stood, stretched and walked out into the room.

Jim had his coat on and was looking down at his phone again with a concerned look on his face. I put my hand on his forearm,

'You off home?' I said.

47

He nodded.

'Aye, I've got to go and give one of my kids a talking to. You all set here?'

I nodded back. 'I'm going to follow-up on local florists first thing tomorrow. Speak to people from her office,' I said, 'I want to know more about her.'

I decided to leave too. I could smell my armpits and felt the desperate, itching urge to change my underwear. I wanted to find him. I needed to shower and sleep. Or at least try and sleep.

'I've also got the behavioural analyst lined up for tomorrow too.'

Jim pursed his lips.

'Who did we get?' he asked.

'Dylan Nicholson, you know him?' I replied.

Jim shook his head. His phone began to vibrate. He didn't even look at me as turned to leave.

'Night, Fletch.' he said.

It really was too late to call Derek. I wanted to tell him that I couldn't continue with his daughter's case. But I knew that if he was anything like my Dad, he would have been one whiskey down by ten pm and either snoozing on the sofa, or locking up the house for bedtime. Besides, I didn't want to worry them. A late night call on a landline was seldom ever good news. I decided to drive home, sleep, and make the phone call the first priority for tomorrow.

6

I woke early, after a sleep punctuated by frequent, agitated turns to the clock. My bedroom was a mess. I hadn't had a proper clear out since Sam had moved her things out. I'd been dropping laundry in a tower in the corner next to an overflowing laundry basket and recently had to dig around at the very back of my drawers to find clean pants.

I gave up on trying to sleep at 5am and decided to clean. I didn't enjoy cleaning. Something Dad and I always left to Mum, who had a very Catholic pride in the way her house looked. I don't think I ever saw the carriage clock on the mantel piece with any sort of dust on it. My approach to cleaning was a rushed face wipe run over surfaces and pushing discarded socks under the bed, but it felt good to throw in a load of laundry. I rifled through my sparse wardrobe and pulled out a shirt dress and an old pair of boots. I should care more about fashion. Sam cared about fashion. I missed her, and how perfectly curated her wardrobe always looked. I should have apologised. I should apologise.

My phone alarm rang as I was brushing my hair, shaking me out of my regret. I put thoughts of Sam aside and decided to head into the station early. But as I sat on the bed and tied my shoes, I realised that my ability to make that switch so quickly was one of the reasons she had left. I guess she had always respected my job, knew how important it was, but it hurt her how much I prioritised thinking about the job when I was with her. She would catch me staring at my phone, or idling over a small task, chewing on my lip and chewing over the details of a case. It hurt her that I couldn't be present. I made the bed, sprayed on my signature perfume and headed to the car.

The early morning was so cold. I decided to call Derek from the station and started up the car.

I could see that the report from the coroners office was sitting as a flagged email at the top of my inbox. I knew Carl would have prioritised it but hadn't expected to see it so quickly. I opened it up, quickly taking in the key details and realising that there wasn't much that I didn't expect to see. Greta was killed by strangulation and the cut to her scalp carried out post mortem. Fuck, I was grateful to see that confirmed. There was no trace evidence found on the body, and nothing currently from any of the foliage extracted from her hair. I knew there would be nothing from the moment I smelled the bleach in her flat. I was hoping that my man might have gotten carried away and secreted some kind of evidence but, again, there was something so controlled about the incision at her hairline that I knew he wouldn't be. My man was too calm for that. I started to build his profile in my head as I stop-started my way along Balham High Road. I thought about my Man. How he might be.

Calm. Strong. Meticulous.

Dangerous, because I knew he wasn't done.

The police station was not much warmer than my car. I sat in my small office and picked up the phone. Derek picked up the receiver after one ring.

'Mr Fox?' I opened.

'Correct,' he answered, 'and may I ask who is speaking?'

'It's DCI Fletcher. Isla.'

'Oh, Isla, hello.' He voice pitched up with an enthusiasm and hope that made me sick to crush, 'how are you?'

I took a deep breath and got ready to disappoint him. My right hand was clenched in a fist so tight that I could feel each individual fingernail against my palm.

'I'm afraid that I don't have an update for you on the investigation,' I said, getting straight to the point, 'but I wanted to ring you in person for a development on the resourcing here at the station.'

The line went quiet.

'I'm sorry to tell you that I have been reassigned. It is common practice for lead detectives to be moved when a more serious incident presents and I'm afraid that I have been asked to work on another case.'

The line stayed quiet.

'But the good news is, is that Jessica's case will be looked after by a very experienced, very capable DC who I have personally handed over to. Your family liaison officer will be in contact with you to sort out a meeting.'

'Derek, I really am very sorry. I know I made promises to you.'

Before I could continue there was a quiet knock on my office door. I moved the phone to the other side of my face and answered.

'I'm sorry Derek. I really am. I can only tell you that the case I have been reassigned to is a homicide.'

I shouldn't have said that.

The knock rapped again. It was tentative.

'One second.' I spoke to the door.

I placed the receiver back to my ear.

'Derek I want you to still call me if you need me, ok? Use my mobile.'

He cleared his throat.

'I will.'

His platitude made the guilt sting. I lowered my voice, 'I assure you. I will keep linked in with the investigation team. Anything I can do to help, I will. And you have my direct mobile number?'

'Yes. It's all written down 'ere.'

North West accent. Not quite Manchester, not quite home.

'Please use it. And if I don't answer then leave a message. I'll get back to you.'

'Thank you, Isla.'

'You're welcome.'

For nothing. For absolutely nothing. I had nothing else to offer.

Derek Fox hung up and I placed the handset back in the cradle. I felt like shit. It was common practice for the SIO in a homicide to be freed up from existing cases. I trusted the investigation into Jessica's assault would be sound, I trusted Jules, the family liaison officer, to keep me updated and I knew that the handover had been thorough. It was not usual, or bloody professional, to dish out mobile numbers to the parents of victims. But I couldn't help it. I'd promised Derek I would find the man who had done that to his daughter, to his first-born baby, and I hated breaking promises.

There was another tentative knock on the door.

'Come in.'

Patrick Ryan opened the door and extended his head around the thin opening.

'Do you have a moment ma'am?'

'Course. Come in.'

He dropped a printed version of the coroners report on my desk.

'The MIR notice board is set up ma'am. I've assigned a logist too. Did you want a coffee?'

'Thanks, Ryan. Latte if you're going.' I asked. 'Could you

also set up a briefing meeting in meeting room seven with everyone? The one with the whiteboard? Just bang fifteen minutes in everyones calendar every morning. Make it for nine forty-five. Give them time to have their caffeine and get their shit together.'

I handed him the list of attendees that I had drafted at three thirty am.

'Yes ma'am. On it.'

He closed the door behind him.

That gave me an hour to get my own shit together. I needed to show Jim that I was capable of running a homicide investigation as an SIO. To showcase professional development from all the bloody manuals I have been reading these last few years. In a society where there a relatively few unusual homicides, as opposed to say domestic or gang homicides, it was difficult to put theory into practice. I had been preparing for something like this for a long time. I loved reading about unusual homicides, I listened to true crime podcasts, watched documentaries. I kept up to date with changing legislations, I read each manual update as they were published. I needed to design and implement the strategy. I needed to assign additional resources. I needed to show that I was ready.

I messaged Jim and told him about the time of the briefing. I also confirmed that I was happy to lead it and that I'd bring a list of investigative actions with me.

So what did we know? What did we need to know?

The morning light was bright and a thick shaft of sunlight cut through the window onto my desk. It was warm on my left arm. I set out to draft the bullet points that would form the briefing meeting. I would set out each of the strands of the investigation and assign owners. I would build the team.

Physical evidence. Obviously Lester and Carl would keep me updated. There was limited information from the physical evidence this far. But that wasn't to say that ore might kick up from the SOCO teams as they process everything from the house. I would ask Ryan to keep working with SOCO to keep me updated but the physical evidence was firmly on the back burner.

The intelligence network. I wanted to focus on this. We needed more information about Greta. The first real action for me, or Jim, was to meet with Isobel and Joachim, her parents. Lucy Graham was the appointed family liaison officer and I'd asked for her to be in the morning brief, assuming she wasn't still with the family. I wanted to speak to the people closest to Greta. To Uma Dixon, her best friend. I wanted to know her friends, work colleagues, people she lived with in the past, people she slept with. The people who shared her stories. The people she loved. I wanted to build a map of how and where she lived her life, and then zoom in on the past few months. I wanted to figure out how had she met my man. I would let Whalley manage the sub-streams here: house to house enquiries, interviewing peripheral witnesses, ANPR and VOC searches. I didn't want to get stuck in the weeds of information and I trusted Ryan to pluck out the plants for me.

This put even more importance on the profile. We could try and paint a picture of him. I hadn't worked with the behavioural investigative analyst before but had heard good things about him. I'd heard lots of things about him. Back in February, I was providing testimony to a grievous bodily harm case. During a break, I was sat reading my emails on the loo when I overheard two junior solicitors involved in another case talking about the hot BIA. One of them had asked him for drinks. I didn't really give a shit about how he looked but the women had also spoken about his insight, his creativity. I was interested to hear what he had to say.

I wanted to build a team with lots to say. I needed different opinions. I wanted the team to challenge each other, challenge themselves, push each other.

I would ask for more resource. We would need to fan out

the lines of witness interviews and try and chase as much information from Greta's network as possible. I would also make sure that I looked after the people on the team. I knew I had a tendency to focus on the investigation and forget about the management. I needed to remind myself constantly of the impact of an investigation like this on the people around me. There might eventually be hundreds of people who knew the details of how Greta Maiberger was killed, what had happened to her body. I had to be sensitive to how upset it would make them too. We needed regular breaks, ways to switch off, annual leave. All advice I would never take.

I wrote my next bullet point: press release. Sophie Lewes, Head of PR, would be at the briefing and I had some key messages to share in the press release. The news last night had made mention of a woman's body being found in Wandsworth but we needed to give them more details. Some but not all. I felt like my man would be listening to whatever we had to say. I would talk with the room about a media appeal. I didn't want to put any strain on Greta's parents but would test the idea with Jim.

I rolled my head in circles, rolling out the remnants of a bad nights sleep. I was also a huncher. The more I stressed, the closer my shoulders got to my ears. I leaned back on the chair and moved my shoulders back in circles. I wasn't going to lead the morning briefing looking like a stooped old woman.

I glanced at the copy of the ACPO (2005) Guidance on Major Incident Room Standardised Administrative Procedures (MIRSAP) on the shelf. As Jim had said at the crime scene. We didn't want any admin cock up to hold us back at prosecution.

I read down my bullets, prioritising them.

There was an assertive knock on the door.

Ryan stood in the doorway. He placed a large coffee cup on my desk.

'I've got the Behaviour fella.'

It was still early. The behaviour analyst was early. Something that ordinarily would have impressed me but today it just pissed me off. That was definitely a weakness of mine. I hated being interrupted when I was in the middle of a thought process. When I was really in it. I was in it too often for Sam. She hated being dismissed when she interrupted me.

'Great,' I said to Whalley. Forcing a smile and pushing down my irritation. I raised my head and gestured towards the end of the corridor, 'Take him through to the MIR. And get him a drink.'

Ryan nodded and closed the door; I watched the two distorted figures strobe away through the frosted glass. I pushed my hair back with my left hand and leant back onto the desk and picked up my pen. I had written a clear set of investigative actions. It was nine forty. Just enough time for a quick hello with the behaviour guy before the morning briefing.

I took two mindful, belly-breaths in and stood up, stretching out the knots in my spine from hunching over a desk. I took three large gulps of the latte and headed out. The air in the corridor felt stuffy from the overzealous heating system. It was either fire or ice in the bloody station.

As I stepped into the hallway my phone vibrated in my pocket. I stopped to check it and saw it was Mum. I sent her to voicemail without a second thought. I didn't have enough patience to speak to her.

I sensed footfall behind me and turned as Chris stood next to me. Not close enough to touch, but close enough that I could feel the air compressed between us. I heard his lips unstick as he opened his mouth to speak but the door to the MIR opened and three uniforms filed out. Chris closed his mouth and walked away quickly.

The door to the meeting incident room stood open in front of me and I could make out the shapes of the information on the whiteboard. Lines of correlation webbing out in red from the blown-up picture of Greta in the centre. A picture given to us by her family of when she was alive. A beaming, happy woman. There was also a picture of the top of her corpse. Of the flowers. A pretty, grim reminder of our purpose.

I glanced at the blurred CCTV images of her boyfriend, Blake Wallder, on Trinity Road and her ex, Max Greenfield, on Wandsworth Common. Notes and images from the coroner now held up with small magnets. Characteristics and case notes scribbled up in blue ink. An attempt to make sense of the chaos.

I moved close to the board and looked at the second picture. Of her face. The pale, peaceful face beneath the gash. The images that Chris had captured at the crime scene. The pastel halo of curls. The flowers. The image itself wasn't without beauty. It reminded me of a print I had hanging in my room at university. A woman draped in white cloth, illustrated with an art nouveau wreath of flowers in her hair. Thinking about it, I'd seen something similar last year in Chris's bedroom. I winced at the thought of him inside me and swallowed a mouthful of coffee too quickly.

'DCI Fletcher?'

I turned to greet a broad, blonde man who shook my hand with a firm grip and smiled, 'I'm Dylan Nicholson. Nice to meet you.'

I swallowed against the dry burn of the coffee.

'You too.' I said, 'I'm planning on running a morning briefing at 945. I'll outline where we are, what we need to do and then I'll introduce you. Do you need anything before we start?'

He smiled again and shook his head. He removed his racing-green jumper and placed it over one of the plastic chairs set out at the periphery of the room. His shirt underneath was freshly ironed and expensive. The material was thick with fragrance. He held in his hand the terms of reference I had drafted, including the revised NDA. I had made it expressly clear that all information disclosure needed to be signed off by me, or Jim. I'd annotated the report with how best to integrate the profiling into the strategy. He was prepared.

In the briefing, I wanted him to talk over the motivational factors and offender background characteristics. I knew that no one became this kind of weird overnight. Perhaps most importantly, I wanted him to talk about the potential series identification. I knew that Jim wasn't with me, but I felt in my stomach that my Man wasn't done. Greta had been, in horrifying terms, a success for him. I knew he would want that high again.

I looked at Dylan and the notes in his hand and I knew there was more to come.

'Before we go into the briefing,' I said. 'Could I ask that we sign the terms of reference document? I'm keeping a close eye on the admin here.'

I motioned to an empty desk space and we both sat. I pulled out two pens from a desk tidy and handed him one. We sat side by side, close enough that I could feel the heat of his thigh next to mine. He skimmed over the revised document, my amendments tracked in red. He furrowed his brow intermittently, squinted his eyes occasionally, but didn't take umbrage with any of my suggestions.

He flicked back to the first page and turned to me. We both signed the document, stood, and I handed the file to Ryan.

I suppose he was handsome.

'I'll walk with you to the briefing. I'm going to give a quick update of where we are and assign action owners.'

'I'll introduce you to the team, if you could give us a quick five-minute overview of your initial thoughts. Give us your steer on the interview and the profiling. I want to get to questions pretty quickly though.'

'Understood,' he said.

We walked to meeting room eleven. It was the largest meeting room in the station and had floor to ceiling glass windows. Sophie, Lester and Lucy sat at the table while Ryan leant over setting up a conference call.

I opened the door as Lucy was mid-sentence.

'—sedate her.'

I closed the door behind us.

'Is that her Mum?' I asked.

Lucy nodded.

'Yes,' she said. 'She has been sedated. Her Dad is near catatonic without drugs.'

I imagined Carl would be dialling in, along with some of the SOCOs. Jim was sat at a desk in the MIR, looking at his phone with that concerned look again. It was nine forty six and I hated running late. Isobel and Joachim needed answers.

(EVE)

At that precise moment, at Suva private hospital, Fiji, Tu'uakitau Caucaunibuca died from what would eventually be categorised as perioperative mortality. The surgeons who removed his tumour three weeks earlier had not flagged Tu'uakitau as being high risk, given his age and general health conditions. Tu, however, had lied about smoking and the increased blood pressure contributed to the hemorrhagic stroke that killed him, aged nineteen, in the waiting room of the post-operative wing. Death came as a dropped, heavy curtain and in his final moment he stared blankly at the football scores on the television screen, forgetting himself in an instant.

Twelve seconds later, Aminata Coulibaly was struck by a machete blade, Aminata was part of a small village living on the outskirts of Sikasso in Mali. Her death was almost as instant as Tu'ukakitau's. She died quietly on the floor as her blood strobed out and soaked into the dust. She did not see the militia men running towards the other villagers.

Death did not come quietly for Kagiso Govender. Kaggie who died face-down in the yellowed grass of a nature reserve on the outskirts of Plettenberg Bay, South Africa. She struggled for air through short, panicked breaths, dusting the inside of her mouth with dry topsoil. The venom from the Eastern Green Mamba continued to course through her body as the pain from the bite throbbed at her swollen calf. The fire of envenomation had spread quickly, stoked by panic and adrenaline as she ran and stumbled towards the edge of the reserve, and the *hope* of her car. The camera had thudded painfully against her sternum as she'd sprinted and lurched over the uneven footpath. The paralysis in her leg eventually stalled her after eighteen minutes and she sat sobbing and resigned. Roaring cries for help. Pain from the growing muscle damage. After twenty-seven minutes, the convulsions began. Respiratory paralysis eventually extinguished her life forty-two minutes after the bite. She died eye-level with a line of double-waisted ants.

7

I was always interested in offender profiling. Something that went back to my third-year forensic psychology module. My lecturer once tried to warn me off a career in forensics. She had judged that I was a young woman and decided that I would one day want children and so she felt honour-bound to warn me off a career in forensics. I remember sitting in her square office as she warned me about what would happen after I had kids, 'you know, when everything changes'. She had quit her own job profiling serial sex offenders after interviewing one paedophile too many. But I knew even then that I couldn't have kids, even if I wanted them, which I didn't. Never had.

But I'd also figured out really early that stating that so bluntly to mothers felt like kicking them where it hurt. Sam hadn't wanted kids either. Something else we agreed on. Not now, Isla.

I finished the grainy drops of coffee and placed the cup down purposefully on the catering trolley. My throat was dry from talking through each bullet point. The meeting room quietened. I sat down next to Ryan, pushing the white board pens from the centre of the table towards Dylan, inviting him to stand.

'Lucy, Sophie, you don't need to be here for this. You've got plenty to be getting on with.'

The women smiled, stood and left the room quietly.

'This is Dylan Nicholson, our behavioural investigative analyst. Dylan is going to talk us over our initial offender profile.' I looked around the room.

'Don't be afraid to ask questions.'

Dylan brushed his hands over the creases on his trousers and blew out his cheeks. He picked up a blue whiteboard marker and scribbled out three words: consistency, sex, now.

He cleared his throat, 'Right. Initial overview. As requested,' He bowed his head in my direction, then turned to the team, 'Consistency. This guy isn't normal, well, normal as we perceive it. Let's focus on what normal might mean for him. What routine he needs to operate. What elements he needs to be consistent.'

'This will help us to build an understanding of what kind of person he is. What he might look like physically and what kind of behaviours he might display. You all know instinctively that we are probably looking at a white male, between 25 and 40 but how else can we narrow that down?'

The room murmured. I glanced over the faces. Not everyone agreed with profiling. I liked how the approach to profiling in the UK focussed on the theory, a regard shared by scant few of my colleagues. The majority of detectives favoured the FBI approach based on tangible police evidence. Not even the research reports could validate it for the doubters.

'We might not know what he looks like facially,' he continued, 'but we know that he must be physically quite a strong guy. If she was bathed after death, arranged. That takes strength.'

'But that doesn't necessarily mean tall,' I interjected.

Dylan nodded, 'And it doesn't mean we are looking for a muscle-man either. But he will be strong. He will be very mentally strong too. Very controlled and measured. We can assume this took a great deal of planning, and we know he took his time.'

Carl spoke up on the phone.

'From her time of death, he also had plenty of time with her after she died.' he said.

'We also know that there was no semen, no sexual interaction. So he is emotionally strong too. He has self control.' He looked back to his three words on the white board and continued, 'But I'll get onto that'.

He tapped on the first word on the whiteboard with his knuckle, 'First. Consistency. If we go down the line of theory that Canter proposes, that of criminal consistency, then how he treated the victim might well play out in his real life. The area, the house, the victim even will be familiar to him. He will have watched her, he may well have even been into her house before. That's not to say she knew him, but he definitely knew her.'

He continued and I thought about the scope of the interview strategy. We needed to speak to more people. I had a list of people I needed to speak to from her office, and her best friend. Greta's keeper of secrets.

'The consistency plays out in his behaviour too. He will, almost certainly be aggressive to women. All women. Try and get a woman in the room whenever you interview anyone new and see how they act. He will also be incredibly neat. It goes back to control. I'd bet clean shaven, well-presented. He is smart too. He might even work in the medical profession based on the confidence used in the incision.'

Whalley looked up from his notes. 'So, you mean interviewing staff at St George's?'

Dylan nodded emphatically.

'Surely, not a doctor?' said Jim.

'Probably not.' said Dylan. 'But let's not rule it out.'

'So looking at all medical staff, then. Plus maybe admins and cleaner?' said Whalley.

'Well, we don't need to go that broad this quickly. We can definitely find ways to narrow this down?' I said.

'Absolutely, but broader than that, remember he had almost certainly been to her flat before. Or at the least, her building. He wants spatial consistency. Somewhere to feel comfortable in. Somewhere, in this case, to work in. And on that note, I'm confident in saying he works locally too. So, St George's fits the bill. But so do local offices, cafes, the driving range on Trinity. Freelancers. He knows the area. What forms her routine? How did he find her?'

He began to lose the collective interest in stating the bloody obvious and tapped his knuckle against the second word: sex.

'What has turned him on here?'

I spoke up, 'The power, the control, and...' I realised as I thought out loud, 'not necessarily her.'

Dylan tilted his head, 'Really? You don't think he found her sexually attractive?'

'No, I'm not saying that. But, as you said, there were no signs of sexual assault, no secretions at the crime scene.'

He pointed at me with the pen in his hand, 'Precisely. So when is he getting off? Where is he getting off?'

Whalley offered an answer, 'Afterwards? Maybe he takes photos?'

'Yes. Or some kind of token. The release comes afterwards, after he has made the perfect scene. His own perfect sort of pornography.'

The thought of the killer masturbating made me feel uneasy. My mind leapt and I thought about Dylan masturbating. That made me feel uneasier still.

Dylan continued, 'This is a man with very specific sexual needs. He is very controlled. He took his time with her but didn't have sex with her, either during or after death. He has discipline. A method,' he drew an arrow from the word sex and wrote: power. He turned back to the team, 'It's the power. That's sexually charged too.'

'He clearly revelled in wielding the power. The power

of taking her life, of making her how he wanted her to be. I wouldn't be surprised to find him in a job without power. A menial role in his mind. Something beneath him.' he said.

I agreed. But I knew my man was a clever bastard. I stood up.

'But smart, remember that,' I added, 'he will have an above average IQ but almost certainly struggled at school. I'd be surprised if ended up with qualifications past GCSE.'

Dylan, who was nodding along, scribbled on the white board: childhood.

'This is a tricky one,' he said, 'as I don't think this kind of mutilation would have been practised. It's so specific that the victim, the muse, needed to be perfect. But he will definitely be in our system, either as a victim of childhood abuse, or as demonstrating violent tendencies from an early age.'

I agreed. But there was one point that wasn't digesting. 'You mention that you think he could be aggressive to women. But there were no signs of rape here?'

'No, but I think this is absolutely a rape fantasy. A sexual motive.'

'There were no signs of sexual assault, or bodily fluids.'

'But, she was tied up, was she not?'

I thought about the delicate bindings at her ankles. The care taken in packaging her up. It felt too gentle to be sexual. Not innocent, by any stretch, but respectful. He had packaged her up as the perfect gift to himself.

'Yes. She was tied up. With parcel twine. It was all post mortem. Before he decorated her.'

'But the ideology is there. It's all present. The ritualistic tying up. Perhaps the fantasy comes afterwards. Or in the planning.'

I'd recently read a report that dispelled the myth that all serial offenders were sexually motivated and something didn't sit right for me. I also knew that calling out a serial offender at this stage was premature. But I knew it, even then. I knew he my man wasn't finished.

'I think we absolutely need to consider a sexual motive, like,' I struggled to remember the name, 'that guy over in Kansas. He strangled his victims and then masturbated into an article of their clothing.'

I could see revulsion on faces. Dylan clearly disagreed.

'And until we have a full inventory,' he said, 'we don't know if any items of clothing have been stolen.'

'But,' I turned to face the team, 'am I the only one who thinks this is more than that?'

Whalley and Ryan nodded. I carried on, 'There may be other psychological factors to consider.'

Behind me, Dylan had branched out a spider diagram with sex at the centre. At the end of each arrow he had written: visionary, mission-oriented, hedonistic and power. He turned back to us and held his hand open.

'Broadly, this kind of motive falls into one or more of these,' he listed them out on his fingers, 'Is it a visionary thing? Has he been demon-mandated to kill? Does he hear the voice of God?'

Next finger.

'Or, has he had instructions from a bigger power, the Government? Has he made the world a better place by killing Greta Maiberger? Was killing her the mission?'

Third finger.

'Hedonist? I'm not sure. Does this feel like lust? It will have been a thrill, but in isolation was the act an act of pleasure?'

Last finger.

'Control.'

He rapped the pen against the photograph of Greta, 'This

took a great deal of control, every single element of this was his design. His intention.'

'And how does this fit with the decoration?' I asked.

'Well, it's further exertion of control. Making her perfect, making her his vision. The perfect sexual object.'

'Agreed.' I said, and quickly added, 'About the control I mean.'

I still wasn't convinced about the sex, but I wasn't going to bicker with the guy in front of my team, so I continued. 'And I think we are dealing with someone very methodic, calm, quiet.'

He kept his gaze on me but tapped his knuckle on the final word: now.

He spoke loudly, 'What do we need to do, right now, to catch him. How do we get him?'

Before we jumped into the timeline, and the lead generation chat I wanted to spit out the gristle that I couldn't swallow,

'I also want us to think about the possibility of a serial offender, we have to consider the possibility that he might need to kill again.'

Dylan's mouth turned down in a frown but he nodded his head. 'We do need to consider that. But my instincts are telling me that this is a very specific crime. A very specific victim.'

'I disagree,' I stood up from the desk I had perched on.

I was going to go on when I noticed PC Davies hurrying towards me through the MIR. I asked Whalley and Ryan to talk over search parameters and interview strategies and for now that was a good use of time. I could always argue with Dylan away from the team.

I stood out, and closed the meeting room door behind me.

Davies, the chubby red-headed guy from the crime scene, pushed past Whalley and thrust a manilla folder towards me.

Beads of sweat glistened on his pallid upper lip and his cheeks looked flushed as he addressed me.

'We just got a download of the images from the victim's phone, ma'am.' he said.

He turned and shook his head at another uniformed officer, Richards. Richard raised his eyebrows and made a smiling gesture at his watch. The download from the phone had taken a long time and he was obviously embarrassed by the delay. Or embarrassed by what he found on the phone.

I opened the folder and flicked through the images. Nothing surprising. Filtered uploads of London skylines, expensive meals and artisan cocktails, a series of failed, pouting selfies that never made the public gaze of instagram. The last set of images were of Blake, of Greta and Blake together. Kissing.

I stopped at the image with a post it sticker next to it. A grey, grainy still with a small video icon on the lower right corner. A bare shoulder, a bare bed. Greta's open mouth over a balled hand, stooped over a lean, male, abdomen. I didn't need to see the video to know what it was. I recognised a blow job. I closed the file abruptly and held it against my chest. I looked up and realised that Dylan was looking directly at me, he looked interested.

Dylan had brown-black eyes that camouflaged the pupil. I smiled at him and he reflected the same smile back at me. The mirroring of facial expressions natural to those who know how to build rapport. I had no idea if it was genuine. He looked away and carried on talking to the team and I opened the file again at the first image. A beaming family in walking boots stood proudly in front of rolling fells; broad strokes of green countryside, weaving stone walls and a remote out building sitting underneath the grey jagged shadow of a mountain. If it wasn't the Lake District, it was somewhere similar. It reminded me of home. My childhood home. I thought back to a similar picture I had tacked to the inner door of my wardrobe. Me, Mum and Dad the day we walked Scar Fell Pike. The summer that Dad died.

The summer I found him in a tangled, bloody mess at the roadside. The first time I saw Mum cry.

My phone vibrated in my pocket again. I answered.

'Isla, it's Mum.'

'Oh hi. Everything ok?'

'Oh yes, love. Everything is great. I just haven't heard from you in a while.'

I rolled my eyes. In a move I felt certain she could feel over the phone. We always fell so quickly into this routine

'Sorry, Mum. It's been really busy.'

'Oh I know, I know. Are you ok though?'

No Mum. The girlfriend, the one that I never told you about, has left me. I haven't been laid in over a month. I fucked up my last case and right now I'm looking at the corpse of a woman. I've seen her skull.

'Yes,' I lied.

'I wanted to ask you about Christmas, dear.'

'Oh yes,' I said. And struggled to find an excuse quickly enough.

'Listen Mum,' I started, 'I don't know my shift pattern so I can't say for sure.'

'No problem,' she answered, 'you take a look at your calendar and let me know. I'll cook lamb if you come.'

'Great,' I said, deciding not to remind her again that I don't eat lamb.

'I'll let you know. And I'll give you a call later this week, I'm just between meetings now.'

'Of course,' she said. 'I'll let you get back to it.'

8

Laughter echoed in from the outside corridor. A faceless uniform with his back to me, Davies and Chris Jeffries stood outside of the incident room. I recognised the shape of Chris through the glass frame, I knew his stature and the bray of his cocky laugh. I couldn't believe I had ever let him touch me.

I'd met Chris in one of the bars in Clapham Junction. He introduced himself as a photographer and we fucked; an average and experimental affair that only lasted for a couple of weeks. I liked how he went down on me the first night we slept together; I hated his political views and how he refused to shop anywhere but the Whole Foods on the high street. One morning over breakfast he made a shitty remark about immigration and I knew I'd had my fill. Of his expensive bread and his cheap opinions. So I stopped responding to his messages. Cowardly, perhaps, but effective. I never had cause to think I would see him again until he turned up at one of the first crime scenes I attended in CID. I somehow managed to avoid him in the lead up to my promotion and when he turned to greet me that morning I hadn't seen him in a year. By that point, I was already seeing Sam and I sensed immediately he was sore about it. In that obvious way he tried to catch my eye when no one else was looking. I shouldn't have played along when he introduced himself, I should have just called him out on it. But instead, I enabled his charade and introduced myself right on back to him. Acted my arse off. Now every time I saw him I felt more and more annoyed at myself for letting him sweat on me.

I left the room and stood directly behind Chris. Davies shuffled to a silence.

'Are you finished up here, Chris?'

'Oh, yes,' He flinched and his shoulders hunched, I had startled him. Good.

'Sorry, Isla, didn't see you there.'

I glared at him, 'Have you downloaded all of your images?'

He nodded eagerly, and looked sideways at Davies, 'By the sounds of it, my pictures aren't the only points of interest?'

His smirk was thinly veiled. Davies flushed and shifted his weight. I lifted my head and took a step closer to him, 'No, that's not accurate. A video of interest, not a picture."

Chris smiled at me and zipped up his coat. Jim was striding towards me. Chris crossed Jim's path in his haste to leave, but Jim looked right through him to me.

'Isla, have you seen that video?'

I nodded. Davies looked sheepish and he bloody should have. It was deeply unprofessional and bloody sexist to laugh about a sex act.

Jim carried on, 'It wasn't recorded on her phone. Downloaded automatically from a Whatspp message apparently.'

So someone sent it to her.

Blackmail?

'Do we know who sent it?' I asked.

Jim shook his head, 'Well. It wasn't the boyfriend'

'How do you know?'

'I've just come from the office. I checked the mobile number he gave us.'

'Might be his work phone?' I asked.

'Not sure a roofer is a blackberry type. But worth checking.'

'In either case,' I said, 'we need him in again. Davies, can you sort that out for tomorrow?'

Davies carried his embarrassment away and I walked with Jim to the kitchen.

Jim stopped, 'we have to assume that this wasn't the boyfriend she was doing that to,' he said, 'and we should work on the assumption that he's not seen the video.'

'You think she cheated on him?' he asked.

'I don't know'. I answered, honestly. 'I haven't spoken to her friends yet. I can't speak to her character.'

'If the boyfriend saw this, he'd be pretty pissed off right?'

I nodded. But.

'Have to be honest, Jim. I don't think this means he did it.' I replied.

'Me neither. But If I saw my missus doing that to another bloke, I wouldn't be happy.'

'Yes. You'd be angry. But that's not what we are dealing with here. This wasn't rage. Plus we don't know when the video was recorded. It doesn't mean she cheated.'

Jim made himself a herbal tea and sipped it gently. I followed suit and made a raspberry tea that tasted as disappointing as I expected. We stood in silence for a moment, drinking the hot drinks in small, loud sips.

Jim set his cup down on the worktop, 'What did you make of Nicholson? Seems a bit up himself.'

'I don't know. We are going to roll out the interviews to St George's. And I want to speak to her ex-flatmates when they get in tomorrow. We definitely need to speak to Wallder about this video. Either way we need to see his reaction.'

I thought back to the crumpled man we had interviewed, to his snotty tissues and broken attempts to hold back tears. He definitely loved her, and I'd ruled him out almost immediately after we had spoken to him.

'I almost hope the poor bastard hasn't seen it.'

Lucy crossed the kitchen, and stepped backwards after

spotting us.

'Are you off to her parents?' asked Jim.

'Yes. They're still not completely with it. I said I'd drop over to their house and chat to them there.'

I nodded and we both continued drinking.

Ryan walked into the kitchen.

'We identified the number from the message. The video was sent to Greta on the 11th October by Max Greenfield. It was sent when Greta was at a client event up in Leicester. Some trade show called Food Fiesta she was working on for one of her clients. A vegan street food company called Wild Grace.'

'Thanks, Ryan. Was there any conversation around the picture being sent?'

'No, ma'am. It was a single message exchange. Looks like the chat was dormant since then. But it does look like there was a long conversation between Greta and Max after it was sent. They were talking from eleven forty-five to half past midnight.'

I looked at Jim. That changed things. In our initial chat with Max he had told us that he hadn't seen Greta since 5th October when they met for a coffee on Northcote Road.

My next step was speaking to Max. Max who got a blow job and filmed it. Max who lied to us.

9

I took Ryan to interview Max at his office, an architectural practice in Waterloo called Driver and Bridge. Ryan drove us into the City and parked up behind the row of pubs on the River. The sky was cloudless and it was bloody freezing. My dry eyes watered from the wind coming off the river.

The architect's office was clean to the point of being clinical. Floor to ceiling windows and bright white furniture. Parquet wood was laid out in thick blocks and an expensive atomiser steamed out the smell of lemongrass. Even the people working behind vast mac screens looked curated: tailored shirts and designer glasses.

Max met us from the lift and walked us through the open plan floor to his office. The office was mostly wood, with an expensive reclining chair in one corner. A series of cacti were arranged on his desk and he had a clear, stunning view of the London eye, Houses of Parliament and the Thames. The river glittered brown under the morning sun.

'What a view,' I said.

Max didn't turn his chair to look at it. He simply nodded once, then invited us to sit across from him with a steady hand gesture.

I sat.

'We are here to talk to you about content we found on Greta's phone,' I said. Cutting out the pleasantries.

His face remained calm.

'Of course,' he said, 'what do you need to know?'

'How often would you say you text her?' I asked.

'Not that often. Perhaps once a week.' he answered.

'Was that after you broke up?' I asked.

'Yes.' he answered. Then wondered what I meant.

'I mean,' he continued, 'I still considered her to be a friend. I wanted to keep in contact.'

He seemed to believe that.

'And can you confirm that the last time you spoke to her was on the 5th October?'

'Yes.'

'And this was at the Flourish and Co coffee house on Northcote Road?'

'Correct.'

'And you hadn't spoken to her since?'

He paused and shook his head.

'So you didn't send her any videos?'

His eyes widened.

'What kind of video?'

I feigned ignorance.

'Any kind I suppose. Any memes or funny Youtube vids?' I asked.

Max relaxed.

'No, never.' he answered.

'Any links to instagram? Snapchat videos?' I asked.

'No.' he answered.

Max looked too relaxed.

'So, no videos of a sexual nature?' I asked.

He clasped his hands together. He didn't answer.

'Can you confirm your mobile number to us?' I asked.

He didn't answer.

'Well, Mr Greenfield I don't need you to answer. Because we know your telephone number and we know that you spoke to Greta on 11th October. After you sent her a video message.'

I opened the folder in front of me, a folder which didn't contain the images, just some typed interview notes. I raised my eyebrow and looked at Max. He definitely sent it.

'You see, Mr Greenfield, we are concerned by a video of sexual nature sent to the victim a week before she was killed. It appears to show Greta and an unidentified male. And we are trying to identify both the man and the person who sent it to her.'

Max's shoulders dropped, along with his gaze. He finally answered.

'I did.'

'Sorry,' I kept on, 'you did what?'

'Send it.'

'Send what?'

'A video.'

'You sent Greta a video file?'

A pause.

'Yes'

'When did you send it?'

'A couple of weeks ago.'

'And why did you send it?'

'I don't know.'

Liar.

'And who filmed the video?"

'I did.'

'Can you please confirm the content of the video?'

He looked pale and the words stuck together in his lips. Adrenaline had kicked in. I ramped it up.

'Mr Greenfield, can you please outline the precise nature of the video that you sent to Greta?

'It was,' he stumbled for a formal way to phrase it, 'oral sex.'

'Oral sex performed on whom?'

'On me.'

'And why did you send it?'

'I don't know, honestly,' he started to shake, then whispered, '*ich weiss es nicht.*'

'Can you tell us when the video was filmed?'

He scratched his face.

'About a month ago.'

'And when did you and Greta end your relationship?'

'About eight months ago.'

'Was she in a relationship with Blake Wallder when the video was filmed?'

He gulped, nodded.

'Was the incident a one-off?'

He paused. Rubbed his face.

'No.'

'Had you been involved in an affair with Greta?'

'No.'

'But you had been sleeping with her?'

'No.'

'Just oral sex?'

'No.'

'Sorry Max. I feel like I'm missing something,' I said placing both hands on his table, 'I guess I'm getting old.'

'We kissed.'

'You kissed?'

'Yes.'

'On how many occasions?'

He looked up, to the left.

'Three times.'

'And on which of those occasions did the oral sex occur?'

He took a deep breath. Looked down.

'None of them.'

'So, truthfully, when was the video filmed?' I was getting annoyed.

His eyes welled. The muscle of his chin trembled. His eyes darted to the office of people.

'When we were together.'

Ryan nodded.

'Had Greta consented to being filmed?' asked Ryan.

Max nodded his head vigourously. It was a good question, but we would have no way of finding that out anyway. What mattered is that he had sent it. Revenge porn was classified as a sexual offence under the Criminal Justice and Courts Act 2015.

'Mr Greenfield. To be clear, you filmed the video when you were together, right. So why did you send it to her after you had broken up?' I asked.

'I don't—'

'I think you do know.'

'To make her remember?' he offered. He was getting flustered. Rosy.

'Really?' I interjected, 'because to me it seems like you sent it to frighten her.'

His eyes widened.

'No...'

'And if not to frighten her, then to embarrass her. To bully her. To blackmail her?'

'No.' He stood up and in doing so the chair wheeled back

and banged into the window.

He scared himself at the volume of his own assertion.

He composed himself.

'I was drunk when I sent it. I would never.'

'Never what?'

'Want to scare her. I loved her,' he bowed his head and rubbed out the tears, 'I wanted her back.'

I sensed that the movements of the open plan office had slowed. People were typing, walking, speaking in very obvious movements to try and disguise their interest in our conversation.

'Did you share this video anywhere else?' Ryan asked.

'No,' said Max. 'I swear.'

I believed him. I didn't believe his motive for sending it. I think he did want to frighten her, but there was no way to prove that either.

'So can you confirm what was said on the call on the 11th October?'

'Yes.' he said, 'although I really was quite drunk. She said that it wasn't fair of me to send it to her. She was pissed off with me. She said that she thought we could have been friends but that the video made her doubt that.'

'I didn't want to lose her from my life completely. I promised to delete it.'

'And did she say anything else? Anything about where she was at the time?' I said.

Max shook his head and then remembered something.

'Yes, actually.' His eyes narrowed as he focussed on the memory, 'she said that she'd had a shit day and that this was the last thing she needed. One of her clients had made a pass at her at some food event. Made her feel weird. She said that she'd emailed her boss to get the account reassigned elsewhere.'

'Can you remember the name of the client?' I asked.

'Yes. It was one of the brothers who own the Wild Grace company.'

Ryan and I looked at each other. We knew that was enough from Max.

'Thank you Mr Greenfield.' I said. 'One of my colleagues will be in contact with you to make an appointment for an official statement.'

I stood and pulled my coat on.

'And I recommend that you tell the truth in that interview.'

Max flushed a deeper pale of pink and gritted his teeth. The muscles on his jaw stood out pronounced.

'Of course.' he said.

He remained seated and made no motion to show us out of his office. Ryan and I walked out through the open plan office and didn't say anything until we got into the lift. As the door closed I wagered that every single person in that office was looking at us.

'Do you think that's everything from him, ma'am?' asked Ryan.

'Yes.' I said.

'But I'm interested to know more about this Wild Grace company. Have you got the notes on them here?'

We walked out onto the cobbled street. Old red-bricked warehouses stood tall. I noticed an artisan coffee cart on the street corner and ushered Ryan towards it.

'What are you having?'

'Oh, a black americano please ma'am. Thanks very much.'

I placed the order. Ryan took out his note pad.

'Wild Grace has been an account for the Sister Marketing Agency since 2008. They started as a cafe in Bethnal Green serving vegan food but then made a market in meat alternatives. Pretty hipster brand. Lots of swearing in their adverts.'

'And the brother that Max mentioned?' I asked.

'Yes. It's owned by Lee and Stephen Grace. Lee is the older one, married with three kids living in Dulwich but based in the food production head quarters in Clerkenwell. Stephen is single and lives in Hackney.' he said.

'And were they both at the food show?'

'That I don't know I'm afraid. I'll look into it now.'

That was the next step. I just wanted to know which way we needed to turn when we crossed the River into North London. Whether we needed to turn West into Clerkenwell or East into Hackney.

I was also eager to speak to the people that Greta worked with. I needed to make an appointment for the team at Sister, the marketing agency where she worked in Shoreditch. I wanted to get a sense of Greta from the people who spent the most time with her. It might have been that she met my man through one of her clients. He might have been one of her clients.

Max might have been an arsehole but I didn't believe that he killed Greta. I didn't believe Blake did either. I knew procedures needed to be followed but I felt anxious. Where did my man meet her? How did he select her? I needed to speak to the people who knew Greta, to get a feel for how she lived. Before speaking to either of the Grace brothers I would start with her work. The people who she spent most of her life with.

That was a depressing truth. That the majority of your adult life is spent with people you don't know, people you don't choose, people you might not even bloody like. At least eight hours a day with perfect strangers. But proximity meant patterns. The team at the agency would know Greta's patterns, maybe even her social patterns too. They'd know how she took her tea, how she reacted under pressure.

It was still cold by the river. My eyes watered against the sharp breeze. The agency where Greta worked was only twenty minutes away in Shoreditch.

Ryan and I drank our coffees as we walked towards his car. He called back to the MIR to try and find out more about the Grace brothers and I checked through my emails. Nothing from Jim yet on his conversations with Greta's parents.

Dylan Nicholson had sent over his preliminary report. I flagged it to read in the car. There were no other emails of note. Nothing more from the SOCOs yet. And no messages from Sam. Part of me had been expecting her to call or message, to forgive me. But nothing. If I wanted to see her I would really need to grovel.

I deleted the spam emails and then scrolled left to read over the latest news headlines.

An earthquake in Asia had killed thousands. A boy beaten to death in Liverpool. An elderly woman found dead by her neighbours. I also saw an advert for the Picturehouse cinema offering a free bottle of wine with the latest premier. A slasher thriller of some kind.

So many deaths in the world. People died every minute. And yet my focus was on Greta, on this single, isolated death. I imagined the faces of Joachim and Isobel Maiberger and I didn't care if I only focussed on one death. One dead woman. Their dead daughter. I would find the answers for them.

Eighty-three year old Hugo Sosa lay in a near-coma state in his family home in Cordoba, Argentina. His breath still tasted of cigar smoke. He snatched at glimpses of his final resting place - the bedroom he had shared with his wife for fifteen years - as he drifted in and out of consciousness.

Chronic obstructive pulmonary disorder had worn down both his bronchial tubes and his spirits for close to two years. There was a pressure on his chest that increased as he fought to draw breath through the decaying tubes. Air croaked over his voice box whenever he mumbled declarations of love to Rosa. He wearily turned his head between the loved ones at his bedside as they tried to decipher the codes of his dying words. But Hugo knew that when his eyes fixed on Rosa, she could see the thoughts that formed and caught behind his mask. He had loved her and would love her always. This was the over-riding emotion. Love.

The moments of his life flickered like a taupe slide show. In conscious moments he saw piles of dog-eared war novels stacked on the old mahogany shelves, the battered antique chair that had acted as mannequin for his old work suit and the scattered photographs that had gradually yellowed behind their frames. In the darkness behind each blink he saw vivid memories of his life; golden shining days with beer, music, and kisses. Torn bread and handshakes. Battered blankets on brown grass. With the final effort to draw open his lids he knew it did not matter now and he fixed on Rosa. The once treacle tendrils of her hair had greyed and now hung loosely above him, occasionally tickling his brow. She had sat at his bedside since his return from the hospital; fetching drugs, broth and water, but had only these past hours climbed under the down duvet. He smiled at her and died. In peace. Loved.

It was only in serene moments like these that Eve remembered herself. A helpless, voiceless prisoner trapped in that final moment of life. It was only such a drawn-out opportunity, courtesy of Hugo, that she had the time to remember. To remember that she had been. That she too had fought and feared. And drank and blinked.

She could feel Hugo because she *was* Hugo; and Hazel, and Clea, and Reggie and a thousand other souls ending a thousand different lifetimes for Christ knows how many years. It felt like thousands of years in the moments where reflection was possible; but between those aching moments of *self* lay alien and terrifying glimpses; pain, terror, screams. Some over too quickly to even understand.

But right now, here she was. Feeling the warm tears falling onto Hugo's face, tracing them down the wrinkles that years of cigar smoking had deepened. She could feel the warmth that he felt for Rosa, understand the words that caught and rasped in his throat. There was no frustration, no rage. She had felt this calmness before and knew the serenity that stemmed from knowing that those words had been said before. There was no urgency in that last breath.

Eve could feel the weight of the goose-down duvet. She could taste the sandstorm breath that rose and fell in his weakened lungs. She felt the final beat of his heart. And when Hugo died, she had a fraction of a second - or whatever measure of time she operated in now - to indulge in her own emotion and she wished that every single moment could be like this. Without fear or anger and with the simple understanding that they were loved.

More than anything, Eve wished that her own death had been like this.

10

It was unclear which brother had been in attendance at the food event so Ryan and I decided to head straight to the agency where Greta worked. The office was just off Bishopsgate, where new, shining towers stood vulgar between old churches and pubs. Her colleagues spoke of her in bold, colourful terms: her ambition, her ability to work with even the most difficult clients, her vision, her creativity. They all displayed the 'correct' level of grief, and invited me to a memorial service they were holding for her. But none of them could offer up any ideas on why someone would want to hurt her. No one had seen her in the week before her death, because she had been on annual leave. I felt like no one in that vast space really knew Greta on any real level. Their admiration seemed so limited to her professional persona. Their grief felt commercial, almost superficial; scripted by their team of in-house copy writers. I knew that if I wanted to understand her in real terms I needed to speak to the people who knew her in real life, the people she confided in. I asked the team at the MIR to arrange a meeting with Uma Dixon. She lived in Clapham Common and I could head there on my way home if the timings lined up.

I sent Ryan to the nearest Pret and loitered on the corner of Bishopsgate and the pedestrianised road down to Spitalfields Market. Crowds of suits had started to filter out from their tall buildings; all walking at the same, above-average speed with the same look of efficiency. I took out my phone and leaned onto the wall of a church courtyard and saw that Dylan had emailed again. He was following up on his earlier report to make sure I had received it, and was keen to know my thoughts.

I messaged back quickly.

'Yes. I looked over in the car but I'm on the road so not able to reply properly. I'll give you a call with any questions later this evening.'

I accidentally put a kiss at the end of the email and then deleted it.

I noticed from the church notice board that it was a catholic church and made a note to bring Mum here next time she visited. It made her happy to see churches in the chaos of City life. Although the older she got the less she visited. The train journey from the Lake District felt too long for her and her appetite for London crowds had never been that strong.

Ryan crossed the busy road holding two baguettes under his arm and a can of fizzy water in each hand. He handed me one and set his down on the church wall.

'I've heard back on the Grace brothers.' he said.

I tore off a huge mouthful of the tuna baguette and spoke over the dry chunk.

'Go on,' I said. I spat a good chunk on tuna out onto my sleeve and laughed. Ryan laughed too.

'My Mum always did tell me not to speak with my mouth open.'

I finished my mouthful in exaggerated chews.

'Right. Go on.'

'Both brothers were in attendance at the event. It was a street food festival for new product releases, mostly wholesale vendors and chefs. The older brother, Lee was there for the morning session but according to the executive assistant, he left the event at midday to make it back for his son's football trial in the afternoon. The younger brother, Stephen was there all day and had a hotel booked in town.'

'The executive assistant told us that Stephen had put through some expenses for the night which looked like a four person dinner, plus drinks back at the hotel bar. I've asked the guys back at the station to get onto the hotel and let us know if any records of that dinner and if there is any CCTV.'

That settled it for us. Bethnal Green it was, and to the younger brother.

In the short drive through East London I called Jim to update him on progress. He had been fielding the questions from the senior management; it was so rare to encounter an unusual homicide like this that there was a very real political interest in finding my man as soon as fucking possible. Jim had also been keeping in contact with the FLO and Greta's parents. They were still in a subdued state of grief, more in disbelief. Lucy was a very sympathetic and caring woman who I had worked with as FLO on a domestic homicide case a year ago and I knew that the Maibergers were in good hands.

Jim was just as interested as me in what Stephen Grace had to say for himself and said that he would give the Sister agency a follow-up call directly to see if anyone else had received advances from him.

It did not take long to drive from Shoreditch to Bethnal Green. We parked on Roman Road, near to the Buddhist Temple and walked to the Wild Grace delicatessen which had been the birthplace for their growing brand. The woman behind the counter had a septum piercing and the music played out in loud, synthetic beats.

I pulled out my identification and placed in on the counter in front of her.

'DCI Isla Fletcher. Could we speak to Stephen Grace please?'

It took her a moment to appreciate that we weren't ordering food or drink. I suspected this was the first time she'd had any sort of interaction with the police. She wiped her hands on the apron and looked a little flustered.

'Yes. I'll go and get him.'

She rushed to the man grinding coffee beans at the end of the deli counter.

'Can you watch the till for a sec?'

She navigated the high tables and bar stools at the centre of the deli and through a door at the rear of the building. It took four minutes for her to return with Stephen Grace.

He strode over to me confidently and shook my hand with a firm grip, following suit with Ryan. He had a tight white t'shirt, a long ginger beard and two impressively full tattoo sleeves.

'Is everything ok?' he said, in a reasonably open way.

'Is there somewhere that we could talk more privately?' I asked.

He seemed taken aback, looking around the deli for a quiet corner.

'Perhaps upstairs?' I offered.

'Sure.' he said, and turned.

We filed up a narrow and steep staircase into a large office space. The rooms were painted dark grey and bold images of the deli, their advertising campaigns and music gigs were hung in vast expensive frames. A speaker system was set up and playing the same house music as downstairs in the deli. Stephen Grace pointed to a large, steel coffee machine and asked if we wanted anything. I declined.

'We are here to ask you about the food show that you attended a few weeks ago.' I said.

'OK.' he said, frowning with bemusement.

'More specifically about a woman you met there called Greta Maiberger.'

His frown deepened. I laid it out.

'I'm afraid to have to tell you Mr Grace that we found Greta's body on Sunday. She has been killed.'

'What?' he said, turning to steady himself on a chair. He sat down. 'Fuck me. I was only emailing her last week. What happened?'

He looked visibly shook. His skin had paled grey against the copper of his beard.

'I can't tell you the specifics but I can tell you that she was murdered. And that's why we are here.'

The grey reddened.

'Huh? What?' he said.

'We wanted to ask you about the food show. About your relationship with Greta and the dinner that you attended on the Friday night.'

'I didn't have a relationship with Greta.' he protested, 'she was my account manager. I knew her through work but nothing socially.'

'Until that night', said Ryan.

'Well, yes. Until that night. She was there with us, and another food and drinks client she had, some gin company I think. But I asked her to come for dinner with me and an old uni mate Ollie. It was a nice night. He brought a woman from his company called Lois.'

'Mr Grace, we wanted to check if you made any sort of advance on Greta that night. We know that you paid the bill at ten forty-five but could you tell us how the night wrapped up?'

He blinked quickly and held his hands out.

'Look, I was shit-faced. I did think she was hot, and I said as much. But she said she had a fella so I didn't push it. Truth be told I ended up shagging that bird Lois. She stayed with me in the hotel and we went out for brunch the next day before I drove back here.'

'And what was her surname?' asked Ryan.

Stephen blew out his breath.

'I honestly couldn't tell you. But I can quickly message

Ollie and ask him?'

'That won't be necessary,' I said. 'we can find that out and check all of these details with her.'

Stephen nodded his head.

'OK. The whole event was run by a company called Lush Green Events. So they'd have a list of all the delegates if you did need it.'

Ryan made a note.

'And can I ask you what you were up to last weekend?' I said.

Stephen paused and then answered confidently.

'I was in Paris all weekend. From Thursday until Tuesday. Went there with a group of mates for the horse racing. Stayed at the George Cinc.'

I knew that hotel from a weekend away with Sam. Not that we could afford to stay there, bloody expensive as it is, but we had gone for a cocktail in the bar after walking from the Louvre to the Champs D'Elyse. The vegan food market must have been doing ok.

'Not a typical activity for a vegan that, is it? Horse racing?' I asked.

'Oh, I not a vegan.' he laughed. 'Lee, my brother is. But it's not for me. I love my meat too much.'

Ryan finished his notes and then closed his notebook.

I didn't see the point of lingering with Stephen Grace any longer. We could fact check his story with this Lois woman, and the George Cinc. I instinctively didn't think that he was in-volved, I mean, I didn't like the guy but that didn't mean he was capable of murder. It was quarter to four and I figured that if we made good time back across the River then we could go and interview Uma Dixon before heading back to Lavender Hill.

'Thank you for your time Mr Grace,' I said. 'We can show ourselves out.'

'Not a problem,' he said, reaching into his wallet and handing over his business card. 'Give me a shout if you have any other questions.'

The card was black with his telephone number and the business card on one side and 'Veg*n as f*ck' on the other side. Good to see he really lived his brand values.

We managed to miss the traffic in the City but we waded into school traffic and the hot breath of buses around Stockwell. Ryan kept focussed on the road and I managed my emails. I rang Jim but couldn't get through so I wrote him a quick status update in case I missed him at the station.

As I was drafting it, I declined a call from Derek Fox. I felt bloody awful for doing it but I needed to get my thoughts down on paper and I didn't want to have to explain the conversation to Ryan. I really shouldn't have given him my mobile number. I added him to the list of people I needed to call when I got home. First Dylan, then Derek. I would need to eat at some point too. I'd only eaten that dry tuna baguette all day. I really should stop existing on the caffeine and full fat milk.

I pressed send on my email to Jim then messaged Dylan and Derek in turn.

Dylan responded quickly, 'No problem and no need to apologise for the delay. Let's chat when you're free. I'm around all night.'

By the time we got to Clapham I had missed the time window that Uma Dixon had given us. I made a note to put her on the network list and would rearrange for tomorrow. I still wanted to speak to her, Greta's parents. I'd also looked over her Facebook page and made note of a few regular interactions. I'd add them to my list.

I thought about the list of people I had interviewed for Jessica, too. How I built a geometrical design in my head of who she was. How the perspectives of each person had added an angle, a line, a connection. I remembered speaking to Derek, how he idolised his daughter. But Derek wasn't my concern right now.

I needed to focus on Joachim and Isobel, the people who made Greta. I thought about them taking the pregnancy test, announcing her birth. It made me sick to think of their grief.

I needed to speak to Joachim and Isobel parents directly. But as this point it made sense for Jim to own that relationship and for me to meet through him. I didn't want them to have to deal with an audience of police officers. When Dad died I remember the theatre of police who turned up and remember how disorienting it felt. To feel so watched as I cried.

Truthfully, I didn't want to tell them about the blow job. I was happy for Jim and the FLO to talk to them in such stark terms about their daughter's sex life. Having a God-fearing mother made me feel very uncomfortable talking about sex to any older parent. Like I was going to accidentally scream out that I enjoyed having sex with men and women, like it was a dirty secret. I guess Sam felt like that. I did keep her a secret.

I wanted to speak to Isobel and Joachim when I had something to tell them, they didn't need my empty promises.

I scanned the list of Facebook friends and asked Ryan to prioritise booking time in with them.

I thought about who might be on that list if I died. Who would people need to speak to paint a picture of me. Colleagues, ex-school mates, family, Sam. There was only one person who truly knew me, Sam. And no one else in my life knew about her.

We finally pulled into the car park at Lavender Hill at half past five. I'd been on shift since seven thirty and decided to just head straight home. I would eat, read the report from Dylan and then sleep.

11

I stood next to my car, fishing around in my handbag for my car keys. The evening sky was now rose-quartz grey. I noticed the throb of eager shoppers heading towards Northcote Road and considered my options for food. And drink. Cold nights always made me crave the warmth of a heavy bottle of red. I wondered whether the shoppers were preparing for Christmas and considered my options; being alone in my flat or just feeling lonely back in the Lakes with Mum.

A voice spoke at me through my thoughts.

'Do you think it's time we talked about stuff?'

Chris was stood three strides behind me. I hadn't see his smug face since he stood laughing over the image of Greta.

'You know what? No,' I held my keys tightly, I had little patience for the prick standing between me and home. 'I have nothing to say to you. But if you make any joke at the expense of a dead woman again, I will definitely have something to say.'

'I didn't make any joke,' he almost whispered. His expression seemed earnest. He carried on, 'You might want to speak to people in your team about jokes.'

He seemed to make a motion to reach out to me, then thought better of it.

'I've missed you, Issy.'

I folded my arms in front of me, tucking my cold fingers underneath the thick crease of the wool coat. It wasn't a nickname anyone but Chris had called me. It wasn't even a nickname. I knew obvious disdain played out on my face but I was too tired to entertain a conversation.

'Are you being serious?' I said.

The grit of the carpark floor crunched beneath him as he inched towards me.

'We could maybe go for a drink or something? I really don't like it being weird.'

'Look. This is not weird. It's ridiculous,' I stepped around him and opened my car door, I flung my rucksack into the footwell of the back seat and turned back to him, 'We slept together for a month almost two years ago.'

He lowered his voice and placed his hand on my hip.

'I think you and I both know it was a bit more than that.'

'It wasn't. We fucked,' I looked down at his hand and he dropped it to his side. He took a step closer, I could smell bourbon on him. That was new. And bloody early, it wasn't even six.

'We could again?' he whispered.

'Wait, we could what?' I said.

He clenched his jaw and I could sense his breathing was heavy.

'Fuck.' he said. Moving his face closer to mine.

I placed a hand on the car and stepped closer to him, knowing the collar of my jacket would be grazing against his chest.

'Go home. And don't talk to me about this again. If you can't respect me, I can always arrange for you to be moved.'

I stood defiant as he tested the conviction on my face. He took two over-exaggerated strides backwards and then walked away in heavy footfalls, the metal heel of his designer boots clicking on the cold ground. I watched him step over the railing at the periphery before I got into my car, I jammed the keys into the ignition then placed my head down onto hands which didn't feel like mine. The adrenaline throbbed in my empty stomach and I worried that I might dry heave. I gripped the hard steering wheel. My heart was racing.

I made a frozen berry protein shake in lieu of any fresh food in the house. I drank it standing next to the sink but felt too tired to read the report. The adrenaline from my conversation with Chris was still agitating in my bloodstream and I still felt light headed after a hot shower. I ran my wrists under the cold faucet, wiped the steam from the mirrored cabinet and stared into my haunted reflection. I couldn't remember the last time I had slept undisturbed for a full night. It was probably before Sam moved her stuff out. I splashed cold water on my face then turned off the tap. I padded to the unmade bed but couldn't face sleeping. I wasn't tired.

I wanted to see Sam. I really wanted to see her. I was ready to apologise.

I pulled on the cleanest shirt I could find and applied a coat of mascara in the hallway mirror. Mostly to draw attention from the circles under my eyes. I rolled on deodorant, screwed on the cap and threw it into the mess of my handbag. I pulled on the camel coat Sam loved me in and grabbed my keys.

On the drive to her flat, mundane chat murmured out from the late night radio. The short news report spoke of more death, an earthquake in Bali, another gang stabbing. The streets were bleak under the orange glow of the street lights. The mile-long journey would have taken twice as long in the day but I pulled up four doors away from Sam's before I had time to figure out what the hell I was going to say. I remembered how she had looked at me the last time we argued. I remembered how the last thing I'd said to her had tasted. Acidic and bitter.

'Stop acting like such a fucking lesbian.'

At that point, the fight had fallen out of her, she'd quietly gathered up her bags and closed the door softly behind her as she left. I hadn't said a word. I just stared at the floor, chewing the knot of skin on the inside corner of my lip. I hated losing my temper but once the rage descended I couldn't stop myself. I could barely think through anger. The full weight of the words hit me the next morning when I woke, shivering in the darkness of four am. But even then, I couldn't face calling her. I couldn't face texting her. And I hadn't quite figured out what to say in the five weeks since; she hadn't contacted me either.

I really wanted her to be at home.

I pressed the buzzer for the first floor flat and stared up at the lamp glow at the bedroom. She might have left her light on and gone out. Shit, she might even be sleeping somewhere else.

Her voice cracked at the intercom. I answered.

'It's me.'

A heavy silence filled two long seconds and then the door buzzed open with a thick click, I heard the sound of her front door being unlocked and placed on the latch. The strip-lighting in the hallway light blinked on as I made my way up the shallow flight of stairs.

I opened the door carefully to stop Colonel from escaping but he hadn't come to greet me at the door either. He sat in the doorway of the bathroom, judging me quietly with his yellow eyes. Sam stood in the kitchen, leaning against the countertop in pyjamas. I laid my handbag quietly onto the hallway floor and stared at her. I still couldn't bring myself to say anything.

The kettle behind her shook as it steamed out. She turned and filled two mugs with hot water. I walked behind her and placed my hands either side of her narrow hips on the cold surface, tipping my head down and resting my lips on the exposed skin on her shoulder blade. The smell of mint steamed up from the tea.

'I'm so sorry.'

Her left hand moved from the red mug and covered my own. She moved her head a fraction to the left and I could smell the marshmallow fragrance of her night cream.

'I'm so sorry, Sam.'

She turned around to face me and straightened up, her shoulders standing slightly above mine. Her long neck craned down, her gaze looking past me, to the tiles.

'Isla, we can't go though this again.'

I leaned forward to look up into her green, freckled eyes.

'I promise. We won't have to. I'll try. I'm a dick.'

She clenched her jaw and avoided my gaze.

'It's Moroccan tea. But I've got wine...'

'Tea is perfect.'

I stepped to one side and grabbed a teaspoon from the drainer. I stirred the translucent, green liquid and fished out the dripping teabags, ushering them into the swing-bin. I carried both mugs through into the small studio lounge. Her macbook shone a blue glow in the corner and white fairy lights twinkled above a huge mirror on the wall. The bed was crisp with white linen, with an inviting mass of soft pillows. She always made a room feel like home. I placed the mugs on the industrial drum she used as a coffee table and sat in the wingback chair where she devoured books.

She stood over me, staring out through the sash window into the street. A motorcycle revved aggressively and roared away. Her hair had grown. It grazed the sharp line of her collarbone; white blonde in the dim light. She tucked the front section behind her ear, peppered with rose gold studs, then moved her finger tips to her lips. She clamped her thumbnail between her upper and lower rows of teeth and took a deep breath. Wanting to say something but stopping herself. She looked thinner too. The curve of her spine looked more obvious, her long abdomen looked leaner. I missed seeing her naked. She turned and faced me, her huge eyes heavy, and sad. The orange light of the street softened the sharp edges of her frame; the thin ridge of her shoulder and the angular curve of her hip. The grey, broad waistband lay flat against her taut stomach and the thin white material of her vest hung loosely from thin halter-neck straps. I reached out and stroked the outside of her hand. I took hold of the little finger on her left hand.

'Can we just sit? And not talk about it?'

She took a deep breath and blinked slowly. She bit her lower lip, nodded and perched on the arm of the chair. I placed my hand on her thigh and stroked the cotton material with my thumb.

I figured honesty was the best option, 'I missed you.'

She touched my face for a brief moment, then placed her hand over mine. Nothing.

I went with honest again, 'I'm so sorry.'

'You look tired, Isla. Have you been sleeping?'

She turned her body towards me. I reached around her narrow waist and pulled her slowly onto my thigh. She drew her knees up and draped her feet over the other arm of the chair, nestling her head into the nook of my neck. Her hair smelled like lavender. We sat in silence, listening to the noise of the street.

The collage of framed images on the main wall of her studio flat had changed too. More landscape photography. A huge black and white image of a vast, still lake. Hills, trees and the kind of isolated house you only got miles outside of London. Sam had such a good eye for photography. From directing the frame of the lens to knowing where to hang the final image. The new print was definitely from the Lakes, where we had both grown up. She must have gone home in the time we'd been apart. We had lived ten miles apart from each other for nineteen years but never met. it was something we laughed about, bewildered, the night we were introduced. The night we stood inches from each other, but not quite touching, in the noisy crush of a Soho bar.

Sam took a deep breath.

'I haven't forgiven you,' she said.

She sat back, looking at me sternly. I nodded. I knew. Sam wasn't the first woman I was attracted to, or the first one I had taken to bed. But she was the first one I'd loved.

'There's no excuse here Sam. I am really sorry.'

'But?'

'But nothing.'

She readjusted herself. She had told her parents she was gay when she was twelve. They hadn't reacted in any way of note, simply told her they loved her, and carried on eating their picnic.

'You can trust your friends, Isla. You can trust Jim. You really can.'

I hadn't told anyone. Because, I'd argued, I wasn't. You know, gay. I had been with men and women, and it didn't seem like it was worth the hassle of labelling it. The relationship I had with Mum was strained enough without having to explain my sexual preferences. I might not always agree with Mum but she was all I had left. Besides, I always figured I'd end up in some God-pleasing marriage, and then all of her heartache and disappointment about me fucking women would have all have been for nothing.

'You have to realise that we work in really different places.' I said.

'Come on! I've interviewed police before. It's not as bad as you make out.'

'Maybe. But our families are very fucking different.'

She smiled. Exposing the gap between her front teeth.

'Not really.'

'Oh really? Remember the Christmas card.'

At Christmas, Sam had received a handmade card from her parents. Her Mum, Lauren, had been on a crafts making course in the Summer. The resultant home-made card remained pinned to the wall: 'To my daughter and her girlfriend at Christmas'.

'Well it's not like I got a card from Isaac,' she argued.

'I know, and I know it's hard. But he is still your brother. It is different.'

Sam had a very strained relationship with her brother. Nothing stemming from homophobia, more born of that friction that arises when one sibling moves away from home. The more time that passes, the more they forget about what they mean to each other. Childhood bonds are quickly forgotten when a parent falls sick. Or if one child has to foot the Mothers Day lunch bill too often. Frictions over responsibility, money, experience; they all mounted. Neither one of them spoke about it, but then again they never really spoke to each other about anything. Their parents acted as a conduit for information between them as they didn't even send birthday cards any more. I knew it hurt Sam, given how close they were growing up but I also knew she was didn't forgive easily. My relationship with my family was very different. I wasn't sure if just one person constituted a family: my relationship with my Mother was very different. After Dad died, she found solace in the Church. I was jealous I suppose, of how much it helped her. Of how each event, mass, prayer seemed to ease her pain. And as much as Dad's death strengthened her faith, it completely destroyed mine. I had never been devout but I always held hope. A hope that died with him, on the bloodied road.

With religion came judgement. Not against me. Not that Mum knew she was being judgemental against me, at least, but in voicing her opinions on marriage, both heterosexual and homosexual, and contraception it became clear to me that I could never really be me. Never share the sides of myself that needed to be sated by sex: sex with men, sex with women, sex with myself.

'But, Sam, I'm still not sure you understand. How much I would love to be able to tell people. Mum's God would never allow it.'

Sam knew all this, of course. She once attended the Carol services arranged by my Mum. Something else we couldn't believe on that night we first met. How closely our lives had come to touching before.

Sam's bond with her parents made it impossible to understand the dynamics between me, Mum and Mum's beliefs. It was one of the reasons we had argued five weeks ago.

'But I'm still not sure it's an excuse. We went to church too growing up, Isla.'

She kissed me briefly with a closed mouth. I hugged her tightly and felt the closest thing to content since I was assigned to Jessica. I felt exhausted. Physically and emotionally wrecked. I pressed a kiss into her hair and squeezed the hard muscle of her thigh.

'Can we sleep? I really am tired.'

She placed her fingertips on my face, pushing a tangle of curls away from my face. She kissed me again, lips open. I pushed up to kiss her back but she held her hand against my sternum.

'Just sleep.'

We slept fully clothed. She lay curled on one side, warm. I draped my arm over the boney jut of her hip and kissed a good-night onto the cool skin of her neck. I pressed the side of my face against her back, using her heartbeat as a metronome for the beat of my breathing.

I woke four hours later, from a dream I hadn't had in

years. In it, I drifted without physical form, up the familiar winding road that led away from the village towards our house. Dappled light tumbled through the broad leaves overhead. As with all dreams, I couldn't hear the noises of the memory, but I knew they played out in my subconscious; midges, birds, the distant roadworks and the rustle of the wind kicking out at leaves. I remembered the sounds of that day so clearly in waking and sleeping moments. And I'd never forgotten the smell of my own vomit on the hooded sweatshirt.

In the dream I was innocent. I had never felt pain. I was naive. I smiled dumbly at the sky, watching the dusted beads of pollen pass through the sunlight. Without movement, but instantly, the sky turned dark and I was over the broken body of my father, staring at the unnatural angle of his spine; the broken hand that tucked beneath his chest and the shard of bone that jutted out at his knee. I hovered, ethereal, over the body as the pool of red, viscous liquid seeped out in strobes. The edges of the dream shrinking as the blood pulsed out, until all I could see and feel was me, looking at him, suspended in the timeless-black void. My mind held me over Dad's body, as it had countless times before, but this time, Dad lurched suddenly from the shoulder and began to turn in jerking, terrifying movements. Bones creaking and breaking, a deep, low moan playing out from the pierced holes of his punctured lungs. His ribs jutted out like fingers from his chest. Violent, loud cracks vibrated out in dream-tangible waves as he turned onto his back and each bone realigned. I knew the sound of each vertebrae stacking as his neck straightened and remained impotent to stop it. His eyelids opened suddenly, and I must have flinched in my sleep since Sam began to stroke the hand draped over her tummy.

But still, I slept, and watched the dead body of my Dad.

I lowered, suspended only inches from the angular corpse, knowing the smell of red wine and decay lingering on his lips. This time, as his eyes focussed, he was no longer just Dad. The skull in front of me had the face of Dad, but at the very same time it also had the stubbled face of Blake Wallder, the sorrow-grey faces of Greta's parents, and the gentle composure of Derek Fox. When the image finally settled as Derek the flesh began to soften and melt away from his bones. I could feel the reassurance of a voice elsewhere in my mind reminding me that it was simply a dream but I could also feel the fear sticking the bed sheets to my skin.

Derek opened Dad's mouth with such force that his jaw crunched open, the softened flesh tore at the cheeks. Wind rushed out of the bloodied abyss of what was once Dad's mouth and I felt the force of them all crying my name. I had sat jerk upright before I was fully awake.

The night air was a bright blue. Scorched still by the daylight. Francisco Quiroga stood under the canopy of the tall monkey puzzle tree, wiping the sweat from his brow. It wasn't hot. He was getting too old for the weight of the chainsaw on top of the weight of too many worries.   He stared up at the thick spiny branches studded with flat triangular leaves and sighed. Great-grandfather had planted these trees. He revved the gas-fuelled chainsaw and steadied his footing, rooting his right heel into a knot of weeds in the dry soil. He didn't care that it was illegal. Few people drove this far out into his land, and he knew enough about police bribes if it ever came down to it. He did, however, care a great deal about his legacy.   He thought about his own grandchildren and what he would leave behind for them. But he needed the money. They all needed the money, and the loggers paid well.

He braced his abdomen and twisted the heavy saw to his right, swinging the shuddering blade through to the base of the tree. It jarred hard into the directional notch and kicked back. His weak wrist buckled under the weight and the roaring chain swung, diagonally, across the front of his body. The teeth of the chain plunged into Francisco's right thigh, severing the transverse branch of the lateral femoral circumflex artery and nicking three perforating branches of the femoral artery. The denim, skin and muscle tissue opened in a shredded gash as he shrieked, then stumbled backwards onto the dusty ground. His cries echoed out into an empty sky. Blood seeped out quickly into the dirt and he fell unconscious in seconds. His brain, frantic from the loss of oxygenated blood, triggered a series of vivid, still images of his life. His first harvest, his first born, his first affair. The pain faded into a dull background noise of nerve damage and he died beneath the tree.

12

The breakout area at Lavender Hill was empty. I dragged a table over to the window, opened it a fraction and hugged the large milky coffee. I stared up at the bright television screen on the wall and read the ticker tape of the BBC news update: tax cut promises by the Tories, a train derailment in India, retailers projected spending for Christmas. I was wearing one of the outfits I had left at Sam's. It smelled of her laundry detergent. We had showered together before I left for the station. My hair smelled of her expensive coconut shampoo.

The cold air hazed as it pushed in from the cold. I sat, drank in small sips and let the air cool my face. Fresh air, caffeine and forgiveness. I felt like this would be a day for breakthroughs.

I sat and read Dylan's report. It covered everything we discussed in the meeting plus more in depth analysis on my man. I had elements that I wanted to discuss with him in more detail. Specifically the point on serial identification. Nowhere in his report made reference to my comments in the meeting about when my man might look to kill again. I dialled the number at the base of his email. He answered in three rings.

'Dylan Nicholson.'

'Oh hi, Dylan, it's DCI Isla Fletcher here. How are you?'

'I'm great thank you, Isla. And you?'

'Good, thanks. Thanks for sharing your report, and sorry again for not calling you last night. I didn't get a chance to digest the details until this morning.'

'Oh no problem at all. I'm always on my phone so call any time.'

'I wondered if you could pop into the station this afternoon? There are a few ideas I want to talk over with you.'

'Yes. Let me double check my calendar.'

He paused, and hummed a low tuneless song as he opened up his laptop.

'Yes, this afternoon is great. Is three ok with you?'

'Yes. Three works great for me. I'll see you then.'

'Brilliant. See you then.'

I hung up and waved to Jim. He looked like he had gotten at least some sleep.

'Are you coming to the briefing at quarter to?'

'I am indeed. Who was that?' he asked.

'The BIA. You around at three this afternoon to meet with him?' I asked.

'Should be,' he said, 'worst case scenario I'm sure you can grill him yourself.'

I spotted the time on the BBC news screen.

'Are you happy for me to lead the briefing?' I asked.

Jim nodded.

'I can't be there, Fletch. I've got another call. Come and find me after it.'

Ryan and Whalley were both leaning over the table, checking the cables leading into the telephone dock at the centre. Ryan was still working as the Office Manager of the MIR but I'd asked him to work with Whalley given he'd been out on interviews with me. Whalley had taken the role of action allocator and analyst manager. PC Jacob Reese was also in the room. He was working as the Outside Enquiry Officer, filtering and reviewing all of the interview notes from neighbours and peripheral friends. PC Davies and PC Regis were also sat at the desk with stacks of folders.

Sophie, our media manager for the case, and Louise, the

loggist, were both sat at the desk. Louise was documenting every decision, action and updating the policy decisions. They all stood as Jim and I entered the room but I motioned for them all to sit.

'Do we have anyone on the line?'

Ryan answered.

'Just Mark on behalf of the coroner's office for now.'

I wasn't expecting a lot of people to dial in. Senior management had been made aware of the briefing but I suspected they would link in with Jim directly to get the updates.

'Morning everyone.' I said. 'I'll get straight into it. I will give you all a brief update on the interviews we have conducted thus far. If we go around the room, and on the line, can I ask you each then to give a short summary on where you are any key findings and then any next steps? Maybe Mark you can go first and then you can drop off the call.'

Mark spoke clearly from the speaker. He had a thick Brummy accent.

'You already had the preliminary findings on cause of death. Strangulation with the very obvious postmortem mutilation. The mutilation, that it to say, the incision along the hairline, was made shortly after death which we have already identified as 5am on the Sunday morning. No other mutilation occurred to the body.'

He took an audible swig of a drink from a plastic bottle.

'The swabs that we took from the body have all come back negative in terms of DNA markers. Greta had not had sex in the previous 48 hours and there was no sign of rape trauma or indeed any DNA markers in her mouth. She had been meticulously washed with bleach postmortem.'

He wrapped up.

'That's the key detail from me, although there will obviously be more content in the autopsy report. And to your last point, I'm afraid other than fielding questions on my report, there are no additional steps for me for now.'

'Thanks for your time, Mark.' I said. 'Please feel free to leave the call.'

'Thank you, everyone. Cheerio.'

I reached over and closed the line.

'Right. I'll go first in the room.' I said. 'Ryan and I spent most of yesterday in Central London. We spoke to Max Greenfield, Greta's ex-boyfriend, with her colleagues at the Sister Agency and with one of her clients, Stephen Grace. Greta attended a food event a few weeks ago where Stephen appeared to have made a pass at her but he has a certified alibi for the entire weekend over her time of death. We have also had confirmation from Max Greenfield's flatmates that he was at Paradox club with them on Saturday night and then all day Sunday. Blake Wallder, the boyfriend who found her, has no one who can account for his whereabouts on Saturday night given he lives by himself. He has not been ruled out.'

'I will share the report from the BIA which shares more insight into the psychological profile. DCI Greaves and I will be meeting with him this afternoon so if you do have any questions then let me know before then.'

'In terms of my own next steps, I am going out to Clapham this morning to meet Greta's best friend - a woman called Uma Dixon - and then I'll be back here to prioritise her group of friends. I have the meeting with the BIA at three but otherwise free either side of that if you find something that you think it important.'

I nodded at Lester, the crime scene manager, to go next. I wanted to keep these meetings to fifteen minutes max.

Lester cleared his throat.

'It's a very clean crime scene. The SOCOs took an extensive, exhaustive haul of information from the site and the process of filtering through everything is still ongoing. Fingerprint evidence thus far is either the victim or her boyfriend, but we expected that. We expected the use of plastic gloves. Footprints I'm afraid come up equally disappointing. Processing ongoing.'

'OK,' I said. 'Sophie, could you go next?'

Sophie leaned onto the desk, clasping her hands over her notepad. Her massive cleavage was making Davies nervous. If she'd noticed she didn't give a shit. She gave a succinct update.

'I've issued a holding statement to the press that we are investigating the murder. Obviously it includes her name but I've not made any reference to the details and asked for privacy for the investigation and for her family. Which, to a large degree, has been respected. I've fielded a couple of journalists digging around for more detail but shut them down. The problems will arise when her family and friends start talking to the press, assuming they find out themselves what happened to her. Speaking to Lucy this morning it looks like the parents haven't actually shared the details of her death with anyone else in the family. I'm keeping an eye on the social media feeds too and there isn't anything of note.'

Sophie leaned back from the desk.

'Thanks, Sophie. Could I ask you to link in with Dylan Nicholson on any future releases? We need to factor in any chance that we are speaking to the killer directly. He might be listening out for us.'

I thought more of it.

'Actually, speak to me if we share anything else to the press.'

She nodded.

'Whalley,' I asked. 'Could you give an update on the house to house interviews?'

'Yes, ma'am' he said, 'there have been twenty two interviews conducted thus far for every neighbour on Crockerton Avenue. A couple of the neighbours remember seeing Blake Wallder around eleven as he headed to the house and one of them actually heard his cries out to the emergency services. Nothing thus far on anyone either the night before or the early morning of.'

I didn't think there would be. I guessed that the Saturday night crowd would be split into two camps: the 'close the curtains get the TV on' crowd who lived for an early night and the 'get shit-faced and head out crowd' who would have missed the time-window of someone breaking into Greta's house at say midnight. Or be too pissed to remember.

Whalley continued.

'There are still plenty of interviews outstanding. So they are the next steps.'

'Great, thanks.' I said, 'And Davies. Anything on CCTV?'

Davies spoke very softly, in an accent I placed somewhere in the West Country.

'The closest CCTV to Crockerton Avenue is from outside the pub on the corner to Trinity Road. Nothing that directly shows who entered Crockerton Avenue on the day before or the day of the murder. We have confirmed Blake Wallder's location based on his statement. There is another CCTV outside the bank on Braemose Road so we are looking into whether we can triangulate the two. Road traffic was busy across most of the night. Lots of ambulances.'

I checked the clock at five past ten. Time to get moving.

'Anything else to add?' I asked.

'Yes, ma'am.' said Ryan. 'I spoke to Lush Green events this morning. They confirmed both Greta and Stephen as delegates. They also confirmed the Lois that Stephen mentioned as a Lois Foster. She works in the Manchester office and lives in Didsbury but they gave me her number and email address so I can validate that element of Stephen's story today.'

'Great. Thanks everyone. Let's wrap it up and I'll see you all tomorrow. Please ring me if anything crops up or if you have any questions at all. And keep the records tidy please. There is going to be a lot of interest in this case.'

Everyone filtered out and heading back to the MIR. Ryan was collecting the papers from table.

'Ryan. Can you accompany me to the Uma Dixon meeting?'

'Yes, ma'am.'

'Brill. Give me ten minutes. I'll meet you at your car.'

I walked quickly to Jim's office, knocked twice and then entered.

'We just had the first briefing. You want the details?'

He shook his head. He was only interested in the leads.

'I'm off down to Clapham Common to speak to Uma Dixon, Greta's close friend. See if I can get more information on her whereabouts, her character.'

'Right,' said Jim. 'I'm going to go and see her parents this morning. I'll do exactly the same, in not so many words. See if there is anything they could add. I'll give them all the details of where we are too, assuming you've got someone who can send me the minutes from the briefing?'

'Yes. I'll get Louise to send them over.'

'I had a call with Detective Chief Superintendent Marshall this morning.' he said.

'I've agreed to keep her updated every day too. She's taking a back seat now as she doesn't want to muddy the waters. But if we don't identify more leads in the next day or two we might need more resource.'

I knew that Jim wasn't trying to worry me. He was just telling me the facts.

I thought back to the twelve days it had taken me to get nowhere for Jessica and felt anxious to get out and speak to Uma Dixon. It reminded me that I needed to return Derek Fox's call too. I would do that after today's interviews.

'Thanks, Jim. I'll keep you posted. And I'll see you back here for the meeting with the BIA. It's looking like the profiling might be our best lead for the time being.'

Jim nodded.

'Catch you later.'

13

Uma Dixon worked for a small graphic designer agency in Brixton but she had taken compassionate leave and was working from her studio flat in Clapham Common. The flat was above an Indian restaurant on a very busy road. Her studio had high ceilings and large windows that were thick with dark grime on the outside. The 155 bus stop was outside her window and every seven to nine minutes we were all eye-level with the whole top deck. Uma didn't seem to mind.

Her hair was greasy and tied up into a messy bun and she was sat cross-legged on a futon sofa. Ryan and I sat on a two-man dining set. The table of which looked just about big enough to accommodate one plate and one glass.

'I'm just so in shock. You know?' she said.

I measured every word I said to her. I needed words with purpose.

'I know. It's really a very difficult time. We are very sorry for your loss. We are doing everything we can.'

She nodded.

'Would you like us to make you a cup of coffee? Or Ryan could pop out and get us some drinks from the coffee shop?'

'No, it's ok.' she said. And smiled. She was ready.

'OK. How long had you known Greta?'

'Eight years.'

'And where did you meet?'

'I used to work for Sister and I went on secondment to the Berlin office. Sister are notorious for paying their staff really badly but they have a great global presence and they are happy to move staff around. I have an A level in German, which actually I didn't need because everyone in the office seemed to speak perfect English. Greta's grammar was better than mine.'

'Greta was an account manager for a drinks client I was working for. We just became friends working together. She offered to show me around and we would go out drinking together.'

'And how long were you in Berlin for?'

'Eight months. But then Greta and I kept in touch on Facebook and we actually met up at some client events in Amsterdam. We just got drunk together. She could drink so much.'

Uma smiled at the memory of her friend.

'When did you leave Sister?'

'About two years ago. I left just before Greta moved over to London. So, yes, about two years. I've worked for Ink design company since then. But I loved it with Greta moved over. I helped her to find the flat in Balham. She wanted to live in Shoreditch originally but I told her you get more value for money here. I'm the reason she lived in that flat.'

She began to cry heavily. Sobbing.

I stood and placed my hand on her shoulder.

'You are absolutely not accountable for any of this. OK.'

She nodded and pulled herself together.

'Could you maybe describe Greta for us? Tell us about her character?'

Uma pursed her lips and blinked back tears.

'She was brilliant. Feisty. She was smart.'

'Did you know her boyfriend, Blake Wallder?'

'Sort of. I met him a couple of times but only when he was dropping her off on a night out.'

'So she hadn't introduced you to him properly?'

'No. I didn't think it was that serious.'

'How about her ex boyfriend? Max Greenfield? Have you met him?'

'Yes. I love Max. We met out in Berlin. I always thought she was crazy for breaking up with him. And I told her so.'

'And how did she take that?'

'She thought they might get back together at some point in the future. She felt like London was a new beginning. She always said she would worry about fidelity. I mean, a relationship, when she was in her thirties.'

'Is Max ok?' asked Uma.

'He is still very shocked,' I said.

'But you don't think he did it do you?' she asked.

'Not at this stage.'

'I might give him a call, she how he's doing.'

'We don't want to keep you much longer. Can you tell us when you last saw Greta? And when you last spoke to her?'

'Yes. We went to the Balham Bowls Club last Saturday and ended up back here with a couple of friends. She got an uber home about half two. I spoke to her last Wednesday to arrange a pub quiz. That was it. We got cut off because she was heading into the Tube and I said I'd text to sort it out.'

She started to cry again. The 155 pulled up.

'Uma thank you very much for meeting with us. We really appreciate it. Why don't we leave you to it and then if there is anything you can think of you give us a buzz?'

She smiled at us.

'Do you have anyone who can come and be with you?' I asked.

She smiled again.

'My Mum is on her way. She only lives in Roehampton so she's been driving over every day to see me.'

'Good. Take care of yourself.'

Uma stood and padded over to the front door. We left quietly and walked to the High Road. The butchers shop on the corner was heaving with people placing their orders for Christmas. I turned to Ryan.

'If Greta's relationship with Blake wasn't serious enough for her to introduce him to her best friend, why did he have a key?'

I was thinking out loud more than anything.

'I think it would be useful to get him back in for a secondary meeting. Can you sort that out?'

'Of course, ma'am. Shall I drive us back to the station?'

I considered it. Looking out onto the flat, green common. It was midday.

'Actually, why don't you take a lunch break and get yourself back there. Take an hour and I'll see you there.'

I decided to take a green short cut through the common back to the station. It was a cold, blue afternoon and I wouldn't get a chance to exercise properly for the foreseeable. If I didn't crowbar in some sort of cardio then I'd go mad.

Ryan turned right, towards his car and I walked onto the Common and took in a lungful of fresh air. Well, as fresh air as I'd felt all day. The common was flanked on all sides by endlessly busy roads. I took my phone out of my pocket and called Sam.

'Hey.' she answered.

'Hey. How's your day going?'

'Good. Have you decided where you want to go on Saturday?' she asked.

'Yes. I was thinking The Prince. The place in Brixton?'

'Perfect.' she said.

After we had sex this morning we had spoken about taking things slowly. Sam didn't want to move in together straight away and I completely respected her caution. I promised that we could date and told her that Saturday night was hers.

'What are you up to now?' I asked.

'Lunch with Mum. She's in town for a bit. She's got tickets for a show in the West End so I've got a half day.'

'Oh lovely, well send her my love.'

'I will. I already messaged her to say we had decided to work things out. Needless to say she's thrilled.'

We both laughed.

'I feel like with Mum you're the daughter she never had!'

'Oh come on, your Mum loves the bones of you.'

'I know. But she is really happy. She wants us to go and stay with them ASAP. She's down here seeing Isaac too apparently. He's decided he wants to set up shop here for a bit.'

'Oh well that's nice. Maybe you guys could meet up or something?'

Growing up as an only child I always wanted a brother or a sister. It felt like the relationship was so sacred that I always pushed Sam to try and make up with her brother. But she didn't bite.

'I'm just crossing Kingsway so I need to get off the phone. But I'll call you tonight?'

'OK sweetie, speak to you tonight.'

I picked up the pace and took off my scarf. It felt good to stretch my legs. If my shirt dress and ankle boots would have allowed it, I would have run there.

Dušan Borislav Loncar assumed that death by hanging would be instant. He had planned the day, and the method, and finalised his business affairs with those pigs at the market. In the last month, he'd sold his television, paid off the debt with his elderly neighbour and bought a length of suitably thick rope. He woke that morning with the concrete resolve that this was the right choice. This was the right day. He tied the noose with a reef-knot and fixed the other end securely to the radiator pipe beneath the window frame. He tugged on the rope and tied a secondary knot to the leg of the heavy oak table, just to be on the safe side. He stood on the ledge of the window and looked vertically down onto the communal car park of the housing block. A brief wave of vertigo caused him to grip the crumbling wooden window frame. He could never have jumped, he knew he needed the rope. Besides, he didn't want the ferals who lived three flights down to find him. He couldn't bear to think of them digging through his pockets. Dušan closed his eyes against the muted rays of sunshine, stepped out, and dropped. The rope was four inches too short to break his neck, instead, the force of his weight fractured his forth cervical vertebrae and he died from the cumulative effect of tracheal asphyxia and venous congestion.

Eve tried to move his arms, to clutch at the gnawing rope. But nothing connected, nothing caught. She could feel the pain and the panic but remained impotent; as she had at the snake bite and at the hot tear of the chainsaw. She swiped and clawed with all of the the will of whatever she was, but nothing. She looked through Dušan's burning eyes onto the brutalist, concrete landscape and felt the heavy absence of hope, both his and her own.

14

I arrived back to the station at half one. The walk had taken longer than originally planned as I took the scenic route around the Lake on Wandsworth Common. I needed more thinking time. I thought about Blake, letting himself into Greta's flat. I though about the report from Dylan, how he had completely ignored my point about a potential series identification. I thought about Sam. About Max, the jealous ex-boyfriend. I thought about the whiskey on Chris's breath, and how he had made about a joke with PC Davies Greta giving a blow job. I thought about Jessica. I played out the next steps in my head: reading the notes from the broader interviews, crystallising the profile. I headed straight to the MIR and took a seat at an open desk. I noted down all of the next key actions and filtered out all of the read messages from my inbox. I liked to keep open emails as live and have everything else filed away. I was always so organised at work, neat even. Such stark contrast to how messy I let my life get outside of work.

I was composing myself for the meeting with Dylan when Jim swung a chair around from the desk next to mine and placed a large coffee cup on the table next to me. He lifted the lid, tipped in a sachet of sugar, and swirled the cup. He took a large mouthful and grimaced from the heat.

'What do you think, Fletch? Do we go after Greenfield for sexual offence?' he asked.

I had thought about it too. I didn't believe that Max had sent the video to Greta as a means to get her back. There was something about it that felt threatening. But a feeling couldn't be proved.

'Not at this stage. I don't think we could prove his motive. And without seeing the context of the message we don't know what he said. We don't know how she reacted. He could argue she'd asked for him to send it.' I said.

It wasn't like Jim to chase an arrest. He looked distracted.

'I've got a meeting at four. Can we wrap it up with Nicholson before then?'

'Yes.' I said. 'Let's head to meeting room seven. He tends to be early.'

I was right.

Dylan arrived at ten to and was shown to the meeting room. I'd kept the attendees purposefully small as I wanted to argue my point.

Dylan set his burgundy designer satchel on the table and pulled out three copies of his profile report. He had gone to the trouble of binding it with a clear plastic sheet.

'Afternoon. How are you both?' he said.

'Well.' I responded. 'And you?'

'Well', he replied, smiling at me.

'Thanks for coming in', said Jim. 'Let me give you a quick status update. Then we can talk over your report. Which we appreciate you knocking out so quickly.'

'No problem. Case like this, you move quickly.'

'So,' Jim started. 'Putting it bluntly we are behind where we would like to be at this juncture of the investigation. The ex-boyfriend has an alibi, there is no physical material from the crime scene. We are looking to interview the boyfriend again owing to some conflicting comments from Greta's best friend. But we need to look at the profiling in conjunction with the interview strategy.'

I could tell from his tone that Jim was sceptical. He didn't approve of a top-down, American-style approach to offender profiling. I don't think over the course of his career that he had found an BIA to offer valuable insight into an open case. Holmes and Holmes, a couple of psychologists, carried out a study in 1996 that concluded that offender profiling was only meaningful in a few specific scenarios; but one of those scenarios was postmortem slashing. I was somewhere in the middle. I felt like offender profiling was more an interesting way to deconstruct the psyche of a criminal after the fact, although I acknowledged that there had been cases of unusual homicides across the world that relied on it to find their perpetrators. I was willing to try anything. I would find answers Greta even if I couldn't find them for Jessica, or Dad.

I knew that Jim wouldn't want to be seen to be missing opportunities either. I could sense that Jim had eyes on him.

I also wanted to challenge Dylan on his assertion that this was an isolated incident. I felt certain my man wasn't done.

'And', I said. 'I disagree with a key element in your report.'

Dylan raised his eyebrows but nodded. He looked open to a challenge.

'Shall we just start at the beginning?' he said.

I opened the report to page 3.

I agreed with the basic social assessment. I knew my man was between 35 and 40. The cleanliness at the scene, and the confidence of the incision felt like it had the restraint of an older man. But there was also a strength in the strangulation, and in moving her that ruled him out being much older than 50. It made sense that he would be white and I agreed that he would be single. He probably had a stable career history but might have struggled to contain his true nature, his anger towards women. He had probably dealt with disciplinary action at work, he might even have been arrested previously for assault towards women.

'All of this I agree with.' I said.

I also agreed with Dylan's' assessment that we were not dealing with a psychopath.

We both turned the page to the geographical assessment. Dylan looked at my report and could see no annotations.

'How are the geographical searches going?' he asked.

'Well.' I nodded. 'We are interviewing staff at St Georges. And local neighbours. We haven't found any overlaps yet, but looking.'

He added.

'I think this guy might have had some degree of medical training. Maybe he trained to be a doctor or a nurse and then dropped out of the system. Or maybe he didn't. My sense is that a practising medical professional wouldn't be capable of this.'

'And the majority of homicides of this kind happen close to home. So if our fella isn't Wandsworth then he's in South London. For a lot of his time at least. He feels confident here.'

We all turned the page. I had a large star next to the categorisation heading.

We differed in our categorisation of this as a sex crime. There was no secreted semen and Greta had not been raped. But there was something sexually motivated here. He had spent a lot of time with her and we hadn't had confirmation from Greta or Blake on whether anything had been stolen from the scene. I looked out in the the MIR and to the image of her pinned onto the board. I wondered whether my man had taken photos too.

'You think this is different kind of sex crime?' Dylan asked, noticing my mark up to his report.

'Yes.' I said. 'Well, ish. I don't know what sort of sex crime it is. But let's keep an open mind to it.'

There are four broad ways to categorise a sexual crime: power-assertive, power-reassurance, anger-retaliatory and anger-excitation.

A power assertive crime is driven by dominance, but it

is often a planned rape and unplanned murder. The scalpel and decorations ruled this out.

In a power-reassurance crime death is not planned either, it is a planned rape: to act out a fantasy. There were certainly elements of that here. The bindings of the twine. But her death was definitely planned.

An anger-retaliatory crime is a planned rape and murder, borne of hatred for a man or woman. This didn't feel like that either. There was anger, but Greta had not been raped. There was something about the placement that was careful.

Anger-excitation, or a lust killing, plans on death and it is the act of killing that brings satisfaction. I felt like my man lived here. It was the killing he loved. He was just controlled enough to hold it back, to save the climax. Savour it and finish it elsewhere.

'Erotophonophilia.' I said.

Jim nodded, resigned.

Sexual gratification from the death of a human being.

'Yes.' said Dylan. 'And there are more strands that we can bring in if we do position this as a sex crime.'

'Such as?' I asked.

'You heard of the STEP conclusion?'

I shook my head. It rang a bell from university.

'The Sex Offender Treatment Evaluation Programme.' he elaborated. 'They had loads of interesting outcomes. Higher IQ in the murderers than the rapists. But we knew that anyway. Our fella is an organised offender, so he's of high IQ. But an interesting outcome in the STEP research is how the male offenders categorised women.'

'As sexual objects?' I offered.

'Sure. That's one of them. But more. They found that women were,' he paused an made quote marks with the fore and middle finger on both hands, 'unknowable.'

I leant closer. Interested.

'So they found in a significant number of the participants that the men described women as inherently unknowable because of their deception. That every woman set out to be deliberately deceptive. A liar. A keeper of secrets.'

I thought about the people who Greta had left behind and wondered if any of them held her secrets for her. Maybe I could find the secret that linked her to my man.

A wrote 'the unknowable woman' on my copy of the report.

'We can use that in our line of questioning with Blake Wallder' I directed to Jim, who seemed to agree.

We all turned the page. Victimology.

'As Jim mentioned', I said. 'We have a pretty large network of people who knew Greta. But we haven't identified anyone in particular we believe might have done this. So we might need to fill some gaps on how he selected her, how he engaged with her.'

'There's a matter of type I guess.' said Dylan.

'What he's just into good looking blondes?' asked Jim.

'Could be.' said Dylan. 'Greta was a distinctive looking woman. To have thick curls like that. But it wasn't just a chance selection either.'

'You both feel like he must have interacted with her? Knew her to a certain degree?'

'Yes'. We both did.

'It's not like you can just pick a victim out of a catalogue.'

'Not that we're aware. We didn't find any dating apps on her phone and she wasn't signed up to any online dating websites. Her instagram profile was private and the Facebook presence was scarce. Her profile picture was her dressed as Batman as a six year old.'

I'd sat and stared at that profile image at 2am in the

morning. Looking at the child who grew up to be killed.

'So we need to identify how he interacted with her. And for how long.'

'We do.' I said. 'But the biggest point I want to cover is how long we think he might take to kill again.'

'We can't be certain —' Dylan started.

I cut him off.

'We can. I just know he isn't done.'

Dylan sat back in his seat. My argument was ready.

'We don't know if he took a souvenir. But my sense is that he did. And given how carefully staged the body was I feel certain he captured the images too. The incision at the hairline was really confident. Steady and it already feels like a signature. A ritual. I just want to know how much time we have.'

Dylan blew out his cheeks and nodded.

'A serial killer will keep killing until one of three things happen. He dies, he's caught or he burns out.'

'And I don't think we are close to any of those things happening.'

I knew my man was on a high. He was hiding, but he was preparing.

Jim closed the report and asked us both.

'Does Blake Wallder fit the profile here?' he asked.

'No.' I said. 'I really don't think so.'

'I want to talk to him about his relationship, because I don't believe Greta was as serious about him as he made out. But. That might not be his fault. Maybe Greta misled him. Maybe she was,' I turned to Dylan and emphasised, 'unknowable.'

'Plus, I don't think he has the IQ of the man we are looking for. He left school with four GCSEs, did an apprenticeship and then worked consistently since then. Yes he lives in Stockwell, but I just don't think it's him. Obviously challenge your assumptions, but what do you think?'

'I'm inclined to agree.' said Jim.

'What about Stephen Grace?' asked Dylan.

'He probably fits the profile more neatly. He's a smart man, few different careers. But he has a pretty solid alibi.'

'Maybe use him as an anchor,' said Jim. 'If Greta socialised with her clients like that then we need to speak to every one of her accounts'.

I nodded and made a note to follow up with Ryan. He was working with Whalley to conduct the interviews and filter out the key information.

'We are also checking if he has done it before. We're working with forces across the country to see if there are murders with similar MOs. It might be that he's tried before but not been as successful.'

'Maybe it's wishful thinking on my part,' said Jim. 'but maybe this was a very specific one off. Maybe the flowers meant something very specific to Greta. Maybe the urge to kill was specific to her. More than that, what if someone wanted to kill her and all this stuff, this decoration is just window dressing. Trying to sell us something we don't want. Someone smart who wants us to think about a serial killer when really they just wanted to kill Greta.'

Valid point. It was important not to go into any investigative action with an assumption or a bias.

Jim's phone vibrated on the table. He looked down and picked it up.

'I need to take this. I'll leave you both to it.' he said.

He opened the meeting room door and spoke back to me. 'I'll catch up with you later, Fletch.'

It closed with a padded thud.

'Fletch?' Dylan asked.

'Yes. But only to him.' I cautioned, smiling.

It was five to four. I had scheduled in a meeting with Ryan at half past and then Blake Wallder was arriving at five. I also needed to work with Jim to give Greta's parents an update. An update that assured them that we were making progress but one that shielded them from the specifics.

'Do you have time to work through an interview strategy for Blake Wallder?' I asked

'Sure. We could work through a couple of scenarios but one should be that this is a one off killing, discrete to Greta. And if he doesn't have an alibi, let's challenge him.'

I agreed.

'I can't shake it though.' I said.

'What?' he replied.

'That he's not done.'

'Should we get a coffee?' I offered.

'Yes.'

We both stood. He gathered up the copies of his report and slid them into his satchel. I noticed a heavy paperback book and turned my head to read the spine.

'You into trashy thrillers?'

'Guilty. The gorier the better.'

He closed the satchel and fastened the buckle. He lifted it over his head and positioned the strap across his body.

I opened the heavy glass door and ushered him out.

'You smell like coconuts.' he said. Sounding surprised.

'Yes. I do.' I said. Puzzled.

In the canteen, Dylan leant across me to pick up two packets of brown sugar. He poured them both into the black coffee.

He lowered his voice.

'I know offender analysis has it's limitations. But I'm here to help.'

'I get it. It's not me you have to convince.' I said, 'I did psychology at uni. So I'm on board. I get it.

'Oh right. Where did you go?' he said.

'UCL.' I replied. 'A nice cheap life as a student in London.'

He laughed.

'I went to Sheffield.' he said. 'Did my undergrad there and then did my post grad at Manchester.' he said.

'But you're not Northern right?'

'Correct. Bath originally. Although the West Country got knocked out of me pretty quickly at boarding school. And you? Northern right?'

'Yes. Cumbria.'

'Nice.' he said, 'so London was a big change. Green to grey.'

'Exactly.' I said.

'Your accent is softer too.' he said.

'Living in London for 17 years will do that. I still can't stick an extra consonant into words though. A bastard is still a bastard. Never a barstard.'

Dylan laughed.

I turned my head over my shoulder to him and smiled. A gesture that I thought about later that night. In bed. When I thought about the case, about Dylan, about Greta. I thought about the cut at the hairline, the blow job, the map of interconnecting friends. I thought about the things I should have written on my to do list, the things I should have said in the briefing. I thought about the interview with Blake. How it hadn't revealed anything other than a man who loved Greta and believed she loved him.

I thought about Jessica, I thought about Derek. But the thing that stood out, the thing that ticked over with each passing minute of *not* falling asleep, was that smile. I should not have done that.

I tried to masturbate and failed.

Irene Diaz died from bone cancer at five am in Upstate New York. She had known for three weeks that death was imminent and all of her affairs were in order. Her grown children were all sleeping in their family home, after saying a heartfelt goodnight and her ex-husband was staying nearby with his new wife. Irene did not fear death. She had no religion. But she remembered an article written in the New York times about how dying of cancer is the best kind of death. She didn't want to suddenly leave her family, she didn't want to fade away under the spell of dementia and she didn't want to be stuck in hospital as doctors tried to fix failing organs. She was glad that she was at home, that her children were happy and she died in a matter of fact way. With a gentle, resigned peace.

Halima Shelton died of bone cancer at two minutes past five am on Vancouver Island. She too knew that death was coming but she pushed against it. She had met with several oncologists and pleaded with them to try new ways, give her new drugs, make it work. She died alone, full of opiates, without pain; but she was not ready.

Maxima Freedman died of secondary bone cancer at nine minutes past five in Baton Rouge, Louisiana. Her cancer had started in her breast, she had a double mastectomy within weeks of diagnosis and then aggressive radiation and chemo therapy. Maxima lived a full, colourful life for two years before the cancer re-emerged in her bones. She refused all treatment and ran towards death with the same level of gusto as she had lived. She sold her car and bought expensive food and drink, she found a new home for her bassett hound and she died at her friends house after a night smoking weed and laughing. She was too stoned to notice death and her dreams simply faded into a void.

15

I fucking knew it wasn't over. My phone rang at 511am and I didn't remember even getting into my car. I realised as I got out of the car that I had buttoned up my shirt in the wrong way. I tucked the extra material into my waistband and fastened my blazer.

I didn't need to see the body. I could tell from the crowd at the periphery of the crime scene, from the faces of the police officers and from the look that Lester shot me as I arrived. He nodded gravely as I caught his eye, then continued with his briefing. Pointing PCs and PCOSs to the network of gardens at the rear and the alleyway that led directly to Common. I had no makeup on. My reflection looked haunted in the rear view mirror.

There was a woman with bright pink hair sobbing next to the gatepost. A young PC had her arm draped around her shoulder, consoling her. I skirted the mansion block using the common approach path, following the noise up the central staircase to the second floor. The white suits of the forensic team busied themselves through the third door on the right hand side but I could see the body from the staircase. She lay in the open plan lounge. Legs tied at the ankle with parcel twine, cotton white night dress pulled down over the hips. As I approached from this angle I could see the small blonde thatch of pubic hair and the bulge of fat at her lower stomach. Her hands had been placed at the centre of her abdomen, folded one over another. Pale blue nails and delicate gold rings. I could smell the flowers this time, aside from the plastic and the everyday smell of a house where a human lived, it was the first thing I noticed. I couldn't smell bleach.

Jim stood across from me, 'You don't look surprised.'

I shook my head slowly as I moved up alongside her body, approaching the wreath of flowers that lay weaved in her tangle of blonde curls. I stopped and crouched next to Jim, looking at the stained halo of blood that had pooled beneath the flowers. I jammed my tongue against the roof of my mouth to stop the acid in my throat from escaping and stood, slowly. Lesson learned from last time. It wasn't like it had been that long. He only waited four days. Four bloody days.

'She can't have been here too long, the blood hasn't even soaked fully into the carpet.'

Jim nodded. 'Lester reckons we are looking at thirty-five minutes. We got bastard lucky. He might not have even had a chance to clean up properly.'

'He was interrupted?'

'By her housemate, Pattie Hayder. Ran full speed at her, she's lucky to be alive, they both fell down the stairs but he ran away.'

'On foot? No car?'

'She can't remember a car. We've got air support working with us just in case.'

I looked at the corpse.

'They look the exact same, Jim.'

He mashed his lips together and nodded quickly with his chin. In a multiple homicide it's not always so obvious that the cases are linked but here, it was like looking at the exact same woman. The flowers, the purposeful mutilation at the hairline, the placement of the body. From the pathologist report on Greta's body I didn't know if we would find trace evidence at the scene but we might be lucky and catch him in the vicinity. My breath caught in shallow tranches in the upper part of my chest. We needed to move quickly.

132

'What do we know?' I asked. Scanning the room. Looking at the body. The flat was obviously a rented flat share. Posters were stuck with blue tack on yellowed walls. Cheap shelves were stacked with cookery books and car magazines. The carpet was threadbare in places.

I knew we wouldn't know much else about her at this point. There were no pictures of her in the lounge and I didn't want to walk around the flat until the scene of crime had been preserved. More cars were pulling up and more white suits were filling out the room.

'Jim, I'm going to go and speak to the flatmate'

I left Jim to man the crime scene, I had questions for the flat mate, who I assumed was the pink haired woman in her early forties sobbing by the crumbling gate post. Overhead, air support whirred. The street was watching from windows.

I walked towards the flatmate. Daly, a matronly PC who was new to the department, had draped a blanket over pink-haired's shoulders and stood rubbing her arm in long strokes. She was stood next to an ambulance, the paramedic stooped over in the back.

'Are you Pattie?'

'Yes.'

Her voice was hoarse. A silver ring sat flush against her top lip from the septum piercing and she had hollow flesh tunnels in both ear lobes. She extended a frail hand and I shook it with both hands, trying to warm them with an act of habitual courtesy.

'Hi Pattie, I'm Isla. I'm a DCI and I'm here to find out what's happened. Is that your flatmate?'

'Yes.'

'And her name, what's her name?'

'Emmy. Emmeline McDonnell.'

'And you found her like that?'

133

'Yes.'

'You didn't move anything?'

'No.' She shook her head, her hands had started to shake and her lips were white. She needed to be seen by a doctor.

'What time did you get home?'

'I dunno. About half an hour ago'

'And is that a typical time for you.'

'No. My shift pattern changed last week.'

'What is it you do, Pattie?'

'I'm a carer.'

'And how about Emmy. What did she do?'

'She worked in a cafe in Brixton. She took photos too.'

'What time would you normally be home?'

'Much later on, I would have been working till eleven today.'

'What happened when you got home?'

Her lips were pale.

'I was listening to the radio on my headphones, just the one ear in. I got the sixty three bus home from Bermondsey and then walked back. Same as I always do. I'd opened the main door to the house and was stood in the hallway wrapping up my headphones. I noticed that the lounge light was on and shouted out. I didn't know if Emmy or Jacob were still up.'

'Jacob?'

'Bloom. He lives with us. But he spends most of the time at his boyfriends so we don't see him that often.'

'And what happened after you called out?'

'I fell. He just ran at me.'

She rubbed her stomach. The adrenaline might have been wearing off, or she might be realising that she was actually in pain. Shock could hide a lot.

'And did you notice anything about him, when he ran at you?'

She shook her head.

'It was so dark.'

She looked panicked.

'If I'd known, I would have ran after him.'

'I know,' I placed my hand on her forearm, 'there isn't anything you could have done. Do you remember anything at all about him? What he was wearing?'

She shook her head again, 'I'm sorry.'

Her breath started to quicken. I didn't want her fainting so told the paramedic to get her to the hospital. The helicopter still whirred and I could hear the radio updates from the ambulance and the cars.

This part of Clapham North was run down. It was in the blurred border into Stockwell. There was a run down pub on the corner and a faded newsagents. The street was low rise ex-council and I bet still cost a bloody fortune to buy. Lights had started to show in more neighbouring windows, people interested in the noise, woken by the sirens or simply people just waking up to go to work.

Jim stood talking to Lester in the doorway, pointing out where the perimeter needed to be set. I thought about the MIR and expanding the profile, we needed a social media strategy. I didn't want to scare the shit out of every blonde with curls in the Greater London area.

I stood in my thoughts in the middle of the road as Jim took out his phone and made a call. I didn't expect that we would find my man like this. I knew he would be running and that he had been interrupted but he was smart. He would have planned for all eventualities and that must have meant a car. If we were lucky, the Old Swan would have it's own CCTV but at this hour we might be able to identify a car leaving the street. We might even be able get ANPR. I was hopeful.

Jim's phone call was brief. We met in the middle of the road.

'That was Marshall. She wants me to be overall officer in charge.'

I nodded. It made sense.

He placed a heavy hand on my shoulder, 'He didn't waste any time.'

'Four days is fucking nothing. I thought we would have had at least a month.'

'Did the housemate give us anything?'

'Sort of. He knew her routine, or at least he thought he did.'

'How so?'

'She was only due home later this morning. He killed her, decorated her, and sat there with her, for over half an hour. He didn't expect to be interrupted.'

'Christ, how bloody long did he want with her?'

I didn't know. I imagined him in the room with her body. The inertia of the corpse. What did he have planned? How long did he draw out the pleasure?

I looked at Lester, who was heading out towards us, 'I guess we can safely assume there'll be no trace evidence in there?'

'Same story,' Lester confirmed, 'she has been bathed, moved, decorated. All seemingly post-strangulation. SOCOs are still arriving.'

He carried on to the team setting out the periphery.

The helicopter circled back overhead but it felt futile. I knew he wouldn't be found like this.

'We need to get back to the station. I want to figure

out where these women might have overlapped. How he found them.'

In my mind, I was already opening out the whiteboard, looking at the background of both women. A woman who worked in an agency in Shoreditch and a woman who worked in a cafe in Brixton. I thought about how their lives might overlap, what he might have seen in them. I hoped to God it was more than just a preference for blondes. They would have both had cause to interact with the public practically every day. I thought about the women waking across London to start the working day. I thought about the countless blondes meeting strangers on the tube, serving strangers coffee, treating strangers' wounds. I thought about the ring of the M25 and felt constricted; Greater London felt too scary a circus to be trapped in. There had to be more to it. I thought about how my man could have met Greta and Emmy. What would link them.

Jim offered to drive us back and jogged over to Lester to let him know. I thought about online dating profiles, local bars; ways he could have found them. I thought about him walking the streets of London, stalking women, planning his art. I felt sick. I thought about Sam, and her blonde hair then felt ridiculous for panicking. Sam was safe.

The cordon of people at the edges of the crime scene had grown as more commuters slowed down to watch. A couple in matching grey suits stood holding gloved hands, drinking from huge paper coffee cups. Three men with expensive looking satchels stood talking with a uniform and a group of school girls stood open mouthed taking filtered videos of themselves with the crime scene in the background.

I addressed a uniformed officer I didn't know.

'Can we get them girls moved on please?' I said.

Cars slowed and neighbours loitered in their doorways. There might well have been someone who saw something, but one of the things I'd learned about London was just how little notice people took of each other. A man running in the early hours would be observed and dismissed as someone trying to get in some cardio before work, someone looking to shape up before Christmas. I very rarely missed home but at least back in the village people noticed a stranger.

I was glad to see the school girls being told to put their phones away and looked back to Jim who was talking on his phone next to his car. I caught the end of the conversation as I moved to open the car door.

'Don't do anything yet. I'll be back in fifteen.'

He gripped his phone tightly and shook his head at me.

'What the fuck is wrong with people?' he said.

'Anything I can help with?'

'Nah. Not even close to being a number one priority right now though.'

I sat into the passenger seat. The leather seat was still cold and his car smelled like cigarettes. I had never known Jim to smoke but he looked worried, distracted almost, so I didn't push it. The radio chirped up as he switched on the engine, I clicked it off and turned up the hot air.

'I'm going to get that Nicholson guy back in.'

'We need Sophie in too. If we don't get the press conference right we might be in trouble.'

'We'll need a social media strategy too. I can just see this becoming a bleeding snap chat story.'

Jim pulled out onto the main road, slowing to allow four teenage boys across the road.

'Bastard kids,' he muttered, 'you made the right choice not having any.'

Jim looked tired. I clicked the radio back on for the traffic updates and we rode the car journey back to the police station in silence aside from the calls that I made to Dylan, Ryan and Whalley telling them all to meet us Lavender Hill.

(EVE)

At thirty one minutes past seven local time, a train travelling from North Lakimpur derailed six miles from Kamakhya, the place named for love.

Fadia, Saat, and Aafia, three sisters from a neighbouring village, were making a pilgrimage to the Hindu Temple of the Bleeding Goddess. They had saved for three months to go and pray at the feet of Bleeding Devi and the ten other tantric deities. While the temple contained no true figurines of any of the deities, there stood a carving of the Yoni, or vagina, of the Goddess, moistened by a natural spring. It was here where the sisters planned to celebrate their own shakti, or power, before Fadia left the family home to be married.

The train derailed because of the metallurgical changes caused by gauge corner cracking, as opposed to excess speed, or negligent track maintenance. Carriage one, where the sisters had sat, was torn from the other carriages when it impacted a free-standing mast. Saat, who was standing to open the window, was thrown through the glass and out of the carriage. She died almost instantly from the trauma of her skull impacting on the hard ground. Her death came as a sudden flash, a still image of the faces of her sisters, then an intake of breath. Eve could taste the impact at the back of her nose as he skull compacted into her soft brain tissue at the base of her cerebellum.

Fadia was crushed between her seat and the metal frame of the row in front of her, she died from hemorrhagic shock, caused by the force of simultaneous internal ruptures. The shock prevented her, and Eve, from overwhelming pain, but she died full of regret: of never marrying, of never leaving her family home, of bringing her sisters with her. She wasn't as devout as her sisters and she wasn't as convinced as Aafia that this life was simply a stepping stone. She would miss this form. She would miss it all. She died looking at the half missing face of her baby sister, ten feet in front of her.

Aafia's last breath felt wet from the blood in her throat,

the skin on her face was shredded by the broken glass, and she felt weak from the gash in her collarbone. Blood cascaded out, over her chest, down her heavy, hanging arms and trickled out of the tributaries of her fingertips. She was suspended face down above the ground by two metal rails that pierced her at the abdomen and the thigh. Hot air steamed around her, fogging the remnants of the window pane below. Sparks and steam, and searing pain. She couldn't see out of her left eye and had no idea where her sisters where. She loved them.

Eve could feel the pressure behind Aafia's eyes and the searing pain radiating out from the impaled metal. She could feel the heat of the missing skin on her face and the simple acceptance that she would not leave this carriage, that she would die here, suspended in the twisted chaos. Aafia tried to move, to free her shoulder so she could see her sisters, but the pain worsened in her abdomen. This was it. The hope deflated from her lungs and her arms fell heavy. Black clouds tumbled. All she could see was her left arm, limp and bloodied, touching the surface of the glass beneath her.

Aafia tried to move her left arm, to slowly extend her long thin fingers. Eve looked out through Aafia's eyes, felt the hot gurgling drag of each breath and felt the desperate struggle to move her hand. Intention matched intention as Eve felt her own impulse connect to the muscle tissue in Aafia's arm. Desire moved along the connective tissue in the forearm. Aafia had no intention of moving her index finger across the glass, but with the twisted remnant of her left hand she reached out to the surface and traced out a letter S in blood and steam. The start of a word she had no intention of writing, in a language she had never written, expressing a sentiment she couldn't understand.

Aafia died confused, but happy, looking at the glass, hopeful about the passing of her jiva, her spirit, onto the next life. She looked forward to the period of recuperation and the recycled use of her energy and wondered about how the next physical embodiment might feel. She died loving her sisters and praying for a beautiful next stage.

Eve felt hopeful too. As Aafia died, Eve stared at the letter in blood. The letter she, Eve, had put there with Aafia's arm. There was still time to make this right.

16

At the station I wanted to get into it quickly. I barked out the questions in the MIR before I had taken my coat off.

'Talk to me about Emmeline. Who was she? Where does she come from? What had she been up to?'

Ryan answered.

'Emmeline McDonnell. 26. Originally from Leicester but moved down here post graduation. Mother deceased. Father, Jeremy Gibson is in Pentonville for armed robbery. Worked as a waitress at a cafe in Brixton for two years but sold art prints online too. No siblings but her house mate confirmed she had quite a close knit group of friends. Mostly female.'

'Right. Jules. Can you get onto the prison and have someone notify Jeremy Gibson? We will assign an FLO just as would any other parent. Tell them to play nice.' said Jim.

'Whalley,' I said. 'Can you compile a list of close knit friends, and her flatmates and get their contact details together? We need to speak to each and every one of them. Find out where Emmeline has been the past few months.'

Elsewhere in the room, questions came thick.

'Does she have any other family members?' asked Jim.

Ryan answered.

'One cousin in South Africa but that's all I could see. Might well be more but I'll ring him this morning and confirm back.'

'Where did she work?' I asked. 'Which cafe in Brixton?'

'The Ace Cafe. The small one just outside the market. It's

pretty famous for it's flat breads and it has live music most of the day. Most of the staff members play a musical instrument so they have them on rotation.' said Whalley.

'And Emmeline?' I asked.

'Guitar.' said Whalley. 'There are pictures of her playing on the cafes Facebook page.'

'And who owns this cafe? Is it doing ok?' asked Jim.

'A man called Devon Powell. According to Companies House the business is in pretty decent shape. He runs a series of businesses in Brixton but lives over in Dulwich.'

Business must have been in pretty decent shape.

'Get his name on the interview list. Lower priority but let's try and speak to him today.' I said.

'Did she go to university?' asked Jim.

'Not that I can see on her profiles.' said PC Davies. 'But we can ask her flatmates.'

Jim spoke up, 'Any fellas? Anyone with a key?'

Ryan replied, 'On 5th October she changed her relationship status on Facebook to 'in a couple'. Tagged a man called Will Locke. Looking at his profile he's a barman.'

'And where is he?' I asked.

'He works at The Anchor on Wandsworth Common.'

A place I knew well. When I first moved to London I lived in a flatshare above The Anchor.

'Has anyone told him yet?'

PC Angela Ellis answered.

'There was no answer on his mobile. And none at The Anchor.'

'Right. I'll start with him. I'll drive out to chat to him once we finish up here.'

I spoke back out to the MIR, noticing that Ryan had logged into a computer and was scrolling through an email with interest.

'Did Emmeline have any other obvious interests? Her flatmate mentioned that she sold photography prints.'

'Yes ma'am.' said Davis. 'Her Facebook page had a link to an Etsy shop. She sold black and white prints of London skylines. Her latest prints were taken in Greenwich.'

I wondered if Greta had any side business. I made a note to double check.

A phone rang in the MIR and Whalley answered it. I checked my phone and realised that I had missed a call.

An unknown London number. I made a note to call them back after this session. I was making so many notes to follow up on. I hadn't spoken to Sam in a day and I hadn't planned Saturday. I couldn't think about her. I was too interested in Will Locke.

This guy worked ten minutes from where Greta Maiberger lived. Next door to the artisan bakery that sold small bunches of flowers. It didn't feel like the kind of violence a boyfriend would commit, but it was the first opportunity we had to find an overlap between the two dead women. What a tragic Venn diagram.

'Jim, I want to go and speak to the boyfriend.' I said.

'Agreed. I'll come with you.' he answered. 'Let's get a holding statement out to the press and then go. I'll drive.'

Four days was too quick a pattern. It indicated an urgency that scared me, especially with the law of diminishing returns. It might not be four days before he did it again.

Sophie stood from a work station in the corner of the room and lifted a print out of the drafted press release towards me. The conference prep might have to wait until after the interview. A bar man who knew both victims was the only living lead we had. Nervous energy twitched in my muscles, agitated by the need to crack on.

'DCI Fletcher, do you want to read this over before we release it?'

'Thanks, Lewes,' I took the double-sided print outs and scanned the contents, 'assume we are holding back pictures of the second victim until all of the family have been notified?'

'Yes, but,' she peered over the edge of the page and pointed to a sentence in bold, 'we are going to be talking about the physical similarity.'

I handed it back to Sophie and spoke to her and Jim,

'I guess there's nothing we can hide here. Let's keep it lean and factual. But we have to honest.'

Jim nodded.

'We can arrange the conference for later this week, thanks,' I leaned onto the desk to my right and interrupted Ryan, 'Can you do me a favour and follow up with the BIA? I left him a voicemail this morning but I'd like his input on this today if he can make it.'

I wondered what impact this would have on the profile. It hadn't impacted my own thoughts about the kind of killer we were looking for but it would be interesting to hear what Dylan had to say. I thought about the neat edges of his ironed shirt, tucked into his narrow waist band.

Ryan was running towards me through the MIR.

'Ma'am. Emmeline attended a trade show with Dylan Powell, her boss on the 11th October. I saw a picture on her instagram feed that looked familiar and I've just checked the delegate list that Lush Green sent over. She's on it. The same trade show Greta attended.'

'Right. Get Lee and Stephen Grace in here. Both of them. Today.' my heart was racing. 'And get Lush Green to send over the full list of delegates' contact details ASAP. We need to speak to everyone who attended. And now.'

I looked at Jim. He knew what I was thinking. The bar

man who worked moments from Greta and who was dating Emmeline or the two men we knew had been in the same trade show as her.

'Let's divide and conquer, Fletch. You take the barman. I'll wait here and field immediate actions on Emmeline. Let's try and both speak to the Grace brothers this afternoon.'

I stopped in the hallway outside of the MIR and messaged Sam.

'I'm so sorry but it's looking like we might not get to meet up tonight after all. I can't share details over text but there has been another killing. I'm going to be in this for the long haul. I'm so sorry. x'

She replied practically straight away.

'Don't worry at all sweetie, just take your time. I'll see if Mum wants to hang out instead. Call me when you can. Hope you're ok. Love you x'

I emailed Dylan and told him not to bother coming into the station, his time would be better served revising his profile to define my man as I knew him to be: a serial.

I needed to grab some sugar and coffee before I spoke to this bar man. I needed time alone to plan out the line of questioning. I planned on heading back to my office but Jules, the family liaison officer in the Fox case, was waiting outside the MIR. Her skin looked ashen.

'I've got bad news.'

In the demi-second that followed, I contemplated all possible outcomes. The series of dead bodies that I would have to deal with. Had something happened to Sam? To Mum? Had my man killed again?

I remembered that Jules was looking after the liaison for Jessica and felt like I knew what was coming. I pictured Jessica, translucent and naked on a silver gurney. Slashed wrists? Stomach full of pills? Fuck. I was certain that Jessica had killed herself.

146

'Derek Fox died this morning.'

The news passed through me like a wall of noise. Tears stung at my widened eyes and I knew my voice would struggle out. I swallowed hard.

'How?' I asked.

'A stroke.'

I thought back to his earnest face. His small pot belly and the neat buttoned up jacket. I thought about the way he pushed his thick glasses up his nose, and the quiet way he had spoken to me on the phone. I thought about the flesh melting from his rotting face and the smell of him screaming my name as I slept. I bit my lower lip hard. I'd only met him a handful of times. I looked frantically for somewhere to hold my gaze until I composed myself. I would not cry at work.

'When?'

'A couple of hours ago. He was taken to hospital but he just didn't make it. I'm sorry.'

Her voice was soothing, her face empathetic. She was definitely in the right job.

'He didn't feel pain in the end.'

I tipped my neck back and stroked my throat. Exhaling out the fumes of rage. He would never know who had hurt his baby. I had broken my promise. I forced a smile at Jules.

'Thank you for finding me. Can you call me on my mobile when they release the body?'

The noise grew in the corridor as the shifts crossed over. I stood still in the commotion of people filing out from the rooms that branched out around me. Jim raised his voice from the empty MIR, 'Fletcher, can I steal you for a sec?'

I closed the door behind me.

'You alright?'

I held the tip of my tongue between my teeth and shook my head. Empathy always made it worse.

'Everything alright at home?'

I smiled, 'Yes. Nothing like that.'

'I'm afraid, there is something we need to be careful with here.'

'Oh, right,' I pinched my eyebrows together, 'Nothing wrong with the investigation though?'

'No,' he sat down and pushed the sleeves of his shirt over the hairy bulges of his forearms, 'We have had to suspend one of the PCs. Sexual harassment.'

'Jesus,' I leant back onto the wrought iron radiator, 'Anyone we know?'

Jim shrugged, 'No. You ever have any interaction with that Davies guy?'

The ginger kid. The chubby one.

'Only limited. He's relatively new, I think,' I thought back to his blushing cheeks and wondered how he plucked up the confidence to sexually harass anyone.

'What did he do?' I asked.

In my experience in the force I had only seen indirect acts of sexism, borne more of ignorance than intention. But I also knew women who had been groped, pestered, leered at. I suppose I was lucky. Harassment was dealt with swiftly, and severely. I had friends who worked in the City for whom sexual harassment formed part of the day job. An old editor at Sam's place used to finalise business deals in strip clubs.

'Love letters apparently. Dirty.'

'Bloody hell,' I couldn't remember the last time I had seen any kind of sexual harassment involving a written note, 'anyone else involved?'

'Not that we know of,' Jim peered over my shoulder to make sure the door was closed, 'Victim is a PC Stiles. She found him rummaging in her handbag. She'd been finding lewd notes for weeks.'

148

Bloody weird. Unpleasant. Truthfully, I felt like it was a better alternative to some kind of physical assault.

'So, I take it he's out? As of now?'

Jim nodded, 'Yep. Just need to make sure we manage the press properly. Could live without a cock up.'

'Not now,' I said, 'especially with the news we are about the send out.'

I went to The Anchor by myself. Ryan was busy compiling the list of interviewees and I could see that every single person in the MIR was busy on something important. Besides, it sort of felt like going home. I knew the route there from the station so well I didn't have to think. I called the coroners office through the handsfree set on the way.

'Carl. Do you have anything on Emmeline?' I asked, over the noise of the road.

'I can tell you time of death was 330am. Give or take 15 minutes. But not much else yet.'

'Thanks, Carl. I won't keep you.'

'Thanks. I'll let you know as soon as find anything.'

I hung up and turned the ignition off in the car.

The Anchor stood on the corner of Bellevue Road and Trinity Road and was an expensive, pretty gastropub. The waiters were hipster, artistic types and the clientele were hedge fund managers, groomed wives, kids with ridiculous names, expensive dogs. There was a bloody mary station with fresh celery for Sunday brunches and a dog treat station at the door. I used to spend a lot of time in this pub when I lived here. I stuck out. I think that's why Bryn and I got on so well. I was nothing like his regular crowd.

I entered the bar and recognised no one. A short woman with half her head shaved shouted over the taps.

'We don't actually open until 11. But if you take a seat I

can and get your order in a sec.'

I took out my ID.

'DCI Isla Fletcher. Is Will Locke here please?'

A tall ginger man walked through from behind the bar. He stooped to swing his arms around the small woman's waist and planted a firm kiss into the side of her neck.

'Will,' she said.

'This detective is here to see you.'

'Will Locke?' I asked.

'That's me.' he said. He moved away from the small woman, who busied herself with glassware.

'Could you come and sit down please?'

He looked like a toddler who had been told what to do and didn't want to.

He sauntered over to me and sat in a leather wingback chair. His legs were wide apart.

'I'm afraid I have some bad news. Emmeline McDonnell is dead.'

He sat completely still.

'I'm sorry.'

He rubbed a large hand over his face and then leant forward, placing his elbows on his knees.

'What? How?' he sat back, exhaling and looking visibly shaken.

'When?' he said. He had turned pale.

'I am very sorry to have to tell you that we believe that Emmeline was murdered. Her body was found this morning. About five am.'

'Fuck.' he said.

'Were you working last night?' I asked.

He looked around anxiously, making sure he was out of ear shot.

'Yes.' he said. 'Until one. I, erm. I stayed at Elle's place.'

Elle, the short woman behind the bar had disappeared into the kitchen.

'And you stayed there all night?'

He nodded.

'We came into work together this morning. You can ask her.'

I lowered my voice. I didn't need a drama to dilute his reaction.

'Does Elle know about you and Emmeline?'

He shook his head.

'Well it might be time to tell her.'

'How was she killed?' he asked.

'I'm sorry I can't give you any details.'

He looked off, wading through his thoughts.

'I think it would be valuable for you to come into the police station this week. Tell us a bit more about Emmeline.'

'Yes, of course.'

'I'm going to ask one more question before I go.' I said.

'Go on.'

'Do you know someone called Greta Maiberger?'

He paused, and seemed to be genuinely considering his answer.

'No. I don't think so.' he answered. 'Should I?'

'No. Thank you, Mr Locke.'

I stood and walked out of the pub, leaving Will and Elle to it. I didn't get a sense that Will was lying to me, but I also got the sense that unchallenged, he would bend and fuck every women he served without any degree of guilt.

I stood on the corner of Trinity and took out my phone. No new emails or missed calls.

I dialled Dylan Nicholson's number.

'Fletch, how are you?' he answered quickly.

'Have you heard the news?' I asked.

'No.' he said. 'What's happened?'

'There has been another one. He's done it again.'

'Shit. Right. OK. Tell me.'

I looked around me and made sure that no one could hear me.

'Emmeline McDonnell, 26. Exact same MO. It's like looking at the same woman.'

'Right. Should I come in?'

'Maybe. We have some important interviews to conduct. Looks like Emmeline attended the same food show as Greta. We've got the Grace brothers coming in and we need to speak to them as priority. It would be good to speak to you but I can't guarantee a time. Are you ok to wait around?'

'Absolutely. I'll come in. You just find me when you need me.' he said.

'Thank you.' I said. It was reassuring to know he would be there.

I drove back to the station in as much a zoned out state as I had driven to The Anchor. I was planning the interview strategy with the Grace brothers, chewing over the weird letter incident with PC Davis. I was genuinely panicked by the speed at which my man had found his next victim. I'd hoped I'd been wrong about him trying again.

By the time I had got back to the station, the MIR had evolved. The dividing wall between the MIR and the room next to it had been removed, opening it out into a vast space. There were more desks, phones, arses on seats. The room pulsed with activity and smelled like collective morning breath.

The two images of Greta and Emmeline were pinned side by side at the centre of the new board. A slight difference in eye colour aside they were very similar women. Pretty, smiling, dead women.

Stephen and Lee Grace were sat in different interview rooms. Both with two different solicitors from the same expensive law firm.

'Fletch, shall we start with Lee?' said Jim.

'Sounds like a plan.' I said.

I hadn't met the older Grace brother and wondered if he was anything like Stephen.

Jim led the way. Most of the interview rooms were in use. Ryan, Whalley and Davis had been busy prioritising the witness lists: focussing on people from the trade show and Emmeline's immediate friends and family. I had told them that if any witness presented any kind of overlap to let me know. Jim and I needed to focus on the people who had touched both woman lives. The Grace Brothers were the first people we had identified to do that.

'Afternoon, Mr Grace.' said Jim.

'Afternoon.'

'This interview is being taped recorded and may be given in evidence if your case comes to trial. We are in meeting room six at Lavender Hill police station. The date is 22nd November 2019 and the time is fourteen twenty seven.'

'I am DCI James Greaves and this is DCI Isla Fletcher. Please state your full name and date of birth.'

'Lee Joseph Grace. 2nd July 1979.'

'Also present is your solicitor.'

The well-presented man leant towards the desk.

'Alexander Luke Bishop, Bishop & Dean solicitors.'

I guessed that this made the other solicitor in room nine Mr Dean. Either the vegan food business was doing extremely well, or the Grace brothers had family money.

'Do you agree that there are no other persons present?' said Jim.

'Yes.' said Lee.

'Thank you. Mr Grace. Can I call you Lee?'

'Yes.'

'Thanks, Lee.'

'We would like to talk to you about the food show that you attended on the 11th October. Specifically, could you tell me your recollection of the event.'

'My brother and I went up to Leicester together on the train the night before. We met with the people from Sister who had been running our collateral for the stand.'

'Who did you meet from the agency?'

'Louise, one of the senior marketing coordinators. And Greta our account manager.'

'And how long were you with Louise and Greta?'

'About an hour. We met at the conference hall so we could see the banners. We left about 6pm and had dinner together at the hotel. We stayed at the Malmaison and both went to bed about 8pm.'

'So you and your brother separated at 8pm. Did you see anyone else after that?'

'No. I FaceTimed my kids at half 8 and watched TV. And then slept obviously. The day of the trade show, Stephen and I left the hotel at 7am. Greta and Louise met us at the conference centre. We set up with them and a man from Lush Green Events, Zach.'

I made a note of the name and would check in with Ryan on whether someone had spoken to him. If not, he needed to go on the list.

'And,' said Jim. 'Did you spend the full day with Greta?'

'On and off.' he replied. 'She had another client at the event and split her time. I'd say she spent most of the morning with us and then the afternoon with them.'

'And the name of that client?'

'Oh I'm not sure. She didn't want to make us feel unloved.'

'How would you describe the dynamics between you, your brother and Greta over the course of the day?'

'Erm. Friendly I guess. We had a laugh, she was funny, you know.' he said.

'So you liked her?' I asked.

'Well, yes, but not in a weird way. She was nice, I was her client. Nothing creepy or anything.'

Jim took a gulp of his coffee.

'So why didn't you go out to dinner with her and Stephen that night?'

Lee looked at his solicitor. Obviously his brother hadn't made him aware of that. Bishop made a note.

'What dinner?' he asked.

'Your brother, a man called Oliver Long went to dinner at the Malmaison on the night of the 11th with Greta and another woman.'

'Well I wasn't invited.'

'So what did you get up to that night.'

'I didn't stay over. I got the train back to London. I had a family commitment.'

We had already checked his son's appointment. The timing checked out.

'Can you confirm where you were on the night of the 10th November?'

'I was on a lads night out in Clapham Junction. We

watched the Arsenal match at The Goat and then stayed out. I've set out a list of mates who were with me and this is the record of the Uber taxi I got home at one thirty am.'

The solicitor slid over two single sheets of paper with details highlighted.

'And where were you between the hours of 130am and 1030am on Sunday 11th?'

'In bed. At home. You can ask my wife. We had breakfast at home with the kids.'

'Thanks, Lee.' said Jim.

Jim closed one folder on the table and pulled out the second from underneath it.

'Let's go back to the trade show. Do you recall meeting this woman?'

He slid across a photograph of Emmeline McDonnell.

Lee looked at the image carefully.

'No. should I?' said Lee.

'This is Emmeline McDonnell. Do you know her? Have you heard her name?' I said.

'No. Sorry.' said Lee.

'And can you account for your whereabouts on the night of the 21st November?' asked Jim.

'What, two days ago?' said Lee.

'Yes, please' said Jim.

'I was at home.'

'Who were you with?'

'No one. My wife is at her folks place in Devon with the kids. I got back from the office at half 7, ordered a takeaway, played xbox and then slept. I went back into the office yesterday about 10am. Can I ask why?'

'Miss McDonnell was killed in the early hours of the 22nd.'

Lee's eyes widened.

'Well I was definitely at home. I played xBox live until about 1am so you can check on that somehow.'

He turned to his solicitor.

'I was chatting to some fellas in the States playing Call of Duty with them. I can get your their game handles.'

'If you could, that would be great.' said Jim.

'I think that is everything we would like to know for now. But could I ask you to stick around until we have spoken to your brother? Just in case.' said Jim.

'That's fine.' said Alexander Bishop, placing his hand on Lee Grace's arm.

In the room next door, Stephen Grace was sat with the other half of Bishop and Dean. A tanned old man with bright white hair. Stephen was sat relaxed back on the chair with his hands clasped in his lap.

He swore he didn't know Emmeline McDonnell and had been on a date over the weekend. In fact, he had been on two dates. On Friday night he met a Cherechi Aremu in a bar in Shoreditch. Cherechi was a trainee solicitor at a magic circle law firm whom he had met on Tinder. He went back to her place on Friday night and then left around midday on Saturday. On Saturday night, he met Felicia Rossi, a dancer in the West End. He had been messaging Felicia through mysinglefriend for a few months and met a couple of times before. She stayed at his place on Saturday night and they went for a walk around London Fields together early Sunday morning. Both Cherechi and Felicia would account for him; although he would obviously prefer it if we didn't mention one to the other.

Lee did not wait for Stephen. They left the station separately.

I spent an hour in my office reading over the interview notes with increasing frustration and I was glad when Jim knocked on my door.

'Everything ok, Fletch?'

I thought back to the face of Jessica Fox, blackened and misshapen and then the face of her father. I thought about his cold body in a hospital mortuary.

'Derek Fox died today, Jim.'

'Fuck. The assault victim's Dad?'

'Yes.'

Jim stood and held my shoulders with both hands. The closest thing to a hug he had ever gotten.

'Let's go and get some lunch. I'm bloody starving anyway.'

The pub wasn't full of arseholes. It was one of those transient pubs where the locals varied from the stalwart old boys who refused to move out of the area and the wanker young professionals who could just about afford the ex-council high rises. This part of Battersea wasn't quite as upmarket as the neighbouring Clapham Junction but it did a good line of ales, and it didn't play any house music in the background. Jim and I would eat lunch here when we didn't want to bump into any of the junior officers down at The Latchmere. When we needed to talk.

The plates of crusts and crumpled napkins lay in front of us. All I could taste was raw red onion. I crunched an antacid in my mouth as Jim pinched up the last remaining chips from the puddle of vinegar and tipped them into his mouth.

'Did she have any brothers and sisters?' he said.

'No. But her Uncle will be taking care of the funeral,

thank God. She's in no fit state.'

'Is she still in hospital?'

'No. With her family in Surrey.'

He took a huge gulp of ale.

'It's shit, Isla. Nothing more to say.'

I loved how bluntly he put the truth.

'We've both lost parents. There's no easy out for her. You have to just let them get on with it. And you can't shoulder it. Not on top of what we are dealing with.'

His words were part guidance, part warning.

I knew. I had to let Jessica and her family find their own path of least resistance to normality. For me, that had meant moving two hundred miles away and leaving Mum with the Church Women's Group. And building an unhealthy tolerance for wine.

A call vibrated out on the table, I turned it over, expecting an update from Jules, but replaced it face down when I saw Sam's name flash up. I decided to call her on the way home.

'You got yourself a secret fella, Fletcher?'

He seem surprised. I finished the last gritty sip of wine and raised my eyebrows, contemplating how best to talk about Sam.

'Not going to answer it?'

I shook my head. Courage, Isla.

'No, I'll give her a call when I'm done.'

Jim looked as disinterested in prying as usual. I remembered my promise to Sam.

'Sam is my girlfriend.'

Jim finished the foamy dark liquid at the bottom of his pint. Zero reaction.

'Well, when you give me the nod, I'll have to get her over for dinner. That'll keep Jean happy,' he wiped the liquid from his moustache with the thick hair on the back of his hand, 'You got time for another before you go?'

It took me a moment to respond, as I imagined taking Sam to Jim's house for dinner. Picking out the wine, talking over politics and listening to The Kinks once he'd had a skinful.

'I was supposed to be running home but guess I can take a taxi. Small red.'

He looked over to the barmaid and indicated the same again. Masha smiled a toothy grin at us and pulled at the ale pump. Her tanned, sinewy arms strained as the warm liquid frothed into the glass. I felt relieved. Which is why I was so pissed off by what he said next.

'I think you need to take the night off, mate.'

My eyes narrowed.

'I'm conscious of the hours you've been putting in. By all means take a look over the notes at home, but I think you would benefit from a night to think, or rest. You need to sleep.'

I looked at him and tried to form an argument behind my very best poker face.

'Don't be annoyed, I'm only saying it because I care.'

'Listen, I know you do and I appreciate it. But...'

He saw right through me and squashed the idea.

'Not negotiable.'

Masha brought over the two drinks and placed a bill down on the table. It stuck to the ring made by his pint glass. Jim smiled up at her and handed over a battered looking twenty.

'Thanks. Keep the change for yourself.'

He looked back and me, smiled and opened his palms in a peace offering.

'Look, Isla, I can see you're pissed off, but you and I both know that you won't be any use to anyone if you run yourself into the ground. I'm having a night off too.'

I looked at him and took a huge gulp of my drink. The warmth of the red wine coated my throat and I felt a little calmer. I felt tired and surrendered.

'Fine. But I'm dialling into the call tomorrow morning, even if I just listen.'

'Deal.'

'And I'm going to speak to Dylan Nicholson about the profile.'

He smiled and picked up the pint of ale; it looked like toy furniture in his giant hands.

I sat in the back of the taxi, although with the it would have been quicker to walk. The rain was falling hard, to the point where I could only make out shapes and lights out of the passenger window. Brake lights shone a red haze through the wind-screen wipers as the taxi driver tutted with each stop and start. At least he didn't try and make a conversation.

That was the one thing I had quickly acclimatised to in London, not speaking to strangers without a reason. I twisted the material of scarf into small knots, picked off a loose thread from my sleeve, pushed the cuticles back on each nail. Bored, I lifted out my mobile and switched on the night mode. If I was going to dick around on social media then I might as well reduce the impact on my sleeping pattern from the blue light. I idly scanned through my own, sparse profiles before searching for each of the victims in turn. I looked through the instagram feed set up by Emmeline McDonnell and the Ace Cafe. I looked at the Wild Grace website. I scrolled through the memorial messages on Greta's Facebook wall then admonished myself. I closed the app and tried my luck with the news; but the comments sections annoyed me too much. More people dying across the world.

I locked the screen then turned the handset over in my hand. I knew messaging would be a bad idea. The car braked again and the driver switched on the radio. Debate raged between the host and a caller with a thick Geordie accent. I couldn't face being drawn into thinking anymore, and even though I could feel the wine blurring my vision, I logged into my emails.

'Dylan. Thank you for your input today, are you able to dial-in to the briefing call tomorrow am? I think we should then maybe arrange a separate session for tomorrow afternoon if you are free?'

I shouldn't have emailed. I should have called him sober. But the wine had done what it always did. And I felt impulsive.

His response came quickly.

'Sure. I'm happy to do both. Does 3pm work?'

So I had totally misread it. No emotion, no flirtation. I resolved to put the phone away, and email my response in the morning, when it buzzed again.

'...are you only just leaving the office? Have you been working since 4am?'

I felt excited. Relaxed.

'Yes. Working hours don't really apply. Although I managed a glass of wine so it's not all bad...'

I added, then swiftly deleted, a winking emoji. I wasn't that drunk. I followed up with, '3pm tomorrow is great, let's grab a coffee near the station?'

I pressed send but our messages crossed.

'I have had a couple of beers too, I met up with a few academic friends after my last meeting. Are you still out?'

Fuck.

I looked at the sat nav on the dashboard of the taxi. I was

a projected 23 minutes away from my flat.

'In a taxi home. An early night beckons...'

I almost added the truth. The sort of truth I only told myself, and acted on, when I was more than two glasses of wine in. 22 minutes from home. The three dots flashed up showing him typing his reply. Then it stopped, disappeared for a while. Then reappeared. I felt the tension of the two halves of my moral psyche: the half that hoped he would push it and the half that knew we needed to stop.

'I could come over? Bring a bottle?'

I knew exactly how that would end. In exactly the way I had wanted it to. I knew the taste of the wine we would share, the taste of it on him, the taste of him. I shifted my weight in the taxi seat, crossing my legs tightly against the idea. I followed a new raindrop as it joined the tributaries running down the window pane. I imagined the weight of him, and how he would feel inside me, how his hands would feel against my face.

19 minutes from home.

I really considered it. The sex, and the goodbye. Holding the guilt from Sam. I wondered how long it would last this time before I could safely cage it away. But Dylan was a colleague, and a really good BIA. I couldn't willingly sign up to an endless cycle of deceit. I didn't want an affair. But despite everything, I couldn't squash it completely.

'That sounds amazing. But I really do need to sleep, and more wine would only get me into trouble tomorrow.'

I lingered over the button before pressing send. But I had started something simple and physiological, and I needed to finish it. I started a new message to Sam.

'Hey sweetie, are you enjoying your drinks? Do you fancy grabbing some dinner?'Sam replied straight away.

'Of course I would. I just bought a round so will jump on the tube in an hour or so. I'll head over to yours? Can't wait to see you. x'

Then before I could reply to Sam, a message from Dylan flashed up.

'Shame. It would have been really good to see you, Fletch. Another time. Sleep tight. x'

Fuck.

18

My eyes scanned over the contents of the fridge without really processing what was in there. I didn't feel like cooking. I wanted another glass of wine. A big warming duvet of wine, then sex and then sleep. But if I had another glass I wouldn't be able to focus on the case notes on the dining table. I text Sam to see if she fancied a takeaway.

The effects of the wine had worn off. I grabbed a bottle of sparking water and peered over the ledge of the glass brick wall that divided out the kitchen. I stared at the papers splayed out on the coffee table. I was resigned to spending the next hour looking over the case but I couldn't stop thinking about the Fox case. I couldn't stop thinking about my dreams and the rotting face of Derek Fox.

I thought about Joachim and Isobel Maiberger and Patrick McDonnell in Pentonville Prison, confined in his grief. Poor bastard. I had seen the horrified faces of two sets of friends. I thought back to the Facebook pages of both women, seeing their lives played out in check-ins and status updates. Between them, there would be more than nine hundred people mourning their loss; sharing memories, creating memorial pages, remembering their smiles. Nine hundred people. I thought about the family, friends, colleagues, happenstance encounters and ex-lovers. The vast social network of two women who had been killed. Nine hundred people, in countless languages, asking why. And if it killed me, I would tell them.

But I could not force my mind to focus. Jim had been right, I needed to switch off.

I knew I'd end up in the police force after what happened

to Dad. Not because I admired the investigation but because it was such a disgrace. Lost case notes. A family liaison officer that didn't give a shit about me, or Mum. Negligent processes. That was when the night terrors began. They eventually diluted down into nightmares as I studied more about the psychology of grief but I never got over the anger at having nobody to answer our questions. I knew I needed to fix it, I knew I could fix it. I knew I could find answers. I would find an answer for Greta, I would find an answer for Emmeline.

I hadn't found one for Derek. I thought back to Jessica's mangled face and slapped my notepad onto the coffee table. That would be the image that Derek took to his grave, that would be how he remembered his daughter in death. Beaten. A familiar rage simmered and I clenched my fists to count down from ten. I needed to either have a drink or punch something, or fuck. I needed to calm down. I pushed the files across the room where they lay fanned on the wooden boards until Sam clicked her keys in the lock.

I was staring blankly at a quiz show repeat with the sound turned down as she swept in from the hallway and dropped the keys into the bowl on the small dining table. She stooped down and gracefully gathered the papers into one pile, tapping the base on the dining table. She leant over and passed me the new pile.

'Hey, sweetie. You alright?'

I swallowed the urge to snap, 'obviously not' and counted my breath.

'Not really. I'm not really getting anywhere with this.' I said.

'Do you want to talk about it? Over dinner?' she said.

'No thanks. I just can't seem to work this out.'

I glanced down and saw that in a making a single pile, Sam had swept up the case notes with the old Jessica file. Brilliant. Just what I needed. It wasn't Sam's fault, I shouldn't have mixed up the cases.

'Do you want to talk it over with me?' she said.

No.

'I don't know if I should.' I replied.

I recognised the need to lash out at her and pushed back. Not again.

'You know everything you say is confidential, right?' she said.

'I know, I know. It's really dark stuff. I don't want you near it.'

'Well, I offered. Are you going to be working for a while? I could always shower or something?'

Her patience was growing thin.

I snapped myself out of it. Determined to have a good night with her. I gave her a hug.

'No, its fine. I'll order us some food.'

I decided to focus on living a life for an evening and pressed the power button on the remote. Music helped. TV just wound me up. Food, wine, music. Sam. I remembered the words of my old therapist and made a conscious decision to 'choose my emotion'. I shuffled a playlist on Spotify through the speaker system and smiled at her.

'You fancy Thai?' I picked up my iPad to find the menu, 'I'll switch my brain off. Promise.'

She straddled me, her knees sinking into the soft cushions either side of me, her groin pressing onto mine. She took the iPad away and placed it next to me.

'Thai works for me.'

She took the glasses from the nest of hair on top of my head and placed them onto my face, carefully positioning the arms behind my ears.

'You like?'

I noticed the newly short hair and the need for recognition. I touched my fingers tips to her chin.

'I really like it.'

'You sure?'

'Yes. It looks amazing,' I gently touched the short strands that fell over her ears, 'You suit it short.'

She half-smiled coyly and tucked the longer strands at the front behind her ear.

'You sure it doesn't look, you know, a bit too, gay?'

I fixed squarely onto her eyes.

'No. I love it.'

She smiled at me. I really wanted her. And I wanted to make her happy. In as equal measure as I knew I couldn't be faithful forever, I really wanted to be.

'And I told Jim.'

She beamed a wide, toothy grin and we kissed. She pushed her lips onto mine in celebration and squealed.

'I'm so happy for you,' she said as she held up my hands, kissed them, then placed them on the small of her back, 'See, baby steps?'

We kissed again. Lips parted. She tasted like cigarettes and negronis and made me miss smoking. Her tongue was slick from an afternoon drinking sugary cocktails. I always loved how she tasted. I slid my left hand to the small of her back and pulled her closer, feeling the heat of her abdomen against mine. She leaned back, untied the knot of the blouse and slipped the soft material over her head. She undid the two buttons at the top of my shirt and traced a fingertip along my collarbone.

'Let's think about dinner a little later on,' she said as she opened the wide button on the top of her black denim jeans, and leaned back onto me, 'afterwards.'

I stared at the constellation of moles at the nape of her neck and blew away the hair clippings that stuck to the dew of her skin. I really did love her. I couldn't remember the last time I felt as happy, or as guilty. Sweet Catholicism making sure I didn't feel too happy without a hearty helping of guilt to balance it out. I brushed off some stubborn strands of clipped hair and ran my fingers over the smooth skin of her back.

I thought back to the clippings of hair that had stuck to Jessica's ears and tried to close away the guilt. A guilt of a different kind, the guilt of Derek's death.

I moved my fingers further down her back.

Sam started to rock her hips back against my fingertips, ready again to be touched. I kissed the nape of her neck, pressing myself against the moan that vibrated in her chest.

But then, in the party of noises – and desire - in my head, I heard it. The voice shouting my name in the busy room. I jumped off the sofa and stood, naked, trying to remember where I had put my notes from the first visit with Jessica. I ran through to the bedroom. I ducked as I realised the curtains were still open and pulled on my cotton robe, picking up the box file as I ran through to the lounge. I thought back to the pictures I had seen of Jessica in her parents house. I had something.

'Are you ok, sweetie?' Sam sat up and pulled the throw around her.

I sat cross-legged on the floor and emptied the file out.

'I think I remembered something important.'

I didn't think, I knew. She sat and watched me, concerned. I finally found the picture I was looking for and stood up, scanning the room for my phone. It rang out four times before he picked up.

'I thought I told you to take a night off?' he mumbled.

'Jim, he has done it before,' I said. 'He's fucking tried it

169

before.'

I was pacing the room, my voice getting louder. Too loud. I could sense from the concerned look on Sam's face. I smiled at her to reassure her. I could hear Jim grunting on the other line. The heavy, dull shuffle of a duvet.

'Hold on Isla, I'm in bed.'

I put the phone on mute and faced Sam.

'We might need to get dressed, Jim might head over here. It's all fine, I'm sorry, I've just realised something.'

I looked down at the image in my hand, a picture of Jessica with her parents taken eighteen months before the attack. In it, Jessica looked completely different, smiling in the sunshine with thick shoulder length hair. Blonde, golden curls. The day before the attack she had volunteered to be a model in a hairdressing competition, resulting in the auburn pixie crop.

'Isla. I'm here. Whats up?'

'The assault I told you about, Jessica Fox? It was him. It was the same guy. Greta wasn't the first.'

19

I nudged Sam awake from where she had fallen asleep on the sofa.

'Sweetie, Jim is almost here. Did you want to go to bed?'

She smiled at me, then slowly hauled herself out of the armchair.

'It's probably best to meet him another time, anyway.' he said.

I hugged her and kissed the slope of her neck. She padded to the bedroom and closed the door behind her. I glanced at the mirror in the hallway and dismissed my grey reflection. I put a straight edge on the lounge, not that Jim ever noticed the difference, and set out the Woodford reserve on the coffee table. I poured a Dad-sized measure over three ice cubes and stared again at the image of Jessica. I had absent-mindedly sunk two fingers before Jim buzzed downstairs. I slid the picture off the table and ran with it down to the front door, thrusting it at him as I opened the heavy door.

'See what I mean?'

Jim scoffed and ran a hand over his bald head. He took the hallway stairs two at a time.

'Give me a bloody minute,' he stepped out of his shoes and threw his heavy raincoat over the door to the lounge, 'I was asleep about an hour ago. Some of us need to sleep.'

I overtook him and refilled my glass. I poured out a second, neat glass for Jim and handed it to him. He sat, looked at it and then set it down on the table.

'I drove here remember?'

I knew he would be here a while. It would wear off.

'Just look at it.' I said.

'Right then, let's have a look.'

He placed the picture underneath the lamp, stared at it hard, then looked back at me.

'What exactly happened to her?'

'He was waiting for her. A Sunday morning. Broke her jaw clean in half.'

'Jesus.'

'I knew it. I fucking knew something wasn't right, Jim. I couldn't figure out why this guy had stopped.'

'No sexual assault?' he asked.

I shook my head.

'Nothing missing?'

I picked up the image of Greta from the table in front of me and held it out against the image of Jessica.

'Its the same man, Jim.'

'But you know the MO is different. We might struggle without forensics.'

'But that's it Jim,' I said, 'It *was* different. Because he was angry. This was rage. He came expecting to find the perfect woman. Looking the perfect way. But instead,' I leant forward and handed a picture of her in the hospital bed with the cropped hair, and the broken face 'he found someone else. Something else. Something imperfect.'

'I see,' he replied, 'so she cocked up his plan,'

'Exactly,' I said, 'But there is more.'

I pointed to the report fanned out next to the bottle, to the lines highlighted in blue.

'I highlighted some lines from the interview. I just didn't know.'

Jim took a large mouthful of his drink and set the heavy

glass down on the wood. I filled it again as he digested the words.

'There were flowers in her flat?'

I nodded.

'And you didn't ask if she bought them?'

I shook my head.

'I just didn't think.'

I glanced down at the image of the flowers from the crime scene. Wrapped in brown paper and twine. Damson dipped freesias, roses, baby's breath. I imagined them rotting. The organic, dying traces of a failed first attempt.

Jim cleared his throat, 'That's why he did it again so quickly.'

Absolutely.

'We need to find out where those flowers came from,' I offered, 'but there is one point I can't quite make sense of.'

'Go on,' he said, hugging the glass to his chest.

'So, we know he is organised, methodical and controlled. And that, given the physicality of the victims, he selects them carefully, yes?'

Jim nodded.

'Jessica had her hair done the day before the attack?'

He nodded again.

'At some point in the run up to the attack, she was selected. The plan was agreed.'

He stopped nodding, narrowing his eyes.

'Then, what? Nothing?' I held out the fingers on my left out, 'He then waited and didn't see her again until the night he had planned?'

Jim drained the whiskey and helped himself to another, larger measure. I could see that he was stitching the strands of the individual investigations together in his mind. I considered the logistics: the MIR, the interview strategy and suspect pool.

We would need Dylan too.

'There is something else we need to worry about, Fletcher.'

I stopped and looked at the man sitting on my sofa. His posture looked tired, deflated. Jim definitely looked thinner.

'This sexual harassment thing is a bigger than I originally thought. More women have come forward.'

'What?' I scoffed, 'the weird notes?'

I couldn't muster empathy for women who had received explicit notes when I was dealing with women who had been strangled and mutilated.

'Apparently two additional women have received them. One of them thought it was her ex-husband.'

'And it's what? Love letters?'

Jim placed his chin on the rim of his glass and murmured.

'Not exactly. Its pretty grim reading actually. We are recommending counselling.'

'Explicit?'

'I guess. It's more the specifics, you know, knowing the details of their lives.'

'So its stalking, as opposed to notes?'

'We think so. But its more that they were written by one of ours.'

I thought to Davies pink flushed cheeks. I still struggled to imagine him scribbling sordid notes. I admit I hadn't given it much thought.

'When was the last note found?' I asked.

'This morning.'

'Shit, so...'

'Yep.'

He finished the whiskey and set it down on the glass counter top.

'It couldn't have been Davies. He's been living with his bloody Mother over in Kilburn for the past three days. Hasn't left the house.'

He looked at the fan of notes on the table and rubbed a hand over his stubbled face.

'But we've got more important things to talk about, right?'

He definitely did look thinner. Gaunt.

'Is there anything else, Jim? Everything ok at home? With Jean?'

He smiled then picked up one of the folders. He flicked it open then looked up at the copper clock on the kitchen wall. It was three am.

'Should we just push through?'

I peeled the skin of my lower back from the leather sofa, stood, stretched and arched backwards. I felt oldest in my bones. I walked to the kitchen, ignoring the reflection in the french doors from the halogen bulbs shining brightly against the thick black morning.

'Coffee?'

I flicked on the kettle and stared into the cupboard.

'Aye. And stodge.'

I took an old loaf out of the freezer.

'Toast?'

He nodded, absorbed in the medical notes I had shuffled to the front of the folder. Even without the coffee I felt awake. Anxious. Ready.

20

I answered the call from Carl in the car.

'Carl, you've got me and Jim on the line. We are on our way to the station.'

'Good. Two birds and all that.'

'What have you got?' I asked.

'Emmeline. There are no signs of vaginal or anal rape. But there are traces of semen, she had unprotected intercourse a day before her death.'

'Do you think it was our man?' Jim asked.

'I couldn't say. All I can say is that it's there.'

'And cause of death?'

'Exactly the same. Death by strangulation, incision made post mortem.'

'Thanks, Carl.'

I pressed red and then called Lester.

'Lester, is there anything from the SOCOs yet?'

'Not yet, but I'm on my way to a meeting now. I should have something for you in the next hour.'

Ryan was my next call. Jim just focussed on the road. I was giddy in the passenger seat next to him and couldn't stop fidgeting. The morning was bright blue and freezing cold. Frost glittered on Clapham Common and the ice on the wing mirror was still defrosting.

'Ma'am.' said Ryan. He still sounded half asleep.

'Ryan we need to build out the MIR this morning. Greta Maiberger was not the first victim. We believe that he tried to kill before. Jessica Fox, an aggravated assault case. Can you pull everything from case B5333 and have it waiting for me and DCI Greaves. Can you integrate the key notes onto the whiteboard?'

'Yes.' he said.

'We will see you there.'

A crowd of people were milling around the MIR. They were all waiting for me to explain. I took my coat off and set it on a desk with my rucksack. Ryan had put an image of Jessica on the board, of her auburn hair. I pulled a folder out of my bag and pulled out the older picture. I walked over to the whiteboard and put the older picture next to Greta and Emmeline. The room murmured.

'This.'

I tapped the board.

'Is Jessica Fox. She was the victim of an aggravated assault on 30th October. She was assaulted in her flat and hospitalised for 5 days. On the day she was assaulted, she looked like this.'

I pointed to the auburn crop.

'But we believe that the man responsible was expecting to see this woman.'

I pointed to the blonde curls.

'We believe that this is our killers first attempt.'

People in the room looked at each other. They looked just as appalled as I felt.

'Now,' I pointed to the image of the incision in Greta's skull. 'We know that he got better. But we need to assume that his anger made him sloppy. We need to revisit every single element of the assault case and we need to figure out what the bloody hell links these three women.'

'We know from the profile that while he obviously has a type, he must have met them. He must have taken the time to get to know these women.'

I faltered and swallowed hard against the lump in my throat.

'There is another sensitivity here.' I said.

'Derek Fox, Jessica's Father, sadly passed away yesterday. He had a stroke. So in every single interaction we need to remember we are dealing with three grieving families.'

The room nodded. It was 9am so I decided to run the morning briefing from the MIR. Everyone needed to know where we were and I needed everyone to act with the same urgency.

'Ryan, can you open the conference call line just in case anyone dials into the call?'

He picked up the handset of his phone.

'Everyone, we have a 915 briefing call for the Maiberger case but I think it would be to everyone's benefit for us to talk about this here. You'll already know if you're in charge of a work stream, and I might well assign other work stream leaders. So listen up but don't be afraid to chip in if you have any questions or any important information.' I said.

There were a great deal more people in the room. A series of three was very unusual in London and there were a lot of people interested in finding my man. It meant I had to delegate, pushed me further away from the details, but I needed to build out the team.

Jim had ordered in at least eleven new sergeants and a couple of administrative staff. DI Gavenas was a short, pale Lithuanian who I had worked with before. I knew no details of her life but knew she was efficient. I don't think many people had warmed to her. But she looked ready. I'd been introduced to DI Basin on my arrival to the station. He had been drafted in from Brixton Hill and had told me that they had more available, should we need it. He had a firm handshake and seemed ready too.

Telephone calls for all cases had been re-directed to another room. There were boxes of reports stacked on desks and Ryan was standing at the whiteboard, still integrating the key elements from the Fox case. I looked at the board, at the three women. I looked at Jessica and felt revived. I'd find answers for her too.

'So let's start from the beginning.' I started.

'Jessica Fox, 26. Assaulted on 30th October in her one bedroom flat on Abbeville Road in Clapham. Jessica is a freelance journalist who specialises in finance. She returned home at 1130am and was attacked by a man waiting for her in her living room. She was badly beaten and strangled but he stopped short of killing her before leaving the flat. What we know now is that he brought a bouquet of flowers with him.'

'We will need to run over Jessica's network and see if there is any overlap at all with either Greta or Emmeline. Whalley, can you lead on that?'

'Second, we need to look at where all three women had been in October, September push it back to August if we need to. Let's see if there was somewhere they might have all visited. Someone they might have all spoken to. Ryan, I'll leave you with that.'

'Third. We need to carry on building out the network for Emmeline McDonnell. The interviewing process has only just started there. We need to speak to Devon Powell, her boss. We need to interview everyone on that street. Her close friends. We need someone up at Pentonville to speak to her Dad. DCI Greaves and I will look at that list this morning and prioritise it. Then—'

I looked around the room.

'DI Gavenas' I said, 'can you run point on interviews?'

'Yes, ma'am.'

'Parish. Can you look at social media? Including phone and messaging content.'

'Do we need to say anything to the press?' asked Sophie.

'No,' I answered. 'Not at this point. As a holding statement we can say we are following other lines of enquiries but I don't want anything to come out before I've had a chance to speak to Jessica or her Mum. I want to warn them.'

'DI Basin,' I continued. 'Can you now take the lead of the work stream with the SOCOs? We haven't had anything back from the McDonnell crime scene. He was interrupted and we might get lucky there. Similarly, look at the notes on the Fox assault and see if there is anything that jumps out now we know it is linked to the Maiberger and McDonnell homicides.'

I carried on but spoke mainly to Jim.

'As I said, I will speak with Jessica or her family and bring her up to date. I will also update the profile with the BIA and share with you all.'

'Which BIA are working with ma'am?' asked Gavenas.

'Dylan Nicholson. He had written a report based wholly on the Maiberger homicide and was working to update it for McDonnell. But this will be another change of direction.'

'Did Jessica Fox have any siblings?' asked Basin.

'No.'

Neither Greta nor Emmeline had siblings either. I wondered if that made a difference.

Whalley stood and handed the crime scene photographs from Emmeline's flat to Ryan, who pinned it to the board.

'Who was the crime scene photographer?' I asked.

'Chris Jeffries.' he answered.

I hadn't seen Chris since the night in the carpark and I was glad I missed him at the crime scene. I was hoping that he was so embarrassed that he would look for a job elsewhere.

'DCI Greaves, anything to add?'

'It goes without saying really, but I'll say it. Make sure that everything you do is run by the loggist—'

He scanned the room. Louise stood.

'We do not want anything falling through the cracks. So dot the eyes.'

'Any other questions?' I added.

Silence.

'Right. Let's use this morning to get our shit in one sock. I will be in my office for the next half an hour.'

Ryan found me twenty minutes later.

'Ma'am, I've got something interesting.'

'August 21st. Jessica attended a journalists event in the City. It was sponsored by a couple of investment management companies. The delegates all went to The Bird for dinner afterwards.'

'Right.'

Maybe Emmeline had waitressed there, or Greta was meeting clients.

'I spoke to the events organiser at Dillingers, one of the investment managers. A man called Boden Short. He said he would send over the full list of delegates for the day, but he also said that because it was a co-sponsored event they contracted the evening event out to a third party. Lush Green events.'

The same company that managed the food event attended by Emmeline and Greta.

'Great work, Ryan. We need a full list of all of their staff going back to July. All of their events and who worked on what. Make that priority.'

I picked up my phone and called Jim. He would want to know.

Next on the call list was Jessica. Or at the least her FLO.

I closed the door and dialled Jules's number.

'Jules? It's DCI Isla Fletcher. We spoke the other day.'

'Yes, DCI Fletcher. How are you?' she said.

'Well. Listen, I'm ringing to sense check something with you. There has been a development on the Fox case. We believe the assailant is the man responsible for two murders. One on the 11th November and one two days. Two women in their twenties, strangled to death and mutilated.'

'Jesus Christ.'

Indeed.

'I want to update Jessica but I don't want to upset her, or worry her. What are your thoughts? Do you think I can go and see her?'

Jules blew into the phone and hummed.

'Honestly. I'm not sure that would be the best idea. She is staying at her parent's house, helping her Mum with the funeral arrangements. Derek's funeral is next week.'

The line went silent as she thought it over.

'But you're right. She should definitely know. Would you mind leaving it with me? I can talk her through it?'

'Absolutely,' I said. 'Let me drop you a quick email with the key information. I appreciate your help.'

I hung up and drafted the email straight away. I wanted to protect Jessica but I didn't want her to see this on the news. After I had pressed send on the email I saw a text from Sam, asking about where we could meet for lunch. Her Mum was in town until mid-December, staying with Sam's Aunt in Battersea and I had told her that I might be able to meet them for lunch but now knew that I just didn't have the time.

'Hey sweetie,' she answered.

'Hey, I'm so sorry but I'm not going to be able to make

lunch.'

Sam took a moment to hide her disappointment.

'OK sweetie, well I know you are really busy.'

'I am really sorry.'

'Honestly, it's OK. Mum and Aunt Mel understand. And I can get by a lunch with Isaac without you.'

'Your brother is going?' I said.

'Yes. Mum managed to convince him to play nice with me. So it'll be interesting to see if he has anything to say for himself!'

'It will. And it might be nice to try and make amends with him. I know he's a bit of a stress head but he is your brother. And family is important.'

'Thanks, sweetie. I'll let you know how it goes. Try and make sure you eat something though.'

'I will. Speak to you later.'

An email flashed in my inbox from Dylan Nicholson. I was about to pick up the phone when Whalley knocked on my office door.

'Ma'am. There is a geographical connection between Jessica and Emmeline.'

'Go on.' I said.

'I was looking back at her instagram pictures and there was a batch of pictures uploaded in July from a friend's 30th party. It was taken in the private room at The Anchor pub. I just spoke to the landlord and checked the work roster and Will Locke was working that day. So it's entirely feasible that he met Jessica.'

And she had her blonde hair in July.

'Right. Excellent. Can you get someone to go and bring him in?'

'Yes, ma''am.' he said. He closed the door behind him and

I heard his heavy footfalls echo away quickly down the hallway.

I felt overwhelmed by the sea of actions, struggled to tread in the water of each new swell of information. I decided to get out of the station and try and get all of my thoughts ordered. I needed to focus them into something tangible. I replied to Dylan's email, asking if he could meet for coffee on Battersea Rise in fifteen minutes.

My phone rang as I walked to the MIR. I answered it without checking the number, thinking it was Dylan confirming our coffee.

'Hello, sweetheart. It's Mum.'

I did love how she always felt the need to tell me who was calling.

'I'm just ringing to see if you've made a decision about Christmas?'

'I haven't. I'm sorry. It's absolutely chaotic at work.'

'OK. Well, I thought I'd put the order in nice and early for food. So I'll factor you in. You can bring someone if you like? If you're seeing someone?'

'No. I'm not at the moment.' I lied. 'It'll just be me' then added, 'obviously if I can make it.'

'OK. Well I've leave you to it.'

'Thanks, Mum. I promise I'll let you know as soon as I can.'

Parish was the first person I saw in the MIR. I told him I wasn't going to be in my office for the next hour and to tell people to call me on my mobile. I grabbed my coat and set out.

Fresh air, caffeine. Thinking time.

-

21

I had chosen an independent coffee shop on Battersea Rise. The majority of the freelancers tended to sit on the tall benches at the windows and the larger tables with the comfy seats at the back were normally only taken at lunchtime. I had ordered two coffees and placed my coat on the chair across the table from me, reserving it for Dylan. He arrived 10 minutes after I got there, jumping out of an uber on the busy road.

'You don't drive?' I asked.

'No, I do. My car is just in the garage.' he said. 'I would have walked but didn't want to keep you waiting.'

'Thanks.' I said.

It was warm in the coffee shop, I took off my blazer and set it on top of my bag next to me. The smell of ground coffee was strong but I could smell Dylan over it.

'We need to revise the profile. And pretty quickly.'

I handed a green folder over to him.

'Take a look at the before and after pictures. This is an aggravated assault case from a month ago.'

Dylan scanned the contents of the folder and caught up quickly.

'He's tried and failed before?'

He was looking down at Jessica's image. At her blackened face.

'Yes.'

I pulled the report over her face. I hated seeing her like that. And I didn't want any member of the public seeing her.

'It makes sense now. The rage.' I said.

'I was working on that case and I couldn't figure out why the anger was so, well, pointless. No theft, no rape, no murder; just pure rage. And now I understood why: Jessica had fucked up his plan. He really had wanted her to die, he had planned on killing her.'

'There was a bouquet of flowers listed in the inventory list of the crime scene, damson-dipped freesias. He had laid in wait with his props, waiting to paint the perfect image in death. To do what he did to Greta. But in changing her hairstyle so dramatically she had ruined the perfect picture of a corpse he had planned on painting.'

'She ruined it for him.' said Dylan, 'the climax.'

'Does that explain the speed he's picked up now?' I asked.

'Potentially.' he said. 'Maybe this was always part of his plan. Maybe he had selected his victims in sequence. It would fit. Being methodical.'

'How does this affect the profile?' I asked.

Dylan thought for a second, rubbing the side of his cheek.

'He's not as controlled as we thought. Or least, he is capable of great control but he's always right there —' he held his thumb and forefinger together '—the anger. He can snap at any time.'

'I suppose that's what makes the killings of Greta and Emmeline all the more successful for him? Holding it together like that.' I said.

'My sense is that it discounts a medical professional too. He might even have had a more peppered career history. Changing jobs or industries quite often. Because of that he might not own his own home. He might actually be more transient than we thought. Move around a bit.'

'So less focus on the geographical identifiers?'

He nodded.

'He will still want to feel familiar. He for sure knows South London. The fact that all three victims lived here is important. But I think he finds a way to know them in different ways.'

'All three had public social media accounts. Facebook and Instagram. Jessica didn't post as frequently as Greta and Emmeline but all would happily check in to locations. They all had jobs where they needed to interact with lots of people. Greta through her network of clients, and their markets. Emmeline more directly in the people she served, less so through her online store, and Jessica would speak to tons of different people in financial services.'

'Has anyone you've interviewed fit this?' he asked, placing his hand on the report.

'No.'

'Blake Wallder, Greta's boyfriend seemed earnest, but lacked the IQ. I have a suspicion that she cheated on him. I don't think she was invested in it as he was.'

'The unknowable woman.' said Dylan.

'Exactly.' I said. 'Her ex-boyfriend, Max, fits some of the elements. He's smart, successful. His career as an architect shows determination, precision. You know, he's a man of method. But he knew that Greta cheated on him and he still loved her. He was heartbroken. And I didn't get a sense that he hated all women. Plus, I truly believe I could take him in an arm wrestle.'

We laughed.

'How about the Grace brothers?' asked Dylan.

'Again, no. I don't like either of them. Stephen is cocky, and cocksure. He sleeps with women at an alarming rate but just because I think he's riddled, doesn't mean I think he's evil.'

'And you think our man is evil?' he asked.

'Don't come at me with your psychology.' I scoffed.

'I did psychology at uni. So I don't need to argue the semantics. I don't believe our man was born evil, I don't necessary believe in the concept of evil. Psychopathy is just the absence of emotion I guess. By evil, I guess I mean capable of evil deeds. And I don't believe Stephen is. And Lee is another cocky bastard who I think is pretty used to buying his way out of trouble.'

'So do you often go with your gut instinct?' asked Dylan.

'No.' I said, then actually thought about.

'Actually, sometimes. I think I do get a sense for people. But I always back it up with facts. Ans Stephen, Lee and Max all alibi out for Emmeline and Greta. We are confirming Blake's. We will obviously check on where they all where when Jessica was assaulted, but—

'You don't *feel* it was them.'

My phone rang. It was Jim. Dylan could see the caller ID and sat back on the sofa across from me, instinctively giving me space but keeping himself open to input.

'Fletch. The DNA has come back from Emmeline. It's Will Locke.'

'He was on the system?'

'Yes, he was tested as part of a date rape case three years ago.'

'Was he arrested?'

'No. He was part of a massive sample. Ruled out without any formal interview.'

I just didn't think that Will Locke was my man. He seemed genuinely shocked by the news of Emmeline's death. And being a cheater did not make you a murderer, Christ I wasn't even sure it made you a bad person. I wasn't a bad person.

'Jim, it's that's not unsurprising. They were sleeping together.'

'Aye. Well I'm working here on the basis that he has a connection to two of the three women and forensic evidence linking him to a corpse. I've just had a discussion with Chief Superintendent Marshall and we agree, we are bringing him in under caution.'

This didn't feel like Jim. It felt rushed, heavy-handed. But I wasn't going to push him. I knew he was under enormous pressure.

'OK. Well I think I should be there to talk over interview strategy. I'm with Dylan so I'll bring him with me.'

Dylan understood, gathered up his bags and then walked to the counter to pay for our drinks.

We walked up the slope of Battersea Rise together but as we flanked the side of the carpark Jim called me back.

'Fletch, there's actually no rush for you to get back here. I can run the lead on the Locke interview. I think it's good for us to cover all of our bases so why don't you crack on as planned with Emmeline's friends?'

'OK. Good plan.'

I stopped and opened my handbag to check I had my car keys. Emmeline's best friend, Zaria, lived in Colliers Wood and I'd already emailed her to see if she could be around this afternoon.

'You fancy a trip to Collier's Wood?' I asked Dylan.

22

The route through Tooting was hellish. The combination of red lights, pedestrians who felt entitled to just step out onto the road and dickhead drivers who just pulled out onto the High Road from the roads feathering away from it made for a stressful journey. I could sense that Dylan found my attempts to control my annoyance amusing.

I stopped quickly to let a BMW out. Not that I had much choice, the prick had pulled out almost half way before looking.

'You're not sure about this Will fella?' said Dylan.

'No.' I said.

'That old instinct again?'

I glanced at him briefly and then looked back to the road. The winter sun had turned the grey concrete bright white.

'No. So looking at it methodically. He has an alibi for the night Emmeline was killed. Granted people can be persuaded, but let's say for the sake of argument he does. He is strong and I believe physically capable of it. But he works as a barman, after living in six different countries. I just don't believe that he hates women. I think his problem is that he bloody loves them too much.'

'Is that why you didn't argue with DCI Greaves?' he asked.

'I guess. I didn't feel like I needed to be in that room. I'd already met the guy. I just —'

'I get you.' he said.

'But, Isla. If you do think you've got him. You need to be in the room.'

'Do you think he views all women as unknowable? Or just the beautiful blondes?'

'I still stand by the fact that he hates all women. This kind of rage —' he looked out of the window, at the crowds of people on Tooting High Road '—this, is hatred.'

'And,' he added. 'I don't think it makes a difference that you're not blonde.'

Zaria lived in a top floor flat on Clarendon Road in Colliers Wood. It was a grand, Edwardian house and the flat had high ceilings, period features and was immaculately decorated. It was a very different house to the one that Emmeline lived in; a run-down house share with damp in the kitchen.

'Would you like a drink?' she asked. She spoke with a soft Indian accent.

'No, thank you very much. Would you mind if we sat?' I asked.

'Please, do.' she said and offered her hand out to one of the deep, cream sofas.

We both sat on the same sofa, the soft padding sank quickly beneath Dylan and tipped my weight towards him. I braced my core to stop my leg from just resting on him.

'How did you know Emmeline?' I asked.

'We met at a photography fair a year or so ago. It was at a pub in Tooting Broadway.'

'And how would you describe your friendship, where you close?'

'Very. She was my closest friend in London. My family live in India and I only have cousins here. Emmy was amazing.'

Zaria steeled herself, sitting perfectly poised on a patterned armchair. Her hands were folded in her lap.

'How would you describe her?'

'Independent. Funny. Kind.' she answered, 'she has been

through a lot. Had been, sorry.'

She looked down briefly, clasped her hands tighter.

'With her Dad being in prison, she didn't have much family either. She made her friends her family.'

'How long had she been living at her flat?'

'Five years or so. I hated it there. So scruffy. But she loved living with Jacob, had such crush on him even if he is gay. And she loved walking to work. Such a luxury in London.'

'Did you know of anyone who might want to hurt Emmeline?' I asked.

'No.'

'Was she seeing anyone? Boyfriend or girlfriend?' I asked.

'No. Nothing serious. She was dating a photographer a couple of months ago.'

'But she wasn't anymore?' I asked.

'No. He got creepy.'

'Creepy how?'

'Asked her to move in with him.'

'And the photographers name?'

'Shaun. Shaun Richards I think, I'm not sure of his surname. He's not on Facebook. His instagram handle is 'shaunthepeep'.'

She rolled her eyes.

'Did she break up with him?'

'They never officially dated. But she told him in August that she didn't want to see him anymore.'

'And when was the last time you saw her?' I asked.

'A week ago. We had a spa day in Clapham and then dinner. We had pizza from the place on the Common.'

I knew it well, Sam and I would get their sourdough pizzas delivered quite often. I moved my leg away further away from Dylan's.

'Had you spoken over phone or social media in between then and now?'

'Yes. I called her on Thursday night. We only spoke for 30 minutes or so.'

'Did she tell you her plans for the weekend?' I asked.

'Yes. She was going on a date on Saturday. Someone she met on mysinglefriend. But I don't know his name. She was meeting him at The Bowls Club in Balham. She was going to text me if it was going badly so I could save her.'

She closed her eyes to compose herself.

'Actually. She sent me this.'

She scrolled through the pictures on her phone and then handed it over to us.

Emmeline was standing in front of the full length mirror in her bedroom, wearing a pair of tight black jeans and a printed blouse. She had an unusual geometric gold necklace on and bright red lipstick.

'She sent it to me to get my opinion on the outfit.'

Zaria looked sad.

'Thank you, Zaria. I'm going to give you my number now, and I'd like you to call me if you remember anything that you think might help us. And could I ask you to send this picture over to me please?'

'Of course. I'll do it now.'

We all stood and Zaria showed us out of her flat.

Dylan and I walked under the bare canopy of three trees to get to the parked car.

'Strong girl.' said Dylan.

'She is.' I said.

'I think we should head back to the station. I want to see if there are any signs of that necklace anywhere. I don't remember seeing it.'

I called Ryan from the car.

'Ryan. Dylan and I just finished up with Zaria, Emmeline's friend. We are heading back to Lavender Hill now. Do us a favour and get onto my single friend and see if we can access the records between Emmeline and anyone she spoke with over the past week?' I asked.

'Yes, ma'am.'

'Have you had the employee list from Lush Green yet?'

'No. But this Zach guy I'm dealing with said that the HR team will send it over today.'

'Has anything kicked out from the Will Locke interview yet?'

'No.'

'He admitted sleeping with her but just reinforced his alibi. The barmaid from The Anchor came into the station with him and confirmed they spent the night together. Gave us graphic detail on what they did. They took videos of the sex, which confirms him being there are midnight through to 330am.'

'Right. Quite the session.'

'Yes. They are definitely taking drugs in the video too. Coke. DCI Greaves is looking at drafting up a class A charge.'

'How is he?' I asked.

Ryan lowered his voice.

'Not happy.'

'Thanks for the heads up. I'll give him a shout now.'

I hung up and turned to Dylan.

'Sorry about this. Just one more call.'

'Don't worry about me.' he said. 'I'm just taking in the

view'.

He stared out of his window at the vast Primark on Tooting High Road. The car hadn't moved in ten minutes.

I dialled Jim.

'Fletch. Tell me you have something?'

'Yes. I think so. I've got a picture of Emmeline on the night before she was killed. She was heading to a date she'd made on mysinglefriend. I've asked Ryan to get access to the messages. She's wearing a gold necklace that I want to check on the inventory. He might have taken a souvenir after all.'

'Good. That's something at least. We've got piss all from this Locke guy.'

'I'm heading back to the station now. Well, I'm trying. I'm currently sat on Tooting High Road.'

'Looking at the time I wouldn't bother, Fletch. Just get yourself home and we can catch up early tomorrow before the briefing.'

'OK. I'll make sure I catch up with all the work stream owners before I switch off. And I'll follow prioritise the necklace too.'

'Good. See you tomorrow.'

Jim hung up. I clicked the indicator on right and turned out of the traffic. I decided to weave up the back roads of Tooting Bec and across Tooting common.

'Where about do you live?' I asked Dylan. 'I can give you a lift home.'

'Or we could get some dinner somewhere? Carry on talking it over?'

At the mention of dinner, my stomach tightened. I hadn't consumed anything since the large latte earlier today and I needed food. I knew I had nothing at home and would just be getting takeaway and carrying on working anyway.

'As long as you don't mind me being on my phone for a bit

first?'

'Not all all. Let's head left on Elmbourne. I know a good pub.'

As it was early for dinner, the pub was quiet. The commuters hadn't made it back from the City yet and the parents who would dine with their kids after the school pick up had already left. It was a large beamed pub with yellow exposed brick and hundreds of black and white photographs of Italy: landscapes, film stars, musicians. I thought about the images pinned on Sam's wall. The curated gallery Emmeline had made on her bedroom wall. The digital galleries Greta, Emmeline and Jessica had posted on Instagram.

Dylan ordered drinks for us at the bar. A large European beer for him and an orange juice for me.

I sat and read the updates in my inbox, emailed Gavenas and Basin. Each of the work stream owners had shared their updates before heading home for the night. Everyone using a lot of words to tell me they had fuck all.

Dylan went to the bathroom and I messaged Sam.

'Hey. I hope you had a nice time with your family, how were things with your brother? I'm going to be working all night but I'll call you in the morning. Ix'

The portly waitress set down two plates of food. A fairly mediocre looking set of fish and chips with dried mushy peas.

I was eating chips with my hands, scooping up a thick coating of ketchup when Dylan sat back down at the table. He poured vinegar and salt over his meal then picked up his knife and fork.

'When did you move down to London?' he asked.

'11 years ago.'

'That explains the accent.' he said.

'It is now. I tend to get more Northern if I'm drunk, or fucked off.' I said

He smiled. I liked how his eyes smiled too.

'Can I make an observation? he said.

'Sure.'

'You're fucked off about the Jessica Fox case.'

'Yes. I am.'

'How long had you worked on it before it was re-assigned?'

'Twelve days.' I said. 'I don't like leaving loose ends. And I felt very protective of her, and her family. Her Dad died last week.'

'Jesus Christ.' he said. 'Not suicide?'

'No, nothing like that. A stroke. Pretty instant.'

The waitress returned to the table.

'Is everything ok with your meal?'

'Great, thanks.' said Dylan. Not taking his eyes off me.

'But this —' I placed my hand on the folders set out on the table. '—this makes me feel better. We can get the bastard.'

'We can.'

'Have you had any more ideas we can add into the profile?' I asked.

'Yes. I wonder if there is an element of the artistic about him. You know. There's a sort of beauty to his work. Don't you think?'

'I guess. Each woman was beautiful. And there was pattern to the placement of the flowers.'

'And the colours. The blood, the white, the flowers.'

'I thought something similar when I first saw Greta.'

'Have you heard of Alphonse Mucha?' he said.

'The nouveau guy? I have.' I answered. 'I thought about him when I saw Greta's body.'

He scrolled through the internet app on his phone. He

clicked on an image and then moved quickly to show me the piece of art titled *The Rose.*

He placed the phone back on the table. He looked at me. He had small black flecks in his left iris, and his stubble spiked grey at the edges. He looked at my lips and then my eyes and blinked away back to the Mucha print.

'It is beautiful.' he said.

My phone vibrated with Sam's response.

'Today has been the best. Like when we were kids. Tell you all about it tomorrow! Love you. Sx'.

I closed the message and put the phone back in my pocket.

'Do you think you will go to the funeral?' he said.

Good question.

'I don't think it would be proper,' I said. 'The FLO might want to go but I'd feel weird being there. Like I was intruding.' I struggled to explain myself and then settled on clear honesty.

'I feel guilty.' I said. 'I promised him I would find the person who did that to his daughter. He died not knowing.'

Dylan placed his hand on my leg. It felt heavy and warm.

'You have to forgive yourself. You didn't do anything wrong. Shit things just happen sometimes.' he said.

I lifted my eyes from the table.

'I know.'

I looked at him, into the blue irises.

'But he could have died with answers.' I said,

'It's not on you.' he said.

His eyes flitted between my eyes and mouth. I could see the intention. And I wanted him to do it, I wanted him to kiss me, even in full sight of everyone in here. I wanted to sit on him, feel the rough bristle of his beard against my thigh, feel him inside me. My heart pounded. I couldn't.

'Don't.' I said.

He smiled, and leaned in.

'Somewhere else?'

I placed my hand on his then moved it to the padded seat next to me. I moved my knees away from him, towards the table legs, and stared out at the people around us. Strangers, staring at the football, drinking in groups, slotting coins into the quiz machine. We were unnoticed.

I took a deep breath. There was still half a pint of lager in his pint glass.

'I think we should go.' I said.

It was a violet, overcast evening. The common was clear.

I turned on my heel, jammed my hands into my pockets and hunched my shoulders up, pulling my scarf up over my face.

'You've got a boyfriend, right?' he said.

'Girlfriend.' I answered.

I could hear that the kitchen door was open and could clearly make out the sounds of the pub staff chatting as they sorted recycling. I didn't want to be seen. By the pub staff, by a friend. I definitely didn't want to be seen by any of Sam's friends. But I did want a drink.

I opened the car.

'How near to Wandsworth Bridge are you?' I said.

Dylan opened his door and answered from inside.

'Two minutes.'

The inside of his flat was clean. It smelt clean. Of cleaning products and deodorant. Masculine. The excitement and guilt had started as I parked my car in his allocated parking space. Our footsteps echoed distinct beats then we stood in the cold lift in near silence. I could feel the tension of the empty space between our shoulders.

His flat was dark. Dark grey with an expensive lamp sitting on a small table in the hallway.

'Red or white? Or stronger?'

'Whatever you have open is fine.'

I was weighing up my options. I could just have one glass, a big pint of water and then be perfectly fine to drive. I would go home, wake up early and go for a run and meet Dylan back in the office tomorrow. I would just have one glass.

He handed me a large, angled glass with a long thin stem. The sticky legs of the expensive red ran long around the edges. He clinked the edge of his glass against mine and took a small sip. I did too. It smelled of tobacco and berries and it tasted heavy. I took the glass away from my mouth and tasted it on my lips. Dylan watched.

I would just have one glass.

He took the glass from my hand, set it down on the mango wood side table, stepped forward quickly and kissed me. Both hands on my face, then one on my back as we pressed into each other. with tongues and chest then hips. He directed me along the hallway, moving his hands down over my breasts to my waist. He breathed with low deep moan that vibrated from my throat to my thighs.

We fucked on his bed. In deep, quick strokes. I came in a way I hadn't in such a long time. He came too, clutching my hair, with his stubbled lips open over my mouth.

He stood naked and walked back to the hallway, returning with the two glasses of wine. We both took long gulps, staring at each other, and then kissed with much less urgency. He stroked my face with the front side of his fingers. I knew we would fuck again once, maybe twice before we slept and I didn't think about Sam at all until the morning.

(EVE)

Under a yellowed moon, twenty longitude east in Mexico City, Mireya Camino Jurado sat shivering and sunburnt. Mireya was one of the most successful women in the Engulf cartel, recruited aged fifteen by Ignacio to be one of his *La Flaca:* skinny girl, killers. The notion of a female killer was not a new one. But in recruiting and training his girls, Ignacio created beautiful, waspish and brutal assassins. Mireya returned to Mexico City that day to collect payment from one of the senior members of the cartel. It was God awful luck that at the exact same moment the cousin of the man she had killed four months earlier saw her through the dusted glass of his windscreen. Javier, acting on impulse and grief, ran her over in his car in the middle of the busy market place and then delivered her bruised body directly to the compound on the outskirts of the city. This is where she had remained chained for the last 9 hours. Hot and shivering, with a dislocated knee and a broken clavicle, she stared defiantly at the smoking watchmen who shouted abuse and threats of rape in intermittent bursts throughout the day. From the moment of consciousness, Mireya knew she could not escape. A thick metal chain, two feet in length shackled her by the ankle to a thick concrete post at the centre of the courtyard. In the moments when the men returned to the house she had pulled and torn at the chain, drawn blood. Junk, car machinery and ammunition skirted the edges of the yard, absolutely out of reach. Machine guns propped up next to rusted BMX bikes and corrugated iron.

It had been fifty minutes in her estimation since the last guard sat and watched her. She heard cars pull up twenty minutes ago - Eduardo, one of the generals in the opposing cartel, must have come himself to make absolutely certain that she was dead.

Eve had felt this hyper alert despondence before. The fight to control the adrenaline shakes. Defiance holding tight in her face. Tears, hot and secret, burning behind her eyes. As Eduardo swaggered into the courtyard and took his quiet, deliberate aim Eve also felt the inevitable submission to the adrenaline, the complete, utter submission to the fear. Eve might have felt the fear before. But she hadn't, in the eternal vastness of however long she had been here, felt her own frantic pull on muscle before. Muscle memory matched muscle fibres. Intention matched intention. Instinct matched instinct. And as Mireya pulled with the entire force of her ninety eight pound body, Eve pulled too. The third link of the metal chain strained and opened and in the slack that fell from the panicked lurching breath, she unlinked it from the second. Mireya sat hunched, staring at the free end of the chain with wide brown eyes. Syrupy spit stringed between her lips as it gaped open.

In the moment between the understanding that she was actually free and the decision to dart sharp right, to the cover of the shed, Eduardo pulled the trigger.

Eve felt it all. The fear, the hope, the bullets. The three-shot burst of the M4 assault rifle, designed for its destructive cavitation shockwave, sprayed 45 rounds in seconds. Mireya herself could not distinguish where the bullets hit first. And neither could Eve. The eleventh and twelfth bullet reverberated within her ribcage, almost completely destroying her heart. But it didn't matter to Eve.

The pain, the cold of the icy waters, the instant blackness of the stroke, the burn of 45 bullets. It didn't matter, because Eve knew that this wasn't over.

This wasn't the end.

24

I left his flat at six. I felt rested and a little heavy headed. It was the first time that I had cheated Sam in real terms. I'd made out with few other women and one man when we first got together and I'd messaged an ex in the Lakes a couple of months in. I had cheated on every single one of my past relationships. Sam deserved better. But she would never know, it could never hurt her; and if it made me feel better, made me stay then surely that's better than splitting up.

I showered at home and missed the first call from Sam because of the sound of the hairdryer. I called her back as soon as I had drank my second coffee. I cleared my throat.

'Morning sweetie. How are you?'

'Great. Just walking to the tube. I've got a ton of client meetings today.' she said.

'How was it with your family?' I asked. 'You made progress with your brother then?'

'Yes!' she shouted, elated. 'We had such a good catch-up. He even apologised. For pretty much everything.'

'Good. He should.' I said.

'And your Mum?'

'Practically bursting. Then she got pissed with Aunt Mel and cried. I left about nine and left them to it. Isaac was staying up in Mayfair for a conference so they all got a black cab and I got an uber.'

'You know your client events?' I asked.

'Yes,'

'Have any of them been run by a company called Lush Green?' I asked.

'No. Not that I'm aware of.'

Good.

'OK. No problem, I'm just interested.'

And I didn't want Sam anywhere near this.

'Did you want me to ask around at the office?'

'Thanks, sweetie. Are you around tonight? You want to come over?'

'Yes. I'll grab us some picky bits for dinner and just head to yours.'

'Amazing. See you then.'

I threw the phone onto the bed and looked at myself in the mirror. I am fucking unknowable.

I finished drying my hair. Ate a banana in silence in my barren kitchen and sent out a series of emails and meeting invites.

I called Jim on the walk to the car.

'Jim, I'm on my way in now. We have the briefing at nine fifteen. I've extended the invitation to the guys from Brixton Hill but I reckon we just hold it in the MIR. Get everyone on the same page?'

'Perfect. I've got a meeting at quarter to nine with Marshall but I'll head straight there afterwards.'

I felt for Jim. He was taking a lot of the pressure from above, and he was dealing directly with the families.

I drove the short distance to the station in silence. Sitting with the experience of being with Dylan, thinking about how he felt. How easily I had slept next to him. How easily I had lied to Sam. The radio told me of more deaths across the world. A bush fire in Australia. I clicked it off.

I didn't feel guilty lying to her. I knew it made me a bad

person but I didn't. I could always distinguish the actions in my head, between my love for her and my fidelity and the desire for Dylan, for someone, anyone else. I had dampened my sexuality for so long before moving to London that I felt like I was owed. In some twisted logic, that it was somehow my right to explore sex with other people. I figured as long as Sam never found out that it would, in some way, actually improve our relationship. I knew I was kidding myself. Lying to myself. And I hoped if we ever got married that it might change it. But I also knew that there would always be a Dylan. A man or a woman I felt attracted to, and feel completely entitled to pursue. It wasn't the best part of me, it wasn't the worst part of me, but it was part of me. I'd accepted it and there would always be a part of me that I kept. An unknowable part.

Maybe Greta, or Jessica had felt the same way. A boyfriend's assertion was not proof of fidelity. Maybe one of them had their own secrets, their own forged rules. I thought back to the conversation with Uma and Zaria. How they were so sure that neither of them had been seeing anyone. But maybe one of them had. Maybe they had been seeing someone in secret. Most of the interview notes that I had read with Greta and Emmeline's network swore on the valour of the dead women; their kindness, grace, faithfulness, sainthood. But maybe they didn't know, or maybe they were lying on behalf of a dead friend. I didn't have a close group of female friends. I didn't have someone to confide in, I held on to my secrets.

I thought about my man, too. My Man with the flowers, holding on to his secrets.

25

The MIR was crowded when I arrived. I scanned the room to check that the new attendees had received my email in time. I should have sent the updated invite out last night but was too busy fucking the BIA.

'Good, looks like we have everyone we should have.' I started.

'Let's follow the same protocol. Quick update, key actions, next steps.'

Everyone in the room was listening. The people standing were in active stances, braced and most of them had notes and pens at the ready. I carried on.

'I spoke with Zaria Bakshi yesterday. Emmeline was going on a date with someone she met online on Saturday night. She wasn't in a relationship outside of that but had finished we a fella at the end of Summer.'

I indicated to Whalley.

'More to follow on him in due course. We are working on a hypothesis that something was stolen. A distinctive gold necklace. We will be looking to check with Greta and Jessica on that.'

I looked at Jules, the FLO for the Foxes.

'DCI Greaves interviewed Will Locke under caution yesterday afternoon because his semen was found in Emmeline. But, they were in a relationship and he did admit that he had slept with her two days before her murder. We have video footage that proves his location elsewhere for the time of the murder and so for now we can discount him. The footage is now with vice for their consideration.'

'I worked with Dylan Nicholson, our BIA, on revising the profile. I'll have a few copies printed and I'll share to this group via email. Have a read, get familiar. And make sure you run any significant witness interview by me. We think it's important that a woman lead the interview. If you've got any questions on the profile then ask me. I'll be around the station today so come and find me with any questions. I'll be reading the notes from every witness statement: starting with the neighbour profiles from Crockerton Avenue and then working through the networks for Greta and Emmeline.'

'Ryan, I know you've already read them. So can you look at the Fox files today and see if anything jumps out? We can meet in the middle.'

Ryan was leaning on the desk, leaning over himself to make a note. He stood and I nodded for him to give his update.

'We can't confirm that anything was stolen from Greta's flat. Her parents don't believe anything has been stolen. Blake doesn't either.'

Basin stood, He clasped his hands together behind his back.

'As DCI Fletcher mentioned, I have been leading mostly on the interviews. Devon Powell, the cafe owner, was interesting. He took Emmeline on a number of work trips and commissioned her to take photos to hang in the gallery at the back of the cafe. He has said that he didn't hit on her because she was too young but I'm checking up to see if there is any trace of something more serious there. He doesn't have an alibi for either Greta's or Emmeline's murder and we are looking to establish his whereabouts on the day of the Fox assault. I'm still extracting themes from the other interviews and I'll work with DCI Fletcher today to set out next steps.'

Whalley remained seated, but span his chair out to address the room.

'I've been over the messages from the dating website. Emmeline was supposed to meet a man called Lewis Jewkes in Balham on the Saturday night before she was killed. I spoke to Lewis this morning and he cancelled via the website app. He is married. Got cold feet.'

'And where was he on the Saturday night then?' I asked.

'With his wife and kids. She can verify.' he answered.

'And do we know where Emmeline spent Saturday night then?' asked Gavenas.

'I checked with HSBC and there was a charge to a delivery service at half 8. So we guess at home.'

He looked down at his notes.

'I checked with Lush Green who have sent over the full list of events for the past six months along with the delegates. They have also marked up which employees worked on which event. So that's my priority for this morning.'

'Good.' I said. 'Whalley, on the point about messaging apps. Can you check on what other mediums Greta and Emmeline had to communicate? Dating apps, message boards, LinkedIn. Just see if they had anything to say to someone that they couldn't say over email or text message.'

I thought to the messages I had sent to my ex when I was with Sam. How I had messaged over Facebook and not over text or email, a medium which had no notifications or any preview that someone looking at my phone might just read.

Sophie stood up.

'Someone from The Guardian has picked up the similarities between Greta and Emmeline. They are pushing pretty hard for information. There doesn't appear to be anything viral on it on the socials. I've said that we will give a statement this evening. Chief Superintendent Marshall is going to run it and I've got a meeting with her and DCI Greaves to draft it this afternoon.'

I looked around the room for someone from the SOCO team, or Lester. I must have missed him, or he was just swamped.

'Ryan, has Lester dialled in?' I asked.

'I haven't heard from him this morning.' he said.

'Can you get him on the phone?' I asked, then turned to the FLO for Jessica, picking back on a thread of thought I almost forgot about.

'Jules, can you check in with Jessica and see if she had any missing jewellery? We think the killer took a necklace from one of the dead women.'

'Of course.'

'How is she doing?'

'She's strong. She's with her Mum, the funeral—'

Ryan interrupted her.

'Ma'am I've got Lester on the phone, they have a print.'

'Put him on speaker' I said.

Ryan pressed speaker and then hung up the receiver. I walked towards it and spoke up.

'Lester, you're on speaker phone in the MIR. We have a full room.'

'Morning everyone.'

'As I was saying to Ryan. We have a fingerprint. One complete and a partial.'

The MIR fell quiet.

'From where?' I asked.

'We have been lucky. We managed to extract a fingerprint from a part of the foliage.'

'How?'

'With organic matter we wouldn't hope to be able to get anything after more than a couple of hours. It's why we didn't find anything from the flowers extracted from Greta Maibergers crime scene.'

'Excellent, Lester. This is really good news.'

'I'll follow up on this on IDENT1' said Ryan. He then picked up the receiver and spoke directly to Lester. I turned my focus back to the room.

'I think it makes sense for us to put a pin in it here. Lots to be getting on with.'

The majority of the room dispersed. I noticed that Jim had not joined us and made my way to his office.

On the way, I saw Davies leaving an administrative office with Chief Superintendent Marshall and two men in suits. I carried on walking and knocked on Jim's door. He opened it straight away and startled me. He was stood next to a tall cabinet next to the doorframe.

'I see Davies is back?'

'Yes. With a full bastard apology.' said Jim. 'It wasn't him.'

He slammed a drawer on his filing cabinet hard, 'It was a crime scene photographer.'

'Chris Jeffries?' I asked. My voice louder than I would have liked.

'You know him?"

'Yes. You do too.' I said. 'You met him briefly. He was at the Greta Maiberger crime scene.

'Oh that prick.'

'Indeed.'

Fuck it. I needed to be honest.

'How did this come about?'

'Someone in the admin team saw him doing it. Saw him rifling through someones bag.'

'Jesus. Sloppy.'

'Yes. And it doesn't reflect well on us that we had Davies out so quickly.'

'Sorry, Jim.'

'You shouldn't be sorry. You had nowt to do with it.'

I knew I had to tell him.

'You should know something Jim. I would appreciate it sticking between us for now, but just in case it comes up.'

'What?'

'It's embarrassing. Really.'

'We've all been there.' he said.

'I slept with him.'

'What?'

Genuine shock pinched at Jim's brow, 'When? What about your new girl?'

I crossed my arms and bit my lower lip, embarrassment warm in my cheeks.

'A long time ago. Almost two years. Before I came here.'

'How long did it go on for?'

'About a month. Nothing serious, not on my part.'

'And nothing has happened since?'

I shook my head slowly.

'And you think he might be responsible for this?'

'I'm not sure. He made some aggressive advances a week ago.'

'Aggressive how?'

'Just posturing. Peacocking.'

'No threats?'

'Not in real terms. He implied he knew about my relationship with Sam. But nothing overt.'

'We will definitely need a written statement. When the time comes.'

Balls.

'Fine. Just let me know.'

'Will do.'

I hadn't spoken to Jim about my sex life in all of the years I had known him and now I'd burdened him with the fact that I fucked women and dickheads. He looked flustered and sat behind his desk.

'How did the mornings briefing go?' he asked.

'Well.'

'Well thats something at least.' he said.

'We have a fingerprint from one of the leaves placed in Emmeline's hair. Ryan is putting it through IDENT 1 now'

'Jesus.'

'So that's obviously first priority. There are also a couple of dating apps that we are looking at. Ways that Greta and Emmeline might have interacted outside of typical channels.'

'I've got a meeting with Lewes to arrange the press conference.'

'She mentioned that. You need me in it?'

'We should be ok. Obviously you're very welcome to join if you like but I'd rather free you up for the key leads. Keep at least one of us out of the firing line.' he smiled.

'But,' he added. 'We could probably use that BIA in the session with us. Can you drop him a line?'

'No problem.'

I thought of the man I had left in bed at 5am this morning. No problem.

There was a sharp knock on the door.

'In you come.' said Jim.

Whalley stood in the doorway.

'I've got something on the messaging front.'

He walked further into the office and shifted his weight between his legs as he spoke.

'It was on LinkedIn. Messages between Greta and Lee

Grace. Two days before the trade show in Leicester they arranged to meet. He mentions that his wife is away and there is a very flirtatious undertone. It even references previous dinners they have been on. A drawn out analogy but I think they slept together.'

I took the print out from him and read over it. They definitely slept together.

'Jim, I'm going to go and speak to Mr Grace.'

I called Dylan first.

'Morning.'

'Morning.' I said, followed quickly by, 'I'm at the station.'

'OK. Everything ok?'

'One of the Grace brothers lied to me about sleeping with Greta. So I'm going to go and speak to him. Jim wants you involved with the messaging for the press conference, can you come in for a meeting this afternoon with him and Sophie? At 2?'

'Yes. I'll be there.' he said.

'Thanks.' I said.

'Will I get a chance to see you today?' he asked.

'I'm not sure. Maybe this afternoon.' I answered. 'I'll send over the meeting invite now.'

I hung up. I grabbed my rucksack from my office and fished out my car keys.

I called Whalley's number.

'Where is Lee Grace now?'

'At home, Handler Road in Dulwich.'

'Right. I'm going there now.'

26

It was a 30 minute drive from Lavender Hill to Dulwich. The landscape changed as I drove East; the flat green of open commons humped and transformed into steep, tree-lined roads with thin tall terraces. The views towards the City glinted stark and bold in the sunlight. I still didn't think that Lee Grace could have been capable of this but he lied to us. Maybe he had lied about something else.

His house was a large period detached. There was a black BMW parked on the road outside with the licence plate GR4CE. Subtle.

He was very surprised to see me when he answered the door.

'I thought we had discussed everything?'

'You had sex with Greta?'

His eyes widened and he flinched to close the door to behind him and stand on the doorstep.

'Are you fucking mental? My wife is in the kitchen.'

'You lied, Mr Grace. I don't care if you lie to your wife, but don't lie to me.'

'I didn't lie. You asked about specific nights and times and I told you the truth. I'd already finished with her by the time the trade show came round. I'd asked the agency for another account manager but they didn't listen.'

'How long where you sleeping with her for?'

'Three weeks. That was it. It ended in September and she was fine about it. We probably only shagged about seven or eight times.'

'Is everything ok, Lee?' a voice echoed through the tall ceilings of his entrance hall.

He opened the door behind him and shouted back.

'Yes, I'm just finishing off something with the police.'

A thin blonde woman opened the door to us. She had the kind of hair that required regular blow drys and looked like she had lip fillers. She smiled at me.

'DC Isla Fletcher.' I smiled back at her. Lee looked anxious.

'Did you want to come in?' she asked.

Lee glared at me and pasted on a fake smile.

'No, thank you.' I answered. 'I just dropped by to double check some dates with your husband but then I really have to rush.'

'OK.' she looked confused but didn't appear to want to challenge either me or him. She padded back away from the front door.

'I'll be through in a sec, love. Just get the boys ready for football.' he said. He turned to me again and the smile fell quickly.

'Did you ever go to her flat?'

'No.'

'Where did you meet then?'

'Hotels. Always hotels. I'll get Bishop to send over the receipts.'

'Why would you keep the receipts?'

'Business expenses.' he answered.

Sure. Make sure he could reduce his tax liability at the same time.

'And you ended it with her?'

'Yes.'

'Was she upset?'

'No. She knew it wasn't going to go anywhere. She'd was with some other bloke anyway.'

'Now I'm being serious, Mr Grace. Is there anything at all that you haven't told us?'

He stalled.

'Because as of now. I don't have to pursue any sort of legal charges. But if there is anything else. Then I need to know now.'

'There isn't.'

I couldn't gauge whether he was lying. I started to walk away.

'Fine. You might want to get that solicitor of yours on the phone, we will need you to come in and amend your statement. Officially.'

I noticed that as I was pulling away he was still stood in his doorway. He was probably working on the story he was going to feed his wife.

Whalley rang me in the car.

'DCI Fletcher we have found something else on the messaging front.'

'Greta or Emmeline?' I asked.

'Neither.' he said, 'Jessica. She was messaging someone from Lush Green events —' His voice broke over patchy phone signal.

'When? Who?'

I knew that at the time of the attack that Jessica was single. We checked on the alibis for two men she had dated in late summer and all of her male network.

'In June. The man —'

He voice broke again.

I pulled over and parked next to greyed cherry blossom tree. The thick roots had caused the kerb to crack and hump.

I pulled the phone out of the cradle.

'Sorry,' I said. 'I missed that.'

'It's the man I was messaging, Zach. Their head of events. He asked her on a date back in June over LinkedIn.'

'And.'

'She turned him down.'

'Nicely?' I asked.

'Yes. Well, I think so.' he said. One sec I'll read it out.'

'So, on 16th June he messaged her and said, 'It was so great to chat to you today. I wondered if you wanted to meet in person? Maybe I could take you out for dinner?'

She then replies on the same day, 'Potentially. There are definitely some events that I could work with you on. But maybe we could meet for a coffee as opposed to dinner?'. He then replies on the 17th with 'Oh, I didn't mean for us to talk shop. I meant it would be great to maybe go on a date'. And then he added a winking face emoji. So she doesn't reply and then he messages her again on the 19th. 'Is this too awkward? Sorry. It would be great to meet and talk events if you prefer??' and then she replies, 'Sorry for the delay in getting back to you - I am really sorry but I have a boyfriend so I can't meet for a date. I'll let you know if there are any events you might be able to help with in the future.' And then she signs off with a smiley face.'

Jessica didn't have a boyfriend but I recognised her white lie. I'd told the same lie before. A deceptive but gentle way to say no was better than a harder, starker truth. But if this Zach guy knew who Jessica was, then he knew she was lying. It would feed into his belief system that all women were liars. That all women were unknowable. I wanted to speak to Dylan, to Jim. I wanted to be back at the station quicker than I could safely drive there.

'Excellent, Whalley. Where does this Zach live?'

'I checked and his address actually isn't on the list of employees that he sent over. And he's not listed as working on any of the events attended by the three women. Even though we know he was definitely in Leicester.'

'Right. Find out where he lives now. And go and update DCI Greaves.'

Jim needed good news.

As I was fixing the phone back into the hands free set on the dashboard, Sam rang me.

'Morning gorgeous.' she said.

'Hey.' I answered. I tried to measure my response, to not sound like I just wanted to get her off the phone so I could get moving.

'Would you be angry if we moved our drinks tonight to tomorrow?' she asked.

'No' I answered truthfully. 'Not at all. What are you up to?'

'My boss has invited me to some awards show for one of the asset managers we work with. I'd ordinarily say no but if might be a good way for me to switch sides and move into a comms role.'

'OK. Well I really don't mind at all. You go and network, sweetie.' I said.

'Thanks. We could meet for a Sunday roast maybe? Let me sit with my hangover tomorrow?'

'Sounds perfect.' I said.

'You're distracted.' she said.

'I am. I'm sorry sweetie.' I said. I hand both hands on the steering wheel. Gripped and ready.

'I'll let you go.' she said, deflated.

'It's not you.' I said. Taking my hands off the wheel and gesturing as if she were in the seat next to me.'

'Listen, I'm sorry. I'm just in it. You know. I think we might have found him. I think he's someone who works at Lush

Green.'

'Lush Green?'

'Yes, the events company I told you about.'

'Oh yes. Well I don't want to keep you.' she said.

'You're not. I hope you have fun, you deserve a few free drinks all the hours you've put in for that paper.'

'I'll message you tonight,' she said. 'You know I like to annoy you when I'm drunk.'

'I do.' I said. 'Make sure you get a taxi home and just make sure you definitely text me when you get home.'

'I will.' she said. 'Love you.'

'Love you too.' I said.

It was true. I really loved her. I rubbed both hands over my face and pushed my hair back with such force that it pulled on my eyebrows. I exhaled at my reflection in the rearview mirror then pulled out onto the road. And within seconds I was calling Dylan.

'Hello again.' he answered.

'Are you on your way into the station?' I asked.

'Yes, I'm walking.'

I could hear the sounds of his breath and the noise of Clapham Junction in the background strobing with his footfalls.

'Before you see Jim. We have someone.'

'Go on.'

'A man called Zach at an events company. He was involved in the event that both Greta and Emmeline attended and he had direct contact with Jessica in June. He omitted his details in the information he sent over to us too. He's trying to hide.'

'So if you get there before me, can you get whatever information you can from Whalley and then I'll jump into the meeting with you, Jim and Sophie as soon as I get back.'

'I will. I'll see you there.'

'See you there.' I said. I pressed the red button.

Cortisol gripped my stomach and I felt wired. It only took me twenty minutes to make it back to the station. I probably could have been done twice for dangerous driving.

27

Jim, Sophie and Dylan were all sat in Jim's office. I must have looked pink, I had practically run through the station.

'Isla, hi.' said Sophie. 'We just finished drafting the content for the press conference.'

'We're not going to mention any person of interest.' said Jim.

'And any other statements?' I asked, taking off my blazer and setting it on the chair across the table from Dylan.

'No. We are keeping it lean. Lean and reassuring.' said Jim.

'Did you have a chance to sense check the messaging to him?' I asked Dylan.

'I have.' he said.

'To be honest,' said Jim. 'We actually aren't giving out that much information. I don't think we will be speaking in any way to him,'

'Oh he'll be listening.' said Dylan.

There was a firm knock and Ryan entered.

'Sir. We sent two uniforms to Zach's address and it doesn't look like he's there. We have sent another car to his office to try and get him there. No answer on his phone which has been switched off.'

I looked at Jim, then at Dylan.

'If he's running?' I said.

'Let's not get ahead of ourselves.' said Jim. 'He might be on the tube and he might be at his office. Let's keep our cool.'

He address Ryan.

'Just keep us posted.'

'Will do, Sir.' said Ryan.

Sophie stood, closed her notebook and pushed her chair out behind her.

'I'll leave you all to it.' she said. 'I'll crack on with the press release.'

Ryan kept the door open for her and then closed it as he turned to walk with her away from the office.

'We need to get our interview strategy absolutely locked down.' I said.

'Agreed.' said Jim. He looked at the clock above his filing cabinet.

'I have a three o clock with Marshall that I would prefer not to move. It will be nice to give her some good news for a change. Can you and I meet at half 3 to run over everything? I'll come and find you in the MIR.'

'Perfect.'

Dylan and I both stood.

'Thanks for your time.' he said, reaching out to shake Jim's hand.

'Thanks for coming in.' said Jim.

Dylan and I left the room, and as the door closed shut Dylan placed his hand on the small of my back.

'Can I see you properly today?' he said quietly.

I looked at him and then checked the hallway. He realised what I was doing and dropped his hand.

'Potentially.' I said. 'Depends on what time I finish up here.'

We both walked towards my office, passed three small windows and at least six different people.

I stood next to the oak door of my office but didn't open it. I stood holding the folder across my chest with crossed arms.

'If I get out of here before 8, I'll let you know. I don't have any plans tonight.' I said.

'Me neither.' He pulled on his jacket and then dropped the long strap of his satchel across his body. 'and you know where I live.'

He walked away and from behind I could see that he was smiling to himself. I knew I shouldn't sleep with him again. I knew that I would.

I spent two hours reading. Reading interview notes and reports and making sure that we hadn't missed anything. I filed and drafted actions but I was grateful when Gavenas interrupted me.

'We heard back from Lush Green, ma'am' she said.

'Zach has apologised for leaving his address off the list. Says it was a mistake. He's given us his address.'

'And where is he?'

'I spoke to the owner of the company and Zach has a client event in Oxfordshire tomorrow so he's booked into the Travel Lodge in Oxfordshire.'

'Right. Get onto the hotel and get them to confirm when he checks in.'

'Will do, ma'am.'

I then sat back at my desk and didn't stand up again until I had read every single interview summary. My eyes hurt.

It was late. No messages from Sam, which meant that she either didn't have any signal, or she wasn't drunk yet. In the first few months of our relationship I would tease her for her drunken messages. Misspelled and fawning. She was embarrassed at first but then just embraced them, arguing that she was just telling me that she was thinking about me and that she didn't care. She was just being honest.

I called Dylan.

'I'm just leaving now. Is it too —'

'No.' he said. 'Just come over. I picked my car up from the garage this afternoon so I don't have a parking spot. But there are always spaces across the road off the common.'

'I know it.' I said. 'I'll be there in fifteen.'

Eve felt a hard stamp on her collarbone and the sharp pain of the fracture. She held both arms up at right angles to protect her face and neck and cried out at the pain. Pain and fear.

She could smell the burnt sulphur of fireworks and the wet grass. She could feel the moisture from the soft mud beneath her seeping into her clothes. Her face felt like it was on fire from the pain; her left eye stung and watered wildly and she couldn't quite see clearly. She pushed into her legs to move away from him but her arms were not strong enough to push her weight. away. She tried to turn to crawl but couldn't move, adrenaline jammed and surged in every muscle but the pain fought back against every lurching movement. The reluctant acceptance that she was going to die caused a massive dose of stress hormones to flood her nervous system and she shook with important panic as he stood over her. He stood over her, a tall, hooded outline in the clouded, indigo sky. Bare trees stood frozen, branches reaching for her.

She could hear louder cries from somewhere distant. Kids screaming.

He sat on her stomach and pinned her arms underneath each hand.

Eve heaved and fought, arching her spine and crying out. Screaming with a voice that wasn't hers. She was aware of the sounds of people nearby and of the low hum of traffic across the plain of grass.

Strong fingers closed around her neck. Cold strong hands. Eve clawed at a stubbled, familiar face.

Golden snatches of twilight in the darkness. That smell. The smell of him.

Darkness.

28

When I woke up in hospital, I remembered the kids. Something about that group of teenagers on the common unsettled me. It was a thickly clouded evening and the amber lamps barely lit the pathways that branched out from the train station. I could see the huddle of kids around the bench in the centre, six of them I think. The glow of cigarettes strobed in their shadowed outlines. Maybe it was the obnoxious laugh that peeled out from one of the girls, or the smell of weed that drifted over. But I didn't feel easy as I locked the car and headed over to the row of shops on Bellevue Road.

The fear was entirely misplaced. If it hadn't been for them, I would be dead right now.

I remember looking at The Anchor, seeing the distant warmth in its windows. I remember hearing the muffled murmur of its patrons but I was facedown on the floor, with him on top of me, before I realised I had been pushed. I don't remember what I shouted. I clawed behind me, trying to get purchase on the taught material over thighs. My legs kicked out pointlessly behind me against the weight of him straddling my lower back. I could smell wet mud, distant fireworks. Cold moisture seeped in through my jacket. He was heavy, determinedly moving my hands beneath the grip of his legs. He remained noiseless. I was cold. He took a fistful of my hair and slammed my head against the hard patch of gravel. My cheekbone and forehead connected hardest but I could taste the pressure of blood in my nose. I have no idea at this point what I was shouting or if I was shouting at all. I remember his hot, strong hands at my neck, struggling to get purchase through the material of my scarf. I think I remember the screams of the kids as they ran towards us.

From there, all I remember is the hallucinogenic dreams of the opiates.

I dreamt about the bright blue day when Dad died. I remembered his twisted corpse, bloodied at the roadside. In vivid snatches between sleep cycles I was myself, sobbing out screams for help; I was Dad, dead in an instant, engulfed in pain; I was the driver at the wheel, shaking and gripping at the leather, listening to the howling cries from the passenger seat. Psychedelic scenery played out in the rear window of the dream, like the split screen of an old movie. I drove maniacally round the bends and turns of my Lake District home, speaking silently to the faceless, black and white passenger. All the while, the neon, jerking, vistas rolled in that rear window: hills, lakes, mountains, trees, hills, lakes, mountains, trees.

When I woke up, it felt like my neck had been stamped on.

I felt heavy and weak, sleepy and sore. I closed my hand feebly around Sam's slender fingers and smiled at her through heavy eyelids. She called out over her shoulder to one of the nurses but kept her eyes locked onto mine. Her pale grey-blue eyes stood out against the bloodshot pink. Long eyelashes. She squeezed my hand back and stood up over me, gently resting her lips on my forehead and whispering out how much she loved me.

My throat hurt. Really hurt. I peeled my tongue from the roof of my mouth, running it over the thick slimy fuzz coating my teeth.

I forced the words over dry lips, half stuck together.

'What happened?'

Jim stood up from the chair behind Sam, holding a cup of tea. Sam sat back as a huge, male nurse stepped in and check me. He smelled like Dad and smiled at me. Jim landed a heavy, bear hand on her shoulder. Well, at least that saved me an introduction.

'You're safe. Just rest.'

Sam poured out a lukewarm glass of tap water and handed it to me. It rippled in the plastic cup as I drank it from her shaking hand.

'How long have I been here?'

Jim checked his watch.

'Not too long. We were told you'd be out for longer.'

Sam wiped the drop that had fallen from my outer lip and down passed my ear. The soft touch hurt. I wanted to see the damage.

'Can I have a mirror?'

She shook her head quickly with panicked eyes.

Jim dragged the plastic chair over the bedside. Even the sound hurt.

'You're not the prettiest I've ever seen you, mate.'

'How bad?'

I trusted him.

'Broken eye socket, fractured cheek bone.'

I swallowed hard down a dry throat.

'Can I have some more water?'

Sam offered the cup back to me. Mascara had pooled in the inner corners of her eyes and the shadow of wiped tears hung low on her cheeks.

'And?"

Jim carried on, 'bruising, severe abdominal bruising but mostly on your neck.' He steadied himself, 'and a fractured collarbone.'

'But that's what saved you,' Sam stuttered out words before leaning back and sobbing quietly behind a screen of fingers held beneath her brow.

Jim leant forward and held my hand. In all the years of

working with him, he had never held my hand. It felt fucking weird.

'He tried to stamp on your neck, but he hit your collar-bone. It took the brunt.'

I glanced down at the ghost body beneath me, numb from painkillers and shock. My right arm was strapped down at a right angle against my chest. My tongue felt alien inside my swollen face. I couldn't feel any real sense of pain, more a dull ache in my stomach and a tension in my neck. Like I'd spent too long looking at a screen.

'Did the kids?' I said, 'Are they OK?'

'Yes,' Jim smiled, 'They are all fine. Two lasses, two lads. We've got their statements, one of the lads got a decent look at him.'

'Can I see the report?'

Sam scoffed, 'Are you kidding?'

I looked at Jim, who knew I wasn't.

'I'll have someone bring them to you. But only when you're at home.'

'Fine.' I answered. 'But can someone at least tell me we found Zach?'

Jim shook his head.

'Fletch. Just get some sleep. There's nothing important to do now. Sleep.'

The nurse took my hand from Jim and carried on his routine. He noted down my readings and handed me the morphine control. Sam unbuttoned her thick woollen cardigan and wriggled awkwardly out of it in her seat. Jim undid his tie and ran a huge hand over his tired face.

'You don't have to stay with me,' I said.

Neither one of them moved. I pressed for morphine.

When I woke again, Sam had tucked her legs underneath her and found her way to sleep. Jim had draped his angular jacket over her and stood talking to the PCs in the corridor. I turned my neck, feeling the sharp sting in my left eye. It watered and blurred my vision as I tried to make out the cards on two bouquets of flowers. The sparse spray of carnations had a blue card that simply read, 'The Boys' but the other, a densely packed bloom of sunflowers had a more floral inscription, 'Get well soon, precious angel, all of our love, Mum, Dad, Geoff & Isaac. And Molly and Trixie.'

I was not surprised by the flowers, or the gushing sentiment. Sam's family had always included me in their thoughts. I loved how they referred to themselves as Mum and Dad and made sure that they included the cats on every card. Sam's Mum would draw a small paw in place of a kiss. It was nice to see Sam's brother on the card too. I was happy that she had made peace with him.

Sam woke with a grunt, took a moment to remember where she was then leant forward to kiss my hand.

'Your Mum has sent a bunch too, sweetie,' she said, 'we are just finding another vase.'

'Did she ask to come?'

'Yes,' she nodded, 'I told her I was your friend. But I knew you wouldn't want her to see you like this.'

She was right. But, honestly, I was relieved. I couldn't lie my way through the Lord's Prayer with this amount of morphine in my system. I could just about recall my own name. Just about. Although in between the hazy dreams, I would have sworn to God my name was Eve.

I pressed the morphine button again and fell into a very deep, very long sleep.

29

When I woke the next day, Sam had gone home to shower and to get a change of clothes. The flowers had wilted a little under the harsh strip lighting on the hospital ward. They stood vibrant next to the clean lines and the pale blue tones of the bedding, curtains, floor. But I didn't need to see them. They just reminded me of the blooms I'd seen woven into the hair of dead women. I shivered and pulled the thin blanket over me, knocking an IV line on my hand in the process and feeling sick at the thought of the long needle sitting inside my vein.

Ryan approached my bed. He was wearing plain clothes, a pair of Dad shaped jeans and a hoodie.

'How are you feeling?' he asked.

'Better. But still feel like I could have been dug up from the ground this morning.'

'Did Jim ask you to come in?' I asked.

'He did.' he pulled out a small notepad and set it out on the table next to my bed.

'We are still looking for Zach Wiseman. He has not been to his office or house in the last 48 hours and his car hasn't moved. His neighbours said that they thought he had a motorbike but there isn't anything registered to his name so we are struggling on ANPR. We are not sure that Zach Wiseman isn't his real name but we haven't figured out how he got through the identify verification process at Lush Green.'

'We've got people interviewing colleagues and neighbours. Struggled to find much by way of social media, he's not on Facebook. His LinkedIn account looks like it was a dummy just to message Jessica.'

Smart. Smart and running. I knew it was my man. I could feel it through the dull ache in my stomach.

'Have all of the families been updated? Is Jessica safe?' I asked.

'Yes.' we have people with Jessica and her family and Sophie is working on the press release now.

'Is that where Jim is?' I said.

'Yes.' Ryan answered. 'Jim is going to announce that we have a person of extreme interest. We are going to warn the public.'

'Did you get any footage from the common? What he did to me?'

Ryan ran his tongue over his bottom lip and shook his head slowly.

'It's hard viewing. You can see what he did, but it was dark and he had his hood pulled up. When the kids got close he sprinted off towards Wandsworth Town.'

'But we know it was him.'

It wasn't a question. It was a statement. I knew it was my man. It was the same rage he directed at Jessica. I could taste his hatred for me. It was metallic and medicinal and putrid. He hated me like he hated Jessica, a fucking unknowable woman standing in the way of his plans. It just meant he had been keeping a closer eye on the investigation than we expected, I had no idea how he knew where I was. But he was much smarter than we set out in the profile.

'Can you make sure all of the relevant reports are duplicated and sent to my address?' I asked.

'Yes. Am I sending them to your place? DCI Greaves said to check.'

'Good question. Actually, no. I'll probably be staying at my girlfriends. Let me write down her address.'

I reached over to his notepad and winced in pain.

'Let me get that.' he said.

As he moved to the bedside, I noticed Dylan at the ward reception desk. I thought back to the shocked face of Lee Grace at his doorstep and realised the same guilt must have danced out on my face.

The nurse pointed towards me and Dylan clocked that I was with Ryan. He waited in the entrance to the ward until I had given him Sam's address.

'I won't keep you on your day off. Thanks for coming in.'

Ryan started to walk backwards. Clearly relieved to be given leave. It must have been awkward for him standing by his superior officer's bedside with her looking like this.

'Get well soon, ma'am.'

He crossed Dylan's path to my bed. They smiled at each other in that half knowing way and Dylan stood at the end of my bed. He softly placed a hand on the metal edge of the bed frame at the top of the bed.

'I came yesterday, but didn't want to impose.' he said.

'Did you say anything to Jim, or to —'

'No. Don't worry. I didn't say anything.'

'Thank you. I've told them I parked to go to the shop on Bellevue Road.'

'I know.'

'Are you working with Jim on the press release?'

'Yes.' he nodded. 'Although I get the sense he doesn't care if I'm there or not.'

He probably didn't.

'When is it?' I asked.

'4pm.'

'Isla. I'm sorry this happened to you. I know it's weird but I just want to be here for you. I—'

'Don't.' I said.

I thought to the shadow of mascara under Sam's eyes. How she had uncurled herself from sleeping on the chair next to my bedside and winced at how much it had hurt her back. I thought about how she cried at books and how she always made sure she set a multivitamin out for me whenever I stayed at her flat.

Dylan took his hand off the bed.

'It was just a one off.' I said. 'Can we just leave it as that?'

He took a moment, then smiled in the same professional way he had when I first met him.

'Yes.'

He steadied himself.

'I look forward to working with you in the future, DCI Fletcher.' he smiled. 'Please rest and get well.'

'I will.' I smiled back at him and watched him walk away from the ward.

I reached for my phone and called Jim. He answered after two rings.

'Fletch, I'm not having it.'

'I'm just ringing ahead of the press confe—'

'No. Honestly, we are taking care of this. Rest. I will call you tonight.'

He hung up and was left looking at a dead phone. The ward was quiet and a cold wind whistled under the thin opening of the window. The curtains carving out temporary boundaries between the row of beds across from me swayed gently. I pressed the morphine button again and slept.

Vadim Kuznetsov died on the banks of the River Volga, weighing three hundred pounds, his passport tucked into the back of his foul-smelling jeans and three bottles of counterfeit polish vodka in his system. Vadim had checked himself out of hospital three weeks earlier, knowing he had nowhere else to hide, knowing it wouldn't be long before the cancer metastasised and cut through his bowels like glass. But he wouldn't go down without a drink. Every day since he had come to this spot to watch the Saratov Bridge. To watch, and to drink. This was the second day on vodka. The first week he savoured the wine, the second week he gulped down the brandy, but now it was time for the vodka. He was tired. His stomach was bloated from the fluid accumulation and he could barely control his own piss stream. It was definitely time for the vodka, and he'd brought four bottles to be on the safe side.

When he finally fell backwards onto the thick wet grass, Eve struggled against the heavy mass of his limbs. She tried to breathe against the thick weight of his visceral body fat. She tried to move his swollen feet inside his rotten brown boots. She reached and grasped for the muscles in his fingers. Like she had before. To finish her words. For nothing.

But something else connected. Somewhere else. In a small cluster of synapses in Vadim's hippocampus, flooded by toxins from the effect of encephalopathy, Eve found a way to see her own life. In living, this was the area of the brain where Vadim processed new memories, the tales of his day, the stories and events that made him Vadim. They were screened here before they were sent off for storage in the frontal sections. Or repressed. Or deleted.

When Vadim died, he could not remember any element of his living self. He had no episodic memories of his own existence, although they still remained, filed away in the booze-burned archives of his medial septum. Eve was completely in control of his memories, his final thoughts, the dream that danced out as he died.

Vadim died remembering a life he did not live, feeling a pain he did not recognise, in a language he could not understand. Shivering nights under a vast starlit sky and whooping, drunken twirling. He died dreaming of sloping verdant hills, glassy blue lakes and grey mountain tops. Vadim died ghost-walking the trails of the Lake District.

30

I was in the hospital for five days. Five quiet days to sit with my thoughts as Jim and team built a case against a fictional man called Zach who they still couldn't find. Jim kept me updated every day but didn't share any specifics. He was protective and made sure that a uniformed car escorted me and Sam home from the hospital.

Sam had moved the furniture around in her studio, to turn the armchair out to face the common. She had new linen on the bed and had propped up support for my back with thick duvets. She had set up a swinging table for my laptop next to the bed, knowing that going home meant the green light to jump into work with as much might as my broken body would allow. Typing was painful, and painfully slow, but I was excited by the prospect of re-engaging with work, the news, the world.

Boxes from the station stood in the corner of the room. I could tell that Sam hated them being in the house. She had re-arranged the furniture, placed the flowers from the hospital in small vases dotted around the surfaces of the flat. Scented candles flickered on a table full of snacks, my reading glasses and medication.

I spent the first day or so just filtering emails and reading case notes. Reading, deleting and ordering. I saw the updated reports from Dylan but just filed them in my inbox under case notes. I filed him in the same way in my head.

Sam worked from home, her work had been very supportive and aside from the occasional conference call she took in the kitchen, she lay next to me and tapped her words out. She also stood in the kitchen whenever she spoke to her family. Her brother was staying with her parents and they were all worried about me.

Sam was making us a fresh cafetiere of coffee when I got my daily call from Mum.

'Hey Mum.'

'Hello my darling. How are you feeling today?'

'Much better.' I lied.

'Is your friend looking after you ok?'

'Yes. I'm very lucky.'

'Do you think I could come and visit?'

'Mum, I'm just getting back into work. And I'm honestly getting much better.'

'OK.' I could tell it hurt her for me to keep her away. But I couldn't face explaining Sam and I didn't want her to see the extent of my facial injuries.

'I've got a ton of annual leave owed to me. So I'll come and stay with you for a bit.' I offered.

'Oh lovely. Maybe you'll be here for Christmas?'

'Maybe.'

'Oh lovely.'

'Mum, I have to dial into a work call. Can I call you tomorrow?'

'Yes. Rest up.'

I had lied about feeling fine and about having a work call. Instead I felt exhausted. I slid down into the soft mattress, set an alarm on my phone for an hour and then fell quickly into a deep sleep.

I had dreamt a great many things in the hospital, and since coming back to Sam's. Huge, vivid, colourful dream. Jessica, Greta, Emmeline. I bounced fat pollen dust and fell through skies filled with over-sized blooms that could have been plucked straight out of Wonderland.

I woke with a thud onto the soft earth of Sam's . When I woke, I woke with the same name on my tongue. Evelyn Mayhill. I had dreamt the name in the hospital. Eve.

I got out of bed, for the first time in a day and gave my legs a chance to deal with the new sensation. Blood flooded the muscles in my thighs. I heaved myself up and then sat back down quickly.

I tried again and made it all the way to the chair. I stood leaning against it and opened the window. It was December and the air was crisp. The green from Tooting Bec common was reassuring. It reminded me of home and I realised that the thought of going home and seeing Mum made me happy. I needed a break from London, from the black pollution I blew out into tissues when I sneezed, from a job where I saw the skulls of dead women.

Jim had emailed to tell me that they had upscaled the manhunt for Zach but still hadn't apprehended him. I was grateful for the updates but being at Sam's had made are realise just how tired I was. I was certain that Zach was my man but I didn't feel the need to find him. I was happy for Jim to take the lead and knew I was safe here at Sam's. I would take time to heal.

But still. Eve. I could not get the word out of my head.

I saw it as I dreamed. Eve. Eve. Eve. And I cursed the power of the opiates, and the power of my imagination. I had always had vivid dreams, scary dreams. And even though this wasn't scary, I was scared. It felt real. Like someone else's memories.

Sam called through from the kitchenette and asked if I needed any painkillers.

'Just coffee please'

I needed to give the painkillers a rest. I hated the dreams. As a girl I was plagued by nightmares and night terrors; nothing more sinister than an overactive imagination but I would spend countless hours under the duvet, glassy-eyed and frozen in the darkness until I eventually plucked up the courage to call out for my Dad.

Sam placed the huge mug of steaming coffee on the coffee table and stooped to help me back to bed. She picked up a mustard yellow cushion and placed it behind my upper back as I strained to sit up to drink my coffee.

'Are you sure you don't want any more codeine?'

'No thanks sweetie. Its not that bad. Not bad enough for the side effects.'

'Are you feeling sick?'

I shook my head and the muscles in my neck cried out.

'No, its the dreams. Its like being back on the patches.'

When I met Sam I was in the process of giving up cigarettes. Nicotine patches helped me to crush a forty a day habit but the side effects were a source of Sam's amusement. She sat next to me on top of the duvet. Pulling it taught over my legs. I leaned my head against her shoulder and she rested her lips on my hair. And that was when the guilt hit me for fucking Dylan. In a way I hadn't felt before. The weight of it felt like a mass of iron in my stomach but I knew I couldn't tell her. I wouldn't share the burden and hurt her. But I decided that was it. It was time to commit to the person I loved and focus on building something real. I closed the notes and placed them on the floor and turned to cuddle her. We lay, perfectly present, and held each other.

31

When I woke, I felt much clearer headed. A blanket had been lifted from the pain but it was starting to feel more discernible. My face had a dull ache and hurt when I smile. My collarbone would occasionally throw a more searing pain if I moved more quickly than I should. It hurt a little to speak. My legs felt heavy from the rest and my ribs were sore. But it was a manageable patchwork of pain as opposed to just feeling pain from the eyeballs down. I would rather stick to paracetamol and not feel wooly headed.

I switched on the news to see the repeat of the press conference. It was weird to see Jim's face on the TV monitor. His bald head glistened under the bright lights and the wrinkles around his eyes looked deeper. He would be dealing with incredible pressure from Marshall, and from the victims families to step up the intensity of the manhunt for Zach. I thought about him. About my man. But in my mind there was a clear boundary; he was outside. Outside of the boundaries of this safe space with Sam. Outside, beyond the uniforms sitting in the car outside the house. Outside, alone with Jim Greaves chasing him.

I really tried to close my mind to the wider investigation but, much in the same way I knew I needed to fuck Dylan Nicholson, I knew I needed to ask the question.

I picked up the phone. Put it down again.

Sam came back through from the kitchen and placed a plate of smoked salmon and scrambled eggs down on the coffee table.

'Morning, sunshine.'

She kissed me gently and stroked my hair.

'Cucumber water coming up.'

No. I knew it would just annoy me if I didn't act. I dialled Ryan's number.

'Ma'am. How you feeling?'

'Better.' I answered. I meant it.

'There's still no update I'm afraid, we have had a few calls after the press conference. It's like he's a ghost.'

'I'm actually ringing about something slightly different.'

'Oh right.' he said.

'Can you pull up the list of everyone we have spoken to for all three cases?'

'Err, yes.' he said. I could hear the muffle on the phone as he tucked it under the crook of his chin and the tap on the keyboard as he logged back into his desktop. 'one sec.'

He murmured as he opened the case folder and clicked into the database of contacts.

'Got it.'

'Can you check if there is an Evelyn Mayhill in the list?'

'Sure. M-A-Y-H-I-L-L?' he asked.

'Yep.' I said.

Sam came back through from the kitchen and set a pair of coffee mugs down beside the plate of food. She padded back to the kitchen.

'Nope.' said Ryan.

'Ok. Any can you look on the delegate list for the events that Lush Green provided?'

'Sure. One mo—'

I heard the shuffle and the click of the mouse. Then the striking of keys. Sam came back from the kitchen and set the coffee down. She poured two black mugs and then sat on an orange pouffe beside the table. She scooped up the Colonel and

243

held him to her face. He purred then protested to be put down.

'No, ma'am. Sorry.'

'And you personally aren't familiar with the name Evelyn Mayhill?'

'No, ma'am. Should I?'

I shook my head and brushed the hair off my face with my good hand.

'No. Don't worry. Thanks for looking.'

I pressed red and then threw my phone across me onto the unmade bed.

I leant back gingerly into the armchair and Sam handed me a mug.

'Why are you asking about that whole thing?'

I blew onto the surface of the hot liquid and then drew in a small sip.

'What whole thing?'

'The Eve thing?' said Sam, tucking her legs beneath her and leaning forward to take a mouthful of eggs.

'What Eve thing?' I asked.

'Oh.' she squinted her eyes and looked out of the window. 'It might have been around the time you were out of school.'

After Dad died, I took three months off. Mum never pressured me to go back but I couldn't face re-sitting the whole year so I worked from home, got notes from friends, and somehow managed to walk away with enough B grades to get into UCL. If I ever got close to believing in God it was then, because I have no idea how I passed those exams.

'What happened?'

'A girl called Eve. I went to school with her. She died. Fell down the stairs. It was massive, we had a service for her and the whole bloody school went.'

'Christ. Sorry you went through that. Were you close?' I

asked.

She frowned a little and shook her head quickly.

'I was only 15, didn't really know her. But it hit Isaac hard. He dated her for a couple of months. He sort of went off the rails for a bit after that. Decided he wasn't going to go to uni.'

'Do you remember her surname?' I asked.

'Yes. that's what I'm saying. Eve Mayhill.'

I leaned forward quickly and landed the coffee mug down with a thud. The pain screamed in my ribs. Black liquid lurched out over the side of the mug, onto the table and the rug.

'Bloody hell, Isla.' said Sam, moving quickly back from the tide of coffee. She jumped up quickly, grabbed a tea towel and pressed it into the rug. Black liquid seeped up into it.

I stood and picked up my phone, searching the internet for the name. Google images presented a sea of different faces. An academic in the States, the twitter profile for a gymnast in Australia. I clicked away from images and back to the search engine. On the fourth search page was a link to an archived obituary hosted from The Cumbrian Bugle. I quickly read over the article; exactly as Sam said, Evelyn Mayhill, 17 died from a tragic fall at her parents house. Service held in the church hall.'

'Jesus.' I said.

I wondered why I hadn't heard about it. In a small town news like that spread. If the lollipop lady had seen you smoking your parents would know about it before you got home. But in the months after Dad died I completely retracted. I was desperate to leave Mum, leave the pain. I had already decided to move to London and I didn't give a shit about anything in the Lakes.

I looked around the room. I couldn't call Jim. Or Dylan. It was madness. I needed to get to the station, to the private information. I needed see a picture of Eve, I needed to see what happened to her.

'OK. Don't get annoyed.' I said.

'What?' said Sam, sensing what I was about to say.

'I need you to help me. I need to stick another top on and then I need you to help me down to the car.'

'Are you fucking kidding me? Absolutely not.'

Sam was on her feet. Furious.

'Listen. This is important.' I tried to bend to open a drawer.

'And you know I'm going to do it whether you help me or not.'

She picked up the two plates of food and carried them through to the kitchen, placing them into the sink with force. It sounded like one of them cracked. I could hear her taking deep breaths and realising I wouldn't take no for an answer.

She helped me to put on an oversized navy jumper, sprayed on some deodorant and then helped me down the stairs to the car outside.

The PC sat in the passenger seat was surprised to see us approaching in her wing mirror and stepped out of the car.

'Is everything ok ma'am?' she asked. The driver was leaning over the gearstick, craning his head to hear my response.

'Yes. Everything is fine. Are you ok to take me to the station? I will only need to be there for a bit.'

They looked at each other and without speaking agreed that I was to obeyed. I could sense that neither of them wanted to be put between the rock and the hard place of me and DCI Greaves.

Sam was stood in the road next to me, shaking her head.

'It's fine sweetie. Honestly.' I kissed her and then hid the pain as I sat into the rear of the car. 'Please just go back to the flat and try not to worry.'

She closed the door gently behind me and jogged back to the flat.

(EVE)

Maia Wentworth stole a razor blade from her fathers bathroom cabinet and ran a bath using all of the hot water in the immersion tank. She sliced both wrists twice, in purposeful movements. It stung as she placed them back in the tub. She lay back and stared up at the black constellation of mould on the ceiling.

'I'm sorry.'

Maia died without ever knowing what she was sorry for.

Changming Zhou stood on the edge of the Wuhan Yangtze River Bridge in Hubei province. He didn't care anymore. He didn't care about the dead bitch he had left in the bedroom, or her castrated lover laying next to her. He was poisoned by hate and rage. But before he took the final step out, he screamed, 'I'm sorry.' He wasn't. They deserved it. And he had never uttered a single word of english language in his whole, bitter life.

32

The guys on the front desk were as surprised to see me as the uniforms in the car. I had caught a glimpse of my healing face in the rearview mirror of the car; bright green and yellow bruising covered the majority of my face and I had giant bags under my eyes.

I entered the station, walking past the interview rooms and ignoring the caravan of people filtering between the MIR and the conference rooms.

Gavenas stopped me. Shock clear on her face.

'My god. Are you ok?' she said.

'I'm not really here.' I reassured him. 'Just picking up some stuff from my office.'

'It's good to see you up and about, ma'am.' he said. 'Do you need a hand at all?'

'Nope.' I said. 'I've got it.'

I tried to walk without struggling, my legs seemed to have forgotten walking.

I held onto the handle of the door to my office, turning and leaning on it as it opened. I took a deep breath, steadied myself and then limped over to the office chair. I rolled myself back to the door to close it, pushing off it to get back to the desk.

I typed my username and password into the PC and waited for it to load. My office was cold and I could hear the muted hum of the activity in the MIR. I knew Jim would call me if they found him. But I also knew that they needed to make the case against him unshakeable. There was a stack of administrative boxes to check for the Crown Prosecution Service. There was no room for error. The longer he evaded Jim, the more time he gave the team to make sure he went away.

It took me a while to access the case notes in the system. There was a clear record of Eve's death. The coroner report stated a broken neck as the cause of death but noted a significant head wound from where she had fallen into a glass table at the foot of the stairs.

I dialled the number associated with the record. It looked like a switchboard.

'Cumbria Constabulary?'

'Hi there. This is DCI Fletcher from Wandsworth CID. I'm after some information was an accidental death that happened in 1996.'

'Of course. Let me direct you to the right place.' she said.

The line buzzed as she redirected me.

'Archives?'

'Oh hi there. I'm looking I'm interested in any images you can provide for case file record number QI7-990-766. I can't seem to see anything online.'

'Oh no. You won't. We only started scanning digital images in 2003.'

'Do you have hard copies?' I asked. Hoping. It was difficult to believe how quickly the world had turned into the digital age. I grew up without social media, emails. I was disconnected. Yet even I took for granted how quickly we could access information now. The idea of hard copy images in an archive was ancient even to me. And I remembered VHS.

'We do. How quickly do you need it?'

'It's part of an ongoing homicide investigation and a nationwide manhunt. So pretty urgent.'

'Oh I saw that!' he remarked. 'My missus told me it was on the news again this morning. Awful business.'

'It is.' I said.

'Right. I can get it to you today. I'll go right now. I'll scan them over to you.'

'Brilliant. Much appreciated.'

'No problem.'

I hung up the phone and drummed my fingers on the table. I didn't want to step out into the MIR. I didn't want Jim to know what I was doing. I had absolutely no idea how to explain why I was asking these questions. No idea how Eve had found her way into my head.

The email notification pinged on my desktop and I clicked on the attached images.

The crime scene images were grainy. But it was clear what I was looking at. A brown carpet with a pattern that belonged in the 90s. The body of a thin woman stacked at the bottom of the stairs. I clicked on the next image. Taken at the foot of the stairs looking into the house. Eve had fallen down the steep stairs of a victorian terrace and into a glass vestibule table. Glass shards lay on the carpet next to her pale face along with everything that had been on the table: a picture of the family, letters and a broken vase of flowers. Roses, freesias, gypsy's baby breath. One of the stems had fallen onto her face and lay bloom-upward next to the deep gash at the top of her forehead. Even through the grainy still I could see the stark white bone of her skull.

This was it. This was how is started.

And this was someone Isaac loved. Sam's brother.

I called her from my desk top. No answer.

She was really pissed off with me.

I struggled to my feet. My options blurred as a carousel in my mind. I had no traceable rationale for looking at this case file. I had nothing I could explain to the CPS. I pressed print on the image and stooped to collect it. I stood and arched my back.

My legs felt better under me. I took a deep breath and headed towards to the MIR.

Ryan, Whalley and Parish all sat at their desks in an open-mouthed shock that befitted a comedy sketch. Jim, however, didn't look shocked. He looked annoyed. His voice was raised.

'Fletcher, what the fuck are you doing here?'

I raised my hands in an act of peace.

'I've got something. I can help.'

'How can you possible have something that we don't?' he asked. His voice was still raised.

'Isaac Tibbs. Can you pull up details of any vehicles registered to him?'

Ryan looked at Jim for confirmation that he could listen to me. Jim looked resigned and then nodded. Ryan sat down to type in his details.

'Who the hell is Isaac Tibbs?' he asked. At least his voice was at a normal volume.

'Hear me out. He's Sam's brother.'

I decided on the version of the truth to tell Jim and handed over the image of Eve's corpse.

He looked at it for a few seconds. He could see the similarity.

'Who's this?' he asked. 'When was this taken?'

'So. I was talking to Sam about the case. About some of the specifics.' I almost interrupted myself by quickly adding, 'Look. I know i shouldn't have.'

It was frowned upon to share details of cases like this with loved ones. But I decided I would rather Jim scolded me for talking about it to Sam than think I had lost my mind with talk of a dead woman having been in my head.

'We were talking about grief. And loss. And she mentioned that her brother's girlfriend had died in an accident. Back when he was 17. He found the body and she specifically said that he had told her about the flowers, and the fact the gash on her head showed her skull.'

'Right.' said Jim, looking down at the picture.

'You have to admit there are similarities?' I asked.

'I guess so.' he turned to Ryan. 'Anything on this Tibbs then?'

'Yes.' said Ryan, 'he has a motorcycle registered to a flat in Earlsfield.'

South London. Familiar to him.

Ryan leaned closer to his screen and focussed his eyes.

'I'm just cross referencing the reg against CCTV data from the morning Greta was killed.'

He could sense that the room was watching him. Even the people who had tried to feign work had given up and were just watching me and Jim.

'Jim. Look South London? He knows it.'

Jim pressed the point of his tongue against his top lip and exhaled.

I thought back to the profile.

'He got good grades at school then after Eve died he didn't go to uni. His Mum always talks about how intelligent he is. And he's had at least three career changes that Sam has told me about, so he can't hold a steady job down. And I know from Sam that he has a fucking temper.'

'Got him,' said Ryan,. He stood quickly and then leant back onto his desk to read the details. 'Six oh three on the morning we found Greta's body. His motorcycle crosses the CCTV camera at the pub on the top of Crockerton Avenue. And then five minutes later he goes past the tube on Balham High Road.'

'That's enough. Send a car to his address now.'

Four people stood immediately and ran out of the MIR.

'Ryan. See if you can place him at the other crime scenes. Get me a complete background on him.'

There was a quiet excitement in the room. My body felt too broken to cope with the stress hormones pumping out from my adrenal glands. I felt a panic agitating in my abdomen, somewhere between my lungs and my stomach. I didn't know if I was going to have a full blown panic attack or be sick.

We finally had my man. I knew it. My man with the flowers. Zach. Isaac.

I sat on the chair nearest to me and leant my head in my hand, stooping over. I took in deep breaths. I was tired.

'You ok, Fletch?'

Jim walked next to me and placed a gentle, heavy hand on my back.

'We'll get him.'

'I'll be fine.' I said. 'I think I should head back home.

'You're not bastard wrong. I mean, look at the state of you.'

We both laughed. Laughed with relief and with the truth of it. I was a fucking mess.

'Let's get you back home.' he said, gesturing with his arm at the PC in uniform who had driven me over to the station.

'Deal.' I said. 'Let me just let Sam know she can stop worrying.'

I took out my phone and called her.

'Hey!' she answered. 'So glad you called. Are you ok?'

'Yes.' I answered. 'I've done what I needed to. I'm coming home.'

I smiled at Jim.

'Amazing.' said Sam.

'And are you ok?' I asked. 'I'm so sorry for leaving like that, you know what happens when I —'

'I'm fine, sweetie.' she said. 'It's nice to have some company.'

It felt like the blood drained from my face in an instant, solidified in my throat and then sank as an iron ball into my stomach.

'What do you mean company?' I asked. My voice was shaking.

'Isaac's here. He popped round just after you left.'

Sam's phone clicked silent and I looked down at my black screen.

I practically screamed.

'He's with her.'

The entire room fell silent, and I vomited a stomach full of coffee and bile into the centre of the MIR.

33

By the time Jim had half-argued, half-carried me to his car we were four cars behind. Jim drove us there with the full blues and twos and I held onto the passenger side door as best I could as he drove at speed though the turns. My entire body ached but I didn't care. When we pulled into my street there was a two car cordon at either end and two cars parked at angles; like loaded guns pointed at my front door. I tried Sam's number three times in the car but there was no answer, it just rang out.

The motorbike registered to Isaac was parked on the pavement outside of the flat.

Jim had called for SCO19 at the station and they were minutes away from arriving. I had never had any cause to interact with armed response in my entire career. I was leaning on the car, shaking, when they arrived.

Two armed response vehicles arrived, with three ARV officers in each. They piled out, carrying self-loading glock 17s. The thought of so many bullets so close to Sam make me feel like i might be sick again. A man built like a concrete mixer ran over to me and Jim.

Jim spoke clearly.

'DCI Jim Greaves.'

'Bailey. SFO. What are we dealing with?'

'Isaac Tibbs. In the first floor flat with his sister, who we believe is being held against her will. We strongly believe that Isaac is responsible for the death of two women in the last month along with an aggravated assault. We know he is dangerous. We just don't know if he is armed. No contact thus far.'

The SFO turned to look at me.

'DCI Isla Fletcher. I live here.' I said.

'DCI Fletcher co-habits with the hostage.' said Jim, 'Sam Tibbs. She has also been instrumental in identifying this man as the person responsible for the death of at least two women.'

'Is there just one flight of stairs up to the flat?'

'Yes.' I asked.

'And no way out at the rear?'

'No. The garden is steeper than out here. He couldn't jump.'

Bailey began to walk back to the ARV when my phone rang. It was Sam.

I answered the phone, and Isaac spoke down the line.

'Only you.' he said.

I had only heard Isaac's voice a couple of times and never met him person. But on both times I heard his voice he sounded warm: Northern and welcoming. This man was different. His voice was flat.

'Is Sam ok? Don't you fucking—'

'You are not in a position to give me orders, cunt. Sam is ok. But I am armed. And if any of you try and enter the building, I will kill her and then myself. Understood.'

'Understood.'

'Good. I will allow only you.'

The phone clicked dead.

Jim and Bailey were both stood watching me, shaking their heads.

'Absolutely not.' said Jim.

Bailey was looking at me. Listening for Jim to give an order.

'Jim, I have to—'

'No.' he said. 'There is only one reason for him to want you up there, and that's to finish what he started.'

'Fine. Fucking arm me.' I said.

This time Bailey was shaking his head. I knew there was no way that would happen.

'Jim, if it was Jean or one of the boys up there.' I pleaded.

'Plus, tactically, there is absolutely no way we can progress without me going in. The minute we breach the downstairs door he has a flight of stairs worth of warning to kill Sam. I could try and get him closer to the window. Try and talk him down.'

I was pacing. Frantic. I felt no pain in my body anymore.

'We could get her vested?' offered Bailey.

Jim looked at me. At the determination on my face.

'Fine. Do it.'

Bailey spoke into his radio and called two ARVs over to the car. They had a with them a tactical vest and body armour. One of them helped me into it, over my fractures. That hurt.

Bailey came and double checked that the armour was fitted and stood directly in front of my eyeline.

'DCI Fletcher, you have one objective here. That is the safety of you and Sam. Do you understand?'

'Yes.'

'We will leave this line open. He placed a radio into the tactical vest. I want you to make an assessment. If you can isolate yourselves then we can enter. If you can get him to the window, great. But that is secondary. Understood?'.

'Yes.'

'For the love of God, Fletch. Take care.' said Jim.

The radios around me fell silent as I stepped into the road and approached the front of the building. I heard the traffic on the High Road and the distant roar of a plane overhead. I heard radios squawk around me and felt the gaze of the fifteen or so police men and women arranged in a U shape perimeter two houses either side of the house.

I walked up the three steps and pressed the buzzer to the flat.

Isaac must have been watching from the window because he buzzed the door open.

My legs felt the strain of every foot fall up the shallow flight of steps. The door was ajar and I could see Isaac stood in the centre of the room. He had perfect posture. I couldn't see a weapon.

I stood in the doorway.

'Where is Sam?' I asked, peering into the flat.

'I'm here.' she said. I walked into the studio and closed the door behind me. I didn't take my eyes off Isaac as I closed the door behind me. I didn't push it all the way to close.

I moved closer to him and could see that Sam was sat cross-legged next to the bed. She had been crying but looked mostly in shock. She didn't look like he had hurt her.

'Are you ok?' I asked her, keeping my eyes fixed on him.

'He hasn't hurt me.' she said.

'But he's lost his fucking mind.' she spat the words out at him with a kind of anger that reminded me of a couple of kids arguing in the street.

Isaac laughed.

'See?' he said to me. 'I told you she wouldn't get hurt.'

I moved slowly towards the bedside, trying to get myself between him and her.

'And what about the others, Isaac? Why did you hurt them? Why did you hurt me?'

'What?' shouted Sam. She stood quickly. 'What the fuck is she talking about?'

At her quick movement, Isaac removed his hands from behind his back, dropping his arms down to his side. In doing so, he revealed a long thin knife that he had in his left hand.

'Sam. Be quiet sweetie.'

I edged closer to her, moving my left arm behind me to hold out my hand to her. To calm her. To stop her from saying something to make him snap.

'Why did you hurt me, Isaac?'

'You were too close.' he said. Calmly.

'I knew you knew about Lush Green. And Zach.' he said.

Sam started crying.

'I was with this one when you called.' he lifted his head to acknowledge his sister.

'And you didn't notice me keeping you company. As you went about your business.'

He fixed his eyes on me. And I wondered if he had seen me with Dylan.

'And what did I stop you from doing?'

'You know.' he said. 'And I'd only just started.'

'You killed those women?' said Sam.

She had took a step forward and was pressed against my back. I held my hand against her stomach, feeling blindly behind me to reach for her hand. But she was gesticulating.

'You fucking killed them? Why?' she sobbed. I could hear the thick heave of cries catching in her throat. 'You did that to them?'

I reached again and caught hold of her wrist. I held it.

'Liars.' he said.

'So they deserved to be killed?' I asked.

He didn't say anything. He showed no remorse. I could hear the police radios from under the thin crack of the window opening. Isaac was stood out of line of sight on the other side of the studio, beneath the gallery of images that Sam had pinned on the wall, of her home, her childhood, her family.

'And what about Eve?' I asked.

'What about Eve?' he asked. His tone shifted.

'Why did you kill her?' I asked.

'No.' whispered Sam.

'I didn't kill Eve.' he said, raising his voice.

'Don't lie to me.' I said.

He took a step towards us. A step closer to line of sight.

'I am NOT lying. She fell.'

'You told us you weren't there!' said Sam, wriggling her wrist away from my grip and pressing into me. She was certain that her brother wouldn't hurt us but I knew he wanted us both dead. He was just talking us through it. I needed him in line of sight.

'She fell. Or you pushed her?' I said. 'I saw the crime scene. The way she cut her head. She must have hit that table with some force.'

Isaac paced along the periphery of the room. Like a caged animal.

'I didn't mean for her to die.'

'Why did she then?' I asked.

'She was leaving me.' he said.

'People break up, you sick fuck.' said Sam. Not fucking helping.

'Not us. Not then. We had PLANS.'

He rubbed his hand over his face. He was a man with se-crets. I felt like a priest taking confession.

'What plans, Isaac?

'She ruined everything. She said she couldn't forgive me.;

'Forgive you for what?' I asked, trying to mask the fear and the hatred in my voice. 'What did she ruin?'

'For the man in the road.' he said, blankly.

At that moment I felt like all of the air in the atmosphere had been condensed and pushed into the room. The pressure in my head throbbed. Sam reached and held my hand tightly.

'What man in the road?'

'He just walked out. It wasn't my fault.'

I stood, gripping Sam's hand. She had understood what he was saying, I was still fighting. Clawing my way through the disbelief.

'Who just walked out?' I asked. The words fought their way out from my dry throat.

'She told me to stop. But if I had it would have ruined everything. But she couldn't let it go. She was going to betray me.'

'How?' said Sam. She had put her other hand on the dip of my waist, gently hooking her hand onto the material, readying to restrain me.

'By going to the police. When she found out he had died. She was going to fucking shop me.'

I was trembling.

Sam spoke again.

'Did you not think of Mum, of Dad? What the hell happened to you?' she asked.

Isaac turned to the table where he had set down a scalpel. He hung his head low and took a deep breath. He picked it up and turned to us. I braced myself.

'It's too late to worry about Mum and Dad now.'

He took two quick strides towards us and I felt Sam flinch as she tugged on my shirt to pull me towards her.

The gun shot was loud and Isaac hit the low coffee table with his right shoulder and then fell to floor, clutching his side. The gun sounded again and another bullet hit his thigh. Disabling shots. I pushed back against Sam, jamming her backwards against the wall next to the bed. Isaac was on all fours clutching the bullet wound at his side.

EVE

Eve felt the laboured, sticky breaths. She felt the rage in Isaac, and the fear.

In panicked blinks she saw the room. Papers scattered over a thick grey carpet. An upturned coffee table. She looked through Isaac's eyes at the two women. She saw the women in the body armour. She looked at Isla Fletcher. At her tall frame and bruised face holding back a sobbing woman. Eve took in the room. The images from the wall, the bed. The smell of coffee.

She looked back at the sobbing woman and recognised her. She, Eve, knew her. Samantha? But older. She remembered her face and it was definitely a grown up Sam.

Isaac struggled to crawl but Eve contained the movement. She looked down and moved Isaac's hand. The blood was thick and dark. He tried to move it back to the wound at his stomach but she resisted. She fought him and forced a slow moving arm up from the wound to a couple of inches from his face. She made him stare at his dark bloodied fingers, knowing that the colour of blood meant he had only a minute or so before he lost consciousness.

But Isaac was fighting. He was rage. He could get to that bitch. The words gurgled at his throat.

'You're fucking dead.'

He tried to move again to his knees but Eve restrained him and he felt her do it. He knew she was there. He was confused and frightened. And dying.

He fell backwards and sideways, lying on his left, facing the two women.

Eve could hear the loud bang of the SFO unit using the battering ram on the front door to the house and the swift footfall of three armed men enter the flat. She could hear the sound of an approaching ambulance.

She stared back at the faces of Sam and Isla, now holding each other as a strange man with a gun put pressure on the two wounds. She felt Isaac cough and watched a thick, bloody sputum fell out across the floor. She fixed back on the bruised woman, and pushed the words out of Isaac's mouth. '

'I'm sorry.'

And with the effort of pushing out Isaac's last breath, Eve Mayhill died. For the final time.

Epilogue

The green always surprised me. Just how green my life had been. Before university, before London, before too many dead bodies. Before I met a dead woman called Evelyn Mayhill.

Sam and I decided to drive up to the Lakes for Christmas, via an overnight stay in a small B&B in Oxfordshire. We set out on the 22nd. I struggled over a short 2km walk but refused to stop. We held hands as we walked muddy trails. We kissed in pubs and ate too much food and tried to laugh.

Sam was still fragile, and sad. Her Mum hadn't got out of bed since Isaac's funeral and her Dad couldn't stop asking questions. I answered every single one as best I could: yes, Isaac's fingerprints had matched one found on a bloom in the hair of a dead girl; yes, one of the teenagers on the Common positively identified him as the man who had tried to kill me. I was thankful he didn't ask any questions about Eve. Because truthfully I wouldn't have known where to start. I felt like I had known her, known her pain. I knew that she had died twenty three years ago but I also knew that I came to know her a couple of weeks ago. I was thankful for her. I owed her. I owed a dead woman.

I didn't dream of Dad anymore. Or Derek. I didn't even dream of Eve. In fact I couldn't recall dreaming since the day that Isaac died. I had been sleeping a solid twelve most nights, with my face pressed against Sam's back.

We drove passed the boundary to The Lake District on the morning of Christmas Eve. It was a clear, cold day and the blue of the sky was vivid in the reflections of the vast bodies of water. The green of the landscape was vibrant and vast, even with the bare trees staked deep into the rolling land. The air felt clean and the sky felt vast and we listened to Christmas songs with the windows rolled down. Two country girls who had lived in the City for so long that the smell of fresh air surprised them.

We decided against a visit to the Mayhills. Sam didn't even know if they still lived in her village. Sam seemed to remember them moving away and away from the pain. She didn't want to ask her parents about them because that would have opened too many questions. I had shared everything about Eve with Sam but not to Jim, or the team. I made no mention of her in my final reports or in the interviews that were conducted by Chief Superintendent Marshall. I was on three weeks of annual leave and while they had reassured me that my job was safe, I was still considering my options. Sam was considering her options too. And something in the way she stared at the rolling hills made me think she might want to move home. I suppose the important thing was that we would make a decision together. We wanted to be together. And London didn't seem quite so important anymore.

I felt grateful that Isaac had died so far away from home. I felt guilty for how he died, I hadn't meant for that to happen; I was just protecting Sam. I think that was the only reason her parents could look me in the face. We decided that it would be best if I gave them space this time to let them get over their first Christmas without him. Sam would be around but we agreed that she could spend some time with me. With me and Mum.

When I had called Mum to tell her that I was coming home for Christmas, and that I was bringing a friend home, she was so happy that she cried. I hadn't heard or seen her cry since Dad died. Since the day that Isaac Tibbs ran him over and then continued driving. I had no way of proving that either, but I knew it was true.

I decided to tell Mum about Sam in person, and then introduce her. I knew that if she could just meet Sam then she would understand. Sam's ability to forgive was the rarest trait in a human and her capacity for love was unique. Sam and I agreed that if it worked out we would try and spend Christmas afternoon together, just the three of us, and the thought of that made me really happy.

Sam pulled the car into the steep, stone-paved drive, lifted up the handbrake and turned off the engine. I looked up to the curtains at the window. I turned and lifted Sam's hand to my lips and kissed it. I was ready.

Printed in Great Britain
by Amazon

42686411R00158